Praise for the work of ,

Blood Money Murder

What a terrific read! Shay O'Hanlon is the kind of person I'd love to hang out with—she's got a big heart and a smart mouth—and her adventures are funny and nail biting (often at the same time). The secrets, insecurities, and deep friendships in Shay's world all come center stage in *Blood Money Murder*— and we get to see Shay go farther than we ever thought possible for the people she loves. Well done Jessie Chandler!

-Clare O'Donohue, author of The Someday Quilts and Kate Conway Mysteries

Crammed with action and excitement, *Blood Money Murder* kept me turning pages at breakneck speed. Shay O'Hanlon is one tough broad, and Chandler's latest takes us with her on a nonstop ride all the way to the delightful conclusion. Highly recommended.

-Alice Loweecey, author of the Giulia Driscoll Mystery Series

Jessie Chandler really knows how to take the reader for a wild ride. *Blood Money Murder* delivers suspense, snappy dialogue, fun, and the host of lovable characters who have become family in Chandler's Shay O'Hanlon Caper Series. ...From the scary scenes to the laugh out loud moments, *Blood Money Murder* is fast-paced and skilled—and the ending comes all too soon.

-Lee Lynch, award-winning author of *An American Queer*

An emotionally-charged roller coaster of a romp jam-packed with hot pursuits, bumbling bad guys, and leprechauns. A sizzler of an adventure!

-Maddy Hunter, author of the Passport to Peril Mystery Series

Secrets, love, crime, and family all vie for center stage as Jessie Chandler masterfully conducts her quirky ensemble cast through the latest installment in the Shay O'Hanlon caper series, *Blood Money Murder*. Fans of Chandler's work will enjoy seeing Shay and her loyal band of cohorts join forces to help one of their own, while newcomers to the series are treated to a rollicking introduction to Shay's world that's sure to have them reaching for all the titles in the series.

-Carsen Taite, award-winning author of
the Luca Bennett Bounty Hunter Series

...*Blood Money Murder* is the perfect afternoon escape from the realities of the world. Fortunately, the end of the novel opens up some new possibilities for Jessie Chandler to explore in future escapades.

-The BOLO Books Review

I always enjoy myself when I'm reading about the capers involving Shay and her friends. ...This series continues to get better and better with each episode told and I'm so happy that Jessie has a new publishing home and I look forward to more adventures with Shay, JT and the gang.

-Dru's Book Musings

It's another rollicking tale that I couldn't put down, and Chandler delivers an absolutely perfect ending that had me cheering out loud. I don't believe this is the last we'll hear from Shay O'Hanlon, and I certainly hope not.

-Rainbow Book Reviews

Shanghai
Murder

JESSIE CHANDLER

Other Books by Jessie Chandler

Operation Stop Hate
Quest for Redemption

Shay O'Hanlon Caper Series
Bingo Barge Murder
Hide and Snake Murder
Pickle in the Middle Murder
Chip Off the Ice Block Murder
Blood Money Murder

About the Author

Jessie Chandler is the author of seven, oops, now eight, novels, including the humorously suspenseful *Shay O'Hanlon Caper Series*. Her crime fiction has garnered a Lambda Literary finalist nod, three Golden Crown Literary Awards, three USA Book Awards, and an Independent Publisher Book Award. As a kid, Jessie honed an interest in crime and punishment by reading Alfred Hitchcock's *The Three Investigators* under the covers with a flashlight. Once in a while you can still find her beneath her blankets absorbed in a good mystery.

Shanghai Murder

JESSIE CHANDLER

BELLA
B O O K S
2024

Bella Books, Inc.
P.O. Box 10543
Tallahassee, FL 32302

First Edition - 2024

Editor: Ann Roberts

ISBN: 978-1-64247-519-7

Acknowledgements

It took a while, but FINALLY Shay and company are back in business! Many, many thanks to my first readers, Judy Kerr, MB Panichi, Patty Schramm, Lori L. Lake, and Josie Jensen. Thank you, Bella Books: Linda Hill, Jessica, and the rest of the Bella crew, for your incredibly hard work, your patience, and your encouragement. A huge shout out to my editor, Ann Roberts, for her careful eye and most excellent suggestions; to my cover designer—who shall remain nameless—you rock the graphics and continue to delight the hell out of me; to the proofreaders, typesetters, and anyone else who's had a hand in the nuts and bolts of making this book come together. Thank you doesn't begin to cover it. Ultimately, the biggest thank-you goes out to my readers. Each and every one of you mean the world to me and to Shay. From our hearts to yours.

Dedication

To Carlee Service, I'm so sorry you aren't around for the release of this book, but I'm pretty sure you're laughing your keister off anyway. Thank you, Josie Jensen, for the connection.

To Pat and Betty Frovarp, two of the most amazingly kind, loving, and loyal people I know. And you're both the very best stand-in moms ever. New beginnings are hard, but they come with a whole lot of hope, and new books, and chocolate. I love you both so much.

CHAPTER ONE

Shay

"Did you know, Shay O'Hanlon, we are flying on a Boeing 737-900ER? ER means extended range! This airplane can go five hundred and twenty-five miles an hour."

Rocky's finger appeared between the seats from the row behind and poked my shoulder. "This plane holds one-hundred-eighty adventurers! So, not including us, one hundred and seventy-three people are going on one hundred and seventy-three different adventures."

"That's a whole lot of adventures folks are gonna have."

"Yes, it is, Shay O'Hanlon. I am very excited to go to PDX. Did you know every airport has a three-letter designation? PDX is for Portland. But not Portland in Maine. In Oregon. Pronounced OR-uh-gun, not ORE-ee-gone. The Oregon Trail game has it all wrong."

Our rather round Rocky was a sprite with savant syndrome and landed somewhere on the less impacted end of the differently abled. He had almost perfect recall and loved to share his knowledge with anyone who'd lend him half an ear.

"Rocky, honey…" Tulip's head popped up beside Rocky's. "It's your turn."

Rocky adored his French Creole wife, and was fond of food, hugs, and aviator hats. Which was fitting, since right now, his fascination was all things aviation. "Oh! Okay. I must go now, Shay O'Hanlon. I am about to monopolize my bride with the Monopoly game application on my very fancy cellular device."

"Go on with your bad self," I told him. A ball of excitement settled low in my belly as the tang of jet fuel swirled into the cabin on the heels of the last of the boarding passengers. I didn't even mind we were crammed in cattle class tighter than the corset on a drag queen. I was even okay with being pickle-in-the-middle, with my six-four, no-longer-chain-smoking-but-still-mostly-vegetarian best friend, Coop, next to the window and my girlfriend, JT, or rather, now fiancée—god I needed to get used to that word—guarding the aisle on my right.

In less than twenty-four hours, we'd be at the biggest fair-trade coffee convention in the Pacific Northwest. Neither tsunamis nor wildfires would stop me from bringing the hottest-selling, new-to-the-coffee-scene Ochoco Creek brand to the Rabbit Hole, my coffee shop in Uptown Minneapolis. Ochoco Creek Coffee was a fast-rising, West Coast cult favorite, and I wanted to bring that sensibility back home with me to shake up the taste buds of our overwhelmingly Scandinavian population.

JT grunted and gave me the side eye as she got her own Rocky finger poke treatment. In hindsight, I should've seated Rocky, Tulip, and Eddy—a mom figure to us all—in front of us instead of behind.

My sister, Lisa, had tagged along for the ride too. She was stuck in the middle seat three rows up, between two behemoth guys who towered over her own six-foot frame, both wearing University of Oregon Ducks football jerseys. From the sound of their extra-loud conversation over the top of poor Lisa's head, they'd come to the Land of 10,000 Lakes to attend the Power Pull Nationals in central Minnesota, whatever it was, and were returning with some supercharged testosterone pumping through their bloodstream.

"Nick Coop."

I felt hot breath on my arm. Rocky's face was now pushed up against the crack between my seat and Coop's. He must have finished his Monopoly turn. "Did you know this flying tubular air vehicle can travel two thousand eight hundred and ten miles under perfect conditions?"

"Nope, I sure didn't know that."

"If you do not know something, Nick Coop, all you have to do is consult the Great and Mighty Oracle."

Coop barked a laugh. "You're so right, my friend." He dangled his hand over the headrest, palm up, and Rocky slapped him five.

The Great and Mighty Oracle was Google, which Rocky loved to access on his brand-new iPhone. He and Tulip had saved long and hard to buy themselves the very latest and greatest in cellular technology, as Rocky would say. Neither had ever owned a cell phone before and they were stoked.

"Hey, Rocky," Coop said, "what do I need a Great and Mighty Oracle for if I have you?" For a moment the sounds of muffled voices and the slam of overhead storage compartments filled the air. I imagined Rocky's frown as he seriously considered the question.

"You are right, Nick Coop. But if I am not around to be your Great and Mighty Oracle, you can use your own Oracle."

"My dearest Rocky," Tulip said, "sit down and buckle your seat belt. You don't want to upset the nice flight attendants."

"Oh, no. No, no, no. I absolutely do not want to upset anyone. I gave the nice flight attendants a bag of Hershey's Minis with Hershey's Krackel, Hershey's Special Dark, Hershey's Milk Chocolate, and Hershey's Mr. Goodbar when we boarded, so I hope they will be happy. They work very hard, and some people are not very nice to them. It is mean not to be nice." Then, in one of his classic lightning-fast topic changes, he added, "Did you know the design of the aviation seat belt hasn't changed since the 1950s?"

"News to me," Eddy said, her voice groggy thick. Talk of safety equipment must've awakened her from one of her not-somicro snoozes. "But I'm glad to know it now." She harrumphed. "We haven't even left the gate and I'm pooped. I need me a gallon of diet Mello Yello, and I think I gotta pee. See? I told you kids I shoulda stayed home."

"Come on, Eddy." I twisted around as best I could. "You're gonna have a great time. You'll be up to your elbows in coffee samples for the next three days. Plus, you wanted to hit Voodoo Doughnuts. Holy mahoney, I can't wait."

Lisa had spent some time in Portland early in her college career. When she learned we were headed to Stumptown, she'd raved about Voodoo deliciousness. After spending some time on the Internet doing a bit of intense doughnut surfing, my eye was on Voodoo's Old Dirty Bastard, a long john-like, chocolate, peanut butter, and Oreo topped creation. Voodoo, hoodoo, doo doo, I was all in. Well, maybe not so much the doo doo part.

Eddy harrumphed again and I resettled myself. For the last few months, Eddy'd been snappish, totally out of character, and had a terrible time staying awake, which was also out of character. She'd lost interest in much of the shizz which usually occupied her time.

Instead of dealing cards with the Mad Knitters, her not-so-much-knitting-but-poker-playing posse, she was asleep in her recliner with the television tuned into some cooking channel instead of avidly watching the crime shows she loved. She wasn't bopping around the Rabbit Hole, helping as she usually did. I'd hunt her down to find she was in her bedroom taking a nap.

When she was awake, she was constantly downing coffee or diet Mello Yello, and more recently she'd added Red Bull to her arsenal. I didn't know how she could stand the god-awful cough syrup taste, but she could guzzle that shit with the best of them. It came as no surprise with all the liquid she poured down her gullet, she had to go to the bathroom practically every ten minutes. Therefore, most of her naps were pretty short.

The situation would be funny if her actions, or rather, lack thereof, didn't worry me so much. All this had come on so gradually I hadn't noticed anything was truly off till a couple weeks ago. I walked into her living room one morning and found her conked out with three empty Mello Yello cans, two equally empty Red Bulls, and a Rabbit Hole coffee cup on a table beside her recliner. A couple more bottles were strewn on the ground beside her chair. I wondered if she'd suddenly come down with a lingering case of insomnia or maybe late-onset narcolepsy.

It was for those reasons I booked her a ticket to come with us to the City of Roses and the famous Big on Beans Convention— better known as BOB—in Portland, at the last minute. I figured a change of scenery would be good for her, and besides, she usually loved to travel. Anywhere. Anytime.

JT's hand rested on my thigh, and I gave her fingers a squeeze. She glanced up from her in-flight magazine and gifted me an affectionate smile.

God, what she did to my insides. I tilted my head toward her. "You notice Eddy's been acting weird?"

The disembodied voice of the airline world's Oz drowned out my words. "Ladies and gentlemen, the captain has turned on the fasten seat belt sign. If you haven't already done so, please stow…" The announcement droned on. I kissed JT's temple and sighed heavily.

She threaded her fingers through mine and held tight. "We can chat once we're in the air after a successful takeoff."

"It's gonna be fine, baby."

"I know, I know. But still."

JT wasn't a nervous flyer except for the takeoff part. Maybe it was because she had to surrender all control and there was no going back once the wheels kissed the pavement goodbye. Whatever the reason, I held tight to the strong, capable, hand of my slightly scared homicide detective and sat back to "enjoy" my flight.

Fourteen minutes and 31,000 feet later, we leveled off. JT had given me my hand back, and now that she'd survived takeoff, she returned to leafing through her magazine. Behind her seat, a loud, sharp snore emanated at regular intervals. For once, Eddy's need to go to the bathroom wasn't enough to keep her awake. Rocky and Tulip continued to duke it out over electronic Monopoly, and Coop's nose was buried in a copy of *PC Gamer*.

"Hey." I nuzzled the soft shell of JT's ear and considered giving her a wet willie, then decided I better behave.

She kissed the tip of my nose. "What about Eddy?"

"I think she's depressed."

"I've noticed she's tired, like *all* the time."

My "Yeah," was punctuated by a particularly loud snort from the person in question. Even the dull roar of the jet's engines outside couldn't completely drown our matriarch out. "I think maybe all the stuff that came out about my mom and her family really affected her. It's not even been three months since it happened."

This past St. Paddy's Day holiday weekend I'd found out what exactly happened the fateful day that had changed both mine and Eddy's lives forever. My mother had been driving Eddy and her son, Neil, to the bus station to send them to family down south in an attempt to help them avoid some seriously big-time trouble. On the way to the station, my mom's car was T-boned by a truck.

My mom was killed, and so was Neil. Eddy dragged me out of the wreckage and held my insides where they belonged until help arrived. She saved my life.

After the accident, Eddy wracked with guilt, had taken over Mom's duties as best she could and helped my dad, who now had to raise a feisty kid along with keeping his bar, the Leprechaun, out of the red. He'd guzzled booze like it was Kool-Aid for as long as I could remember, and after my mom died, he doubled down on the escape juice. I hated his drinking. He hated the fact I wasn't straight.

Eddy was our peacemaker, often mediating when things between us went south, which tended to happen when he was tanked. Over the years, he and I had come to a wary truce. As I grew older, I better understood his need to drown out the pain. Eventually my father began to work on curbing his liquor intake, and while his truce with alcohol sometimes fell apart, he was doing better, and that's what counted.

Plus, not so long ago, he finally chilled about the gay thing and had actually accepted JT into the family. The passing of time was good for my old man.

Unfortunately, the years hadn't eased a bit of Eddy's guilt. Guilt I never knew she harbored. She never once stopped blaming herself for what had happened, although I could tell she was relieved when the truth came out and I didn't hate her, or worse, turn my back on her.

Like I'd ever do a thing like that. The woman meant everything to me.

Once we'd made it through the revelations and confessions, Eddy had begun sinking. Even dealing with half of those events would take any regular person down. But all of it at once? Eddy was one of the strongest people I knew, and if anyone could survive, it was her. But I knew strong people could also be depressed people.

JT peered out the oval window and I followed her gaze. The sky was a rich blue. Bright sunlight reflected off the metallic surface of the wing, making me squint. She said, "Thinking about it, you're right. She hasn't been to the Lep to play five-card stud for weeks—I forgot your dad mentioned it when I helped him with inventory day before yesterday—and I don't think I've seen her around the Rabbit Hole in the mornings when I've stopped by. Or Agnes either, for that matter. You think they had a falling out?"

Agnes was Eddy's closest friend and coconspirator extraordinaire. "They bicker all the time, but I can't ever remember them getting mad enough they stopped talking for more than one day. They've been besties forever."

"What about the not-so-much-knitting, more often pokering Mad Knitters? Has she been meeting with them?"

"Not really, I don't think." I felt somewhat alarmed and a little ashamed. I'd been so busy with the Rabbit Hole and the efforts Kate—café co-owner and great friend—and I were making to expand our product base I hadn't paid the kind of attention I should've. I should have seen this happening and said something before it ever got to this point.

JT caught my eye. "Babe, don't."

I scrunched my nose at her. Easier said than done. I leaned over to Coop. "Hey," I whispered, "has Eddy been to any Mad Knitter meetings lately?" He was a metro kinda guy, happy to play poker with women three times his age, and even willing to suffer through a knitting or crocheting lesson on occasion.

He blinked then blinked again as he struggled to shift his brain from gaming mode to the present. "Maybe a month ago."

"Was it at her place?"

"Yeah. Why?"

I gave him the rundown of our depression diagnosis.

"You going to talk to her?"

"Yeah, I guess I better." So not what I wanted to do. Sorting through emotional crap was not my idea of a pleasant time. He was right, though. When Eddy and I had a moment alone this weekend, I'd pin her down for a chat. I knew she'd feared I'd hate her. But I could never, ever feel that way. She was as close to a mother to me as my own mom, and nothing could change my feelings for her.

Personally, I thought I'd dealt with those revelations pretty damn gracefully, but maybe Eddy hadn't fared so well in the reprocessing of those dark bits of history.

"Hey, Shay." Tulip's quiet voice slid through the gap between the seats.

I cranked myself around again. "Yeah?"

"Did you guys pick out a wedding date yet?" She gave me a wide-eyed, come-on-already smirk.

I glanced at JT and she shot me a silent expression of panic.

Not long ago, in a rush of emotion after I'd almost been blown to smithereens in a meth lab explosion, and when the truth came out about Eddy and my mother, I'd asked for JT's hand in holy matrimony and bliss. JT gave me the thumbs-up, which, to this day, still surprised me.

Since then, we'd talked about it a little, but both of us were overwhelmed with the entire idea. What do you wear to a wedding when you hate dressing up? Who do you invite? Who don't you invite? Then you had to mess around with writing invitations, and then there was the catering. And flowers. Did all weddings have to have flowers? I felt a little sick when I considered the implications. We didn't have a lot of money and neither did my father. JT's folks were an unknown. One good thing was my dad offered up the Lep as the venue, shocking the shit out of me.

"Tulip, great question. We're still working it out."

"Okay. But you better hurry up cause one day you might be expecting a bundle of joy too. Come on, Rocky." She gave him a nudge. "I'll let you win another game of Monopoly."

I gaped at JT.

She whispered, "Did you hear that?"

"Yes!" Holy shit on a shingle. Were they gonna have a baby?

CHAPTER TWO

Shay

"Tulip," Rocky said, "please do not go to the Witch's Castle. It is a very, very scary place."

"It's not scary, Rocky. It's old and has moss all over it."

"I have seen pictures. It is too dangerous. Something bad could happen." Beneath his aviator hat, Rocky's face was flushed, and the tip of his nose glowed like an oddly shaped maraschino cherry.

"Oh, Rocky." Tulip sat beside him on the rumpled motel bed by the window, an arm around his shoulders. Late morning sunlight cut a swath across her lap. I'd been hoping to get a jump on the convention, but sleep had won out. "I promise it will be okay. Pretty Boy Robbie and Scary Mary said it's a Portland must-see."

JT, Coop, and I had wedged ourselves into Eddy, Rocky, and Tulip's fine Eastside Lodge guest room as we waited for the debate to wind down. Rocky wasn't usually a worrier, so this whole scene was out of character. Maybe it was because he was in a different state and nothing was familiar.

Or maybe it was because Tulip was knocked up.

Holy hot sauce on a hot dog. Tulip pregnant? I couldn't wait to tell Coop. Did Eddy already know? She would've said something about it if she did, wouldn't she? These days, who knew? I really needed to find time ASAP to talk to her. The worry monster inside my stomach gave me an ominous love tap.

Rocky's eyes were wide and wild, and his lips were pinched. "My most lovely Tulip, I do not care what Pretty Boy Robbie and Scary Mary say. I know they are your friends from New Orleans, but I do not know them."

I momentarily wondered if he was jealous, but it wasn't like Pretty Boy Robbie—what kind of name was that anyway?—was coming alone to see Tulip. Besides, Rocky had never displayed any kind of overboard "you are my woman and mine alone" caveman baloney.

"I promise they're really okay, Rocky," Tulip said, her voice gentle. "They came all this way to visit. I'll bring you back a Voodoo Doughnut if we're lucky enough to stop there. We should be back by seven. And you can still come with, you know."

She dropped her arm and laid a hand on his knee. He covered it with his own, his fairness in sharp contrast to her warm sepia.

"No. But thank you, my darling. I want to stay with Ms. Eddy. I know I should not be poopy. You should spend time with your friends." He nodded once. "All right. I will stay, and you will have fun with Scary Mary and Pretty Boy Robbie."

"Rocky," Eddy, who was propped against a couple of pillows on the bed nearest the bathroom, said, "don't forget Tulip will have her Oracle, and you can call her any time."

"True, Ms. Eddy. I can."

Tulip laid a big fat one on Rocky's cheek, and he beamed.

Meltdown averted. Tulip was good for Rocky in so many ways.

The tension in the air dissipated and conversation shifted to what we wanted to do for supper, because of course, grub always made this crew happy.

"The food carts in Portland are legendary," I said, "and Lisa mentioned she knew the location of some super special secret ones."

"She's talking my foodie love language," Coop said. "Speaking of Lisa, where is she?"

"Oy. I forgot." From the nightstand Eddy grabbed a liter bottle of diet Mountain Dew that was lined up beside two unopened Yellow Edition Red Bulls. "She stopped by early this morning. Said she had some errands to run and would check in with us later tonight."

Weird. She'd talked about going to the Big on Beans Convention. But then again, she probably had friends out here she might want to see or whatever, and I needed to remember not everyone was as into coffee as I was.

Eddy opened the Mountain Dew, tipped the bottle to her mouth, and gave it a good shake. She recapped it, and with a flick of her wrist, sent the bottle sailing.

JT ducked and the bottle ricocheted off the wall and landed on the floor. She scooped it up and deposited it in the small wire garbage can beside the desk, then caught my eye with a WTF look. I raised my brows. Definitely not an Eddy move. She was way too neat to play basketball with the trash. Especially when she was so bad at it.

"Thank you, JT." Eddy yawned. "Don't know why I can't stay awake. Went out at six this morning and tried to find diet Mello Yello. They apparently don't carry Mello Yello in this burg. So got me some of this Mountain Dew business and this here yellow go-juice." She grabbed one of the cans.

I wondered if the yellow version of the Bull tasted any better than the original.

As if reading my mind, she said, "Dew will do, but Mello is king. Let's see how this here Yellow Edition is." She popped the top and proceeded to chug the entire contents, then stifled a burp with the back of her hand. "Huh. Kind of tasty."

A knock sounded at the door. Since Coop had filed in last, he answered.

For a second the doorway was empty. Then a hand encased in something appeared at chest level and a disembodied voice said, "Hello!"

It took me a second to fathom the object was a hand puppet. A black pointy hat sat on the puppet's bright-green head, and the rim shaded its crooked, bright-purple nose. "We are here to conjure up a great time for Tulip. Is she here?"

"Scary Mary!" Tulip leaped off the bed and made a beeline out the door onto the third-floor walkway. Coop, JT, and I sidled out of the room, followed by Eddy and then Rocky.

A woman with wild, shoulder-length, blondish hair in a scrubby tie-dye shirt had Tulip in a bear hug, and a guy dressed all in black stood off to the side with a hand on the railing.

Pretty Boy Robbie. In his case, Pretty Boy was a misnomer. Dude reminded me of Ichabod Crane, at least six-five if he were an inch, bony-thin, with an Adam's apple the size of an orange.

"Hello." Ichabod Pretty Boy's voice came from somewhere below his ankles, and his Adam's apple bounced around in an oddly mesmerizing way.

I expected Eddy to take the lead, but when I glanced her way, she'd disappeared back into the room. Probably to hit the john after that energy drink.

Five awkward minutes and a rocky Rocky goodbye later, we regrouped inside with Eddy, who'd resumed her semireclined position on the bed.

Coop briskly clapped his hands together twice, reminding me of my kindergarten teacher. "Time for a last technology check before we hit the show. Everyone pull up Trip a Go Go."

We did as we were bid. Before we left Minneapolis, Coop had downloaded onto all our devices an app called Trip a Go Go. Users created what TAGG defined as a "crew," which was a group of friends or family—hopefully with permission from all parties—who were able to track each other in real-time, as long as we had cell service or the net. He was worried if we got separated, we wouldn't be able to find each other. Leave it to our very own techie to help keep us together.

Eddy, the reformed luddite of the group, had finally caved and gotten a smartphone when Rocky and Tulip had, so she was able to play along. Thank flipping god. At last, the woman was dipping her big toe into the twenty-first century. In less than three months, Ms. "I'll Own a Cell Phone Over My Creaky, Deceased Corpse," had conned Agnes into buying one, and they were now faster texters than I was.

Coop confirmed everyone's apps were working. "Let's get going on our third adventure."

"Nick Coop," Rocky said, "we haven't started our first adventure yet."

"Sure, we have, Rocky." Coop tapped a finger against his bristly chin. "Actually, now that I think about it, this is our fourth adventure."

"Nick Coop, you are funny."

"No, seriously. Adventure number one: leaving home, dropping off Dawg and Bogey with Pam Pine, going to the airport, making our way ever so slowly through security, and finally finding the right gate. Adventure number two: the perfect takeoff, the awesomely smooth flight, and, Rocky, you and Tulip were bestowed with an extra Biscoff cookie—"

"Yum! It is because, Nick Coop, we gave the crew most delicious Hershey's candy bars."

JT laughed. "I think maybe it's because you and Tulip are some of the kindest humans on the planet."

Rocky's face reddened but the smile accompanying the flush was dazzling.

Coop held three fingers up. "Adventure *numero tres*: finding our luggage and riding in the zoom-up-to-the-stoplight-and-slam-on-your-brakes Uber to our motel. Adventure four: scoring our motel rooms. You and Tulip got to pick out which of the three rooms you wanted."

"Hmm." Rocky squinted as he considered Coop's words. "You are right! This will be adventure number six. Because adventure five was meeting Scary Mary and Pretty Boy Robbie, who was not too pretty at all."

Coop stifled a laugh. "You're right. I forgot to count meeting Tulip's friends. That was most certainly an adventure. Okay, folks, everyone back to Trip a Go Go."

I had to admit TAGG was creepy yet fascinating. Tiny bubbles with pictures of our faces floated above a map and it kept track of everyone's battery levels as well. Talk about a full-service app.

"Look." Rocky pointed to one bubble head moving away from our five tightly grouped bubble heads. "It's Tulip."

"See, Rocky," Eddy said, "you check TAGG and you'll know where Tulip is. Okay. Let's get this chaos on the road before I need another nap."

It was almost noon by the time we got our shit together and pried Eddy out of the motel room. We made it as far as the parking lot before she remembered she'd forgotten her fanny pack and phone. I hustled back for the items and then we trudged the half mile to the Oregon Convention Center. The convention had begun at nine, and I was suffering a serious case of FOMO. Usually, I didn't have a fear of missing out, but this time it was full-on ants in my pants.

We navigated Couch Street, pronounced Cooch, thank you, according to the guy working the motel desk. One example of the "Keep Portland Weird" mentality. I was struck by how similar Portland seemed, at least on the outside, to Minneapolis. Lots of pedestrians and bikes rolled around a bustling, pedestrian and bike-friendly urban center. Probably the biggest difference was the cost of living and the number of cars on the road, with Portland taking the cake on both.

At Northeast Grand we made a right, and after ten minutes and a couple of twists and turns, we ran smack-dab into the "A" entrance of the conference facility. Looming over the building like encased scaffolding gone wild were the two famous spire towers the center was best known for. A backlit sign outside of the doors directed BOB Con goers to Exhibit Halls C and D.

JT almost peed her pants when she saw the Stumptown Slime Convention occupied Exhibit Hall A. The coffee and Slime crowds shared space with a Clergy Couture Convention, located in Exhibit Hall B. What was Clergy Couture? High fashion for the religious leader set?

We filed inside and were immediately enveloped by the scent of coffee. My insides jangled happily.

"Okay, java hounds, I'm outta here. Slime's calling my name. I'll check in later." JT peeled off and made a beeline for the SSC.

"Holy moly, Shay O'Hanlon." Rocky sniffed the air. "It smells like one hundred Rabbit Holes."

"Sure does." Eddy fanned a hand in front of her face. "It's a tad overwhelming. Who's selling beans with the highest caffeine content? I need them stat and I need a bathroom."

I gave her the side eye. "I'm sure we'll find you something." I didn't have the heart to tell her all beans carried about the same amount of caffeine. In fact, a light roast had a little more caffeine than a dark roast because the beans were denser and hadn't been roasted as long.

The hallway funneled us into the Pre-Function A section of the convention center. A red carpet with repeating blue and black plus signs dominated an open space sizeable enough that I would've called it Great Ass Big Lobby A instead of Pre-Function A. The lobby title was reserved for a teensy-weensy corridor located directly opposite the exhibit hall, leading to a bunch of meeting rooms.

Coop studied the building map in the convention program I'd printed out. He pointed across the spacious non-lobby. "I think the pendulum thing you've been talking nonstop about, Rocky, is right over there."

Rocky caught sight of a ball slowly swaying twenty feet above the floor and his eyes grew wide. "Yes! There it is! *Principia*." He spoke the word with reverence. "The world's largest Foucault Pendulum. Do you know it is pronounced foo-koh?"

"Yes, Rocky," we intoned, practically in tandem. He'd pondered pendulum mechanics since he looked up the convention center on his Oracle.

"I will wait for you there." He bolted as fast as his stubby legs would carry him toward the rather vicious-looking contraption.

We trailed along at a more leisurely pace, moving with the flow. Some people strolled while others scurried past. Almost everyone had a lanyard around their necks with an attached nametag.

"Ah-ha!" Eddy exclaimed. "I spy a room of rest. Thank the potty gods. I'll meet you at the swinging doodad." Off she darted. Good thing she was wearing her neon orange high-tops, because she dodged and dipped around the flowing mass of conference goers like a basketball player making a drive for the hoop.

A circular terrazzo floor was installed below the slowly swaying ball. An orange crescent was wrapped around an offset, blue-specked, sphere-shaped universe inlaid with concentric gold-colored metal rings. The center of the universe was a brass disk maybe two feet in diameter.

Rocky stood completely still, staring up at the slow-motion action. Coop and I pulled up beside Rocky, who in a reverent voice, said, "The big ball up there is called a bob. It hangs from a cable seventy-feet long. Not sixty-nine or seventy-one. Seventy. That is very long."

"Yes," Coop said, "it sure is."

"The circular thing under the bob is forty feet in diameter." He glanced at me. "Diameter is the longest distance across the circle."

I was horrible at math, and Rocky liked to help me understand that kind of thing.

"Those scary, dagger spikes are knocked over by the bob when they are vertical. They tip horizontal as the halo rotates around the pendulum with the movement of the Earth. It is amazing."

I peered up. "It's definitely something else." The terrifying gizmo was striking, no pun intended.

Rocky radiated as much excitement as a kid who finds out they're going to Chuck E. Cheese for their birthday. "The bob is made of bronze and is exactly thirty-six inches around. It makes a fifteen-foot arc every fifteen seconds."

My neck was becoming crinked. "If the halo thing fell, those spikes look like they could kill."

"Could be a medieval torture device," Coop said, then pointed at the floor. "What are those round things? They look like planets."

Rocky pried his gaze from the swaying ball of death. "Nick Coop, you are sort of right. Those are planets made of pretty rocks." He swept his arm to encompass the entire terrazzo. "This whole floor is a solar system, but one that is made up. It is not like our Earth's solar system. It is pretend."

A puffing Eddy emerged from the hoi polloi. "What'd I miss?"

Coop glanced down at her. "A little history lesson on the pendulum and the cool but fake solar system below it."

"I see."

"Oh, Ms. Eddy! I am so glad you came back. Guess how far it is from here to the ceiling where the cable for the bob is secured with a strong metal plate and many screws."

"Young man, I have no idea. Is that bob thing named after the Big on Beans Convention?"

"You are funny, Ms. Eddy. The bob is not the BOB. This bob is the big round swinging ball. It is seventy feet from the ball all the way up to the ceiling."

Eddy gave Rocky a side-hug. To me she said, "Why don't the two of you go on to the BOB. Rocky and I will wander around."

Rocky's face brightened. "That would be wonderful, Ms. Eddy. I want to show you every piece of art in this amazing building. The fine art hanging in this wonderful establishment is worth two million dollars. That is a whole bunch of greenbacks."

Holy crap. A lot of art and a whole lot of dough. If I were a thief, what a heist this place would be. But probably a million bucks worth of safeguards had been installed, and any potential robber would wind up skewered by one of those aforementioned stakes above our heads.

"Sounds good, Eddy," I said. "Text when you want to meet back up, okay?" I figured it would be no more than twenty minutes before she'd poop out and want to head back to the Eastside for a snooze.

"Yes, child, I will. Now you two go on. I need to find me some pop with gas in it."

"Going." Relief flooded my system to finally get my butt to the convention, but I was still worried about Eddy. My head knew she'd be fine, but my gut wasn't listening.

As we made tracks, I heard Rocky say, "Come on, Ms. Eddy, let us get some gas and then I want to show you the dragon boat!"

Coop and I picked up our registration information and lassoed ourselves with those ever-present lanyards. As we walked away from the desk, he glanced down at his name and frowned.

"What's wrong?"

"It says I live in Minneapolis."

"You do."

"North Carolina."

"Seriously? Minneapolis, North Carolina? I had no idea there was a Minneapolis in North Carolina."

"Me either. I'll have to investigate if I like where I live or not. Maybe it's a good place to settle down and smell the tulips."

"Ha ha ha. Tulips. Oh, shit. Come with me." I dragged Coop out of the two-way river of people to an unoccupied spot along the wall. "I need to tell you this before I get so caught up wrangling coffee for the Hole I can't think of anything but little brown beans." I leaned closer. "You'll never guess what Tulip told me on the flight here. I think it might be why Rocky's freaking."

The happy melted off Coop's face. "What? Is something wrong?"

"No. Well, maybe." I took a breath. "Coop, I think Tulip's pregnant."

For a moment there was no reaction. Then Coop's mouth caught up with his brain. "What?"

"I am not kidding."

"OMG." He put his hands to his head and spun a circle. "Holy shit. Holy *shit*. Okay. We can figure this out. Right?"

"Right." My voice wasn't as reassuring as I would've liked. I tried again. "Yeah, we can. But I'm not sure if I'm ready to be an aunt."

"I'm not ready to be an uncle."

I looked at him. He looked at me. We both snickered, and the snicker became hysterical almost immediately.

After what had to be a full minute later, Coop swiped at his eyes. "Tulip actually told you—spoke the words—she's pregnant?"

I put a hand to my cheek, which was on fire from our runaway mirth. What exactly had she said to me? "It was something about—JT and me—could be 'expecting a bundle of joy too.'" I didn't bother to tell him the comment came during a discussion about wedding plans, or lack thereof. Tulip wasn't the only one after us about setting a hitching date. From the moment the question of "will you" fell out of my mouth, Coop and my father began cooking something up. The not knowing freaked me the fork out.

He straightened. "The 'too,' that's what clued you in." His straw-colored hair was in wild disarray, exactly what it'd look like if he tried to screw his finger into a light socket.

"Yeah. I haven't heard a thing from anyone else, not from Rocky or even Eddy, who you'd think would be the first to know about something like…that."

"No matter. We'll handle it like we always handle dropped bombs."

I could have kissed him. Coop was true blue. "I love you, man."

"Aw shucks. I love you too, woman. Come on. Let's do this coffee thing." We gained admittance to the Big on Beans Convention and slid into the low roar of hundreds of overly caffeinated people milling about a massive space. The aisles were packed, felt as crowded as the Minnesota State Fair on Labor Day.

We shuffled in slow lockstep with about ten million other like-minded coffee-heads up one aisle and down another, passing booth after red-draped booth, collecting samples, business cards, and free pens as we crept toward my java Valhalla. Some of the vendors even offered tours of their factories and shops. So cool. I glanced at the semi crumpled vendor map I clutched in my sweaty little hand. The Ochoco stand took up three spaces and was located less than halfway down the next corridor.

The aisle ended and round we went. After passing a couple stands, I caught sight of a three-by-five-foot, hand-carved, wooden sign towering above a triple wide booth: Ochoco Creek Coffee—The Fairest Trade of All.

Even at five-eight, all I could see from my vantage point behind the wall of Ochoco wanna-haves packed ten deep was a partial view of bookcase-type shelves made of rough-hewn planks stacked on Ochoco Coffee crates. Various roasts and flavors of prepackaged, sample-size Ochoco Coffees lined the uppermost rack.

Excitement flared and I felt kid-giddy. "What do you see, oh tall one?"

Coop stood on his tiptoes. "Not much."

"What?"

"Cut-in-half whiskey barrels, you know, the kind you can buy at Home Depot to use as planters? They're arranged in an arc from one end of the booth to the other. But they're empty. So's all the shelving except the stuff on top. But two coffee slingers are writing up orders, so at least that's good."

Vendors typically had display products and might even give out samples, but they usually brought enough to last more than the first four and a half hours of a convention. Ochoco was hot, and maybe the booth had been even busier than I'd expected. I was looking forward to a sample or two myself, but whatever. As long as I could place an order at discounted convention rates, I'd be a happy coffee camper.

We waited a few more minutes and moved a layer closer as potential customers filed out and away from the booth. My belly grumbled, and I tried to ignore it. It creaked again, and then my stomach cramped. In a moment, I understood how Eddy felt when she needed the bathroom. As in, right this second.

"Coop."

He was too busy watching what I couldn't see to pay attention to me.

"COOP!" I bonked him on the arm.

"Ow." He rubbed his bicep and glanced at me. "What?"

"I gotta go."

"But we just got here."

"No." The gurgling gurgled louder. "I need to go. To the bathroom. Now." I raised my brows and bug-eyed him for emphasis.

"*Oh*. Uh-oh. Lemme look." He glanced the way we'd come and then the opposite direction, down a very long line of booths to the opposite side of the massive ballroom. "Okay. I see a sign for restrooms down there. But it's gonna take you forever to fight your way through the hoard."

My stomach informed me I better get moving in a hurry, or I was gonna be ankle deep in in a very unfortunate situation. "I should never have had the greasy burger and fries for breakfast from that food truck near the motel."

"Deliciousness has its downsides."

I'd taken one step when Coop caught my arm and hauled me back. "Wait, wait. The booths are set up back-to-back. There's probably storage rooms behind each booth, maybe a walkway between them." He pushed me in the opposite direction, against the flow of traffic. "Go. I'll keep your place."

I pushed my way through the surge, feeling more panicky by the second. I didn't usually have this kind of plumbing problem but traveling and eating different food was sometimes big trouble.

Why did my gut have to pick now to uncork itself?

I made it to the end of the aisle and scooted around the corner. Sure enough, a gap between the booths was cordoned off by two stanchions connected by a retractable belt. A sign attached to the belt read NO ADMITTANCE.

Screw that. This was an emergency which could result in serious embarrassment for all concerned, especially me. Teeth gritted, I squeezed my butt cheeks together and ducked under the nylon cordon. Boxes of product or advertising what-have-you were stacked against the heavy red curtains serving as makeshift walls on both sides of a narrow aisle.

I trucked past the rear of one vendor, then another. At the third booth, which should've been the Ochoco stand, I came across a near blockade. Their storage room's back drape rested on top of an uneven row of boxes—hinged, wooden coffee crates— maybe twice as big as a shoe box, emblazoned with Flying High Coffee's red-and-blue logo. Had to be thirty or forty crates. The Flying High brand was the West Coast's answer to Folgers, and flouted the tagline "Coffee your Grandparents Would Love. Economical, Plentiful, and Tasty."

The containers were stacked roughly chest level. Whoever'd carted the crates to the booth had been in such a hurry they couldn't be bothered with moving them three more feet into Ochoco's storage area, and out of the three-foot wide aisle. Instead, they left about a foot gap for people to try to squeeze through. But why would Ochoco use Flying High boxes for transporting their stuff to the convention? Besides, if Ochoco had this much product, why was much of the display area bare?

My stomach creaked louder. I didn't have time to care about the whys and wherefores of the organization of a coffee company's booth. I squeezed my cheeks tighter and carefully picked my way around the roadblock. Once clear I scooted the rest of the way through what felt like a twenty-three-mile obstacle course. I popped out the far side, and damned if I wasn't directly across from the restroom Coop had spotted. Thankfully, the Gods of Flush were smiling down on me and created a timely gap in the cross-aisle gridlock. I took advantage and zipped into the facilities.

When I finished taking care of biz, I washed and dried my hands, trying to decide the best return path. Didn't take a genius to realize my best bet was to simply backtrack. Poor Coop was probably close to the front by now, and no way did I want to miss out on my ordering window.

Apparently, the Gods of Flush had decided their job was finished, and now the cross aisle was practically impassable. Welcome to a live game of Frogger, I thought, as I ping-ponged my way across the pedestrian superhighway into my secret passage. As I passed behind the Ochoco booth, a harsh, angry whisper from behind the red curtain caught my attention. I put the brakes on when I caught the words "…and how the fuck did you manage to ship the fucking wrong crates to the fucking wrong location with the fucking wrong contents?"

My curiosity quotient—what Eddy liked to term unduly dangerous nosiness—kicked in. I leaned forward, propping myself against one of those haphazardly piled stacks of Flying High coffee to hear more clearly through the thick curtain. The boxes were situated more unevenly than I thought. One moment I was politely eavesdropping, and the next I was falling, along with the crates, as they slid out from under me and crashed into the Ochoco storage area. Horrified, I tried to regain my footing, but I was too far out of balance. Luckily, the curtain pinned between my elbows and the containers came down without much resistance. I could've accidentally dragged the entire framework for the booths down with me, and then I'd really know what idiocy felt like.

I sprawled awkwardly over the tumbled crates and tried, in a panic, to figure out how to extricate myself from the mess I'd created.

As I shifted to crawl off the wooden boxes, the lid of one of the crates came loose. Kleenex-sized cardboard boxes tumbled onto the floor, and the impact broke some of them open. Small metal objects rolled out of them and rolled around the floor.

I'd lived with JT long enough to know bullets when I saw them, and that's what was scattered all over the polished concrete.

What the holy hell?

I tried again to lever myself off the wreckage, but before I could accomplish the task, someone grabbed me by the scruff and yanked me to my feet.

Fact. The barrel of a gun doesn't look very big until it's pointed at the space between your eyes. Then it looks like the freaking tunnel of doom.

CHAPTER THREE

JT

The entry fee to the Stumptown Slime Convention cost all of ten bucks, a price JT was happy to pay. Little kids outnumbered adults six to one, but that didn't deter her from finding a Make Your Own Slime Station and pulling up a kid-sized chair to a kid-sized table. When had slime become a thing again? Then again, maybe it had never stopped being a thing.

JT remembered playing with slime as a tot, the kind of slime in a bright green trash can. One time she got the glop stuck so thoroughly in her hair her mom wound up cutting the lumps out with a pair of scissors. The next day she was a half-bald flower girl at a cousin's wedding. The slime versus hair battle royal hadn't phased her love of the slippery goo. Nothing was better than pulling it. Poking it. Popping it. Squishing it and making juicy farting sounds.

She hadn't thought about slime in years, but one day a few weeks ago, she'd popped into Eddy's place on an errand and found Eddy and Tulip making a big batch of homemade slime for a birthday party Tulip was working. She'd had no idea the stuff could be made from household ingredients. Tulip had given her a jelly jar of her very own purple slime, and she kept it in her car for late-night stakeout entertainment. The life of a cop didn't leave a lot of time for such silly endeavors, but occasionally she felt compelled to throw her arms in the air and embrace her inner child, something she never would've contemplated before Shay came along.

Now, the only thing she was missing, she mused as she mixed glue and baking soda together, was the person who'd rekindled her playful side. She and Shay would've had a great time creating some of the slick stuff, but the coffee convention was her partner's priority.

As she watched the kids around the table concentrate on their creations, she tried to imagine Rocky and Tulip taking care of a youngster of their own. They'd be great with a baby, but would no doubt need help. Which would be okay, because they had Eddy and Shay, Coop, Lisa, and herself to assist. Kate and her sister Anna would pitch in, too, of course. But sheesh, kids were a lot of responsibility. She'd never envisioned herself with any mini-devils, and never felt the maternal tug to have one of her own.

Yet, anyway.

She and Shay had never seriously talked about having kids. Frankly, the thought was enough to give her the heebee hives, but she supposed she owed it to Shay to at least broach the subject.

The kid sitting next to JT tapped her forearm. "Here's the thick-making stuff." He handed her a white bottle of saline contact solution. "Don'tcha think you're a little old to be makin' slime, lady?"

"Nope," she said. "Sometimes big kids need to play too."

He shrugged. "'Spose."

For a couple of minutes the table was silent. JT adjusted her mixture until it was acceptably slimy. Bottles of food color were clustered in the center of the tabletop. She grabbed bubblegum pink and added a few drops.

"Hey," the boy said, "you should put more color in there unless you don't want it too bright."

"Bright's good." She squirted more hot pink on top of her slime and tried to mix it in with a plastic spoon. "What's your name, kid?"

"Charlie." He pointed at her spoon. "That'll break. You gotta use your hands." His own hands were stained every shade of the rainbow and his slime was beginning to take on a muddy tinge.

Might as well embrace her inner brat. She sunk a hand into the slop and worked the food color in. The slime oozed nicely between her fingers; fingers which were probably going to be stained glowing pink for the foreseeable future.

Charlie grabbed a Ziploc from a box on the table and stuffed his sickly brown creation inside. "It was good to meetcha, lady."

"You too, Charlie. Thanks for the slime color advice."

He waved and skedaddled to another project station.

Ten minutes later, as JT worked on her second slime mixture, Coop sat down beside her. "Hey."

"Hey. Bored of the coffee con?"

"Not exactly. You seen Shay recently?"

JT gave him a sideways glance. "No. Isn't she with you?"

"She was."

Her purplish fingers stilled over her bowl. "She *was*?"

"Yeah. Went to the restroom and never came back."

"What?" JT began to scrape off the oozy glop. "Is she sick?"

"I don't think so. The breakfast burger apparently did her in. I held a place in line for her at the Ochoco Coffee stand while she hit the john. After fifteen minutes, I got worried and tried to text her, then attempted to pull up TAGG, but reception sucks in this joint. So, I went looking. She wasn't in the bathroom, unless she was hiding from the eighty-six-year-old lady I paid ten bucks to go in and check for me. There's so many people in that convention it's next to impossible to find anybody. Then I thought I'd check in with you and see if she'd hunted you down for some reason."

JT stood. The lady running the slime table handed her a wad of paper towels. "Thanks," she said as she tried to wipe off the goo and then gave up. "Here, sweetheart," she said to a curly-haired, gap-toothed girl sitting across the table and slid the partially finished slime toward her. "Have at it."

"Thankth, lady." She dumped JT's purply-blue slime on top of her own green concoction.

Paper towel lady pointed across the room. "There's a hand washing station over there."

JT flashed her a smile.

"Wanna meet me outside the entrance when you're unglued?" Coop asked. "I snuck in without paying, so I should probably sneak back out."

"Don't want the slime police to bust you?"

"Nope. No slimy jail for me."

"Okay. Lemme take care of this mess and then we'll go find our missing barista."

Forty minutes and a whole lot of skulking where they didn't belong later, JT and Coop regrouped near the Foucault Pendulum. The one place they hadn't checked was the Clergy Couture Convention, but unless Shay had suddenly taken up the preaching mantel, JT knew she wouldn't have gone anywhere near the Triple C.

"This makes no sense," she said. "Why would Shay leave you stranded at the one place she was dying to go? I don't know if I should be worried or pissed." She put a hand to her head, where a persistently sharp pain was developing. Had Shay said or done anything in the hours before they'd arrived at the convention that would explain her seemingly bizarre behavior? No. Her girlfriend had seemed fine when they'd gone their separate ways earlier.

"You know Shay doesn't do this." Coop's frown accentuated a deep forehead crease. "She doesn't up and disappear."

JT hit him with a "you've got to be kidding" stare. Shay was nothing if not impulsive.

He had the presence of mind to look mildly chagrined. "Okay, you're right. But there's got to be a logical explanation."

"I know. There's about a trillion people in here. We easily could've missed her and she's looking for us as hard as we're looking for her. We didn't even run into Rocky and Eddy while we scoured the place. Try TAGG again."

"Okay." Coop did his thing. "No go. I'm downgrading the reception in the building from crappy to zipola. Let's find the Legend of Sleepy Hollow and her sidekick. With luck, maybe Shay's with them."

They found the Legend in the Slime Convention sitting across from Rocky at a round table by the concession stand. Rocky was busy snarfing down a bowl of creamy white jello speckled with black clods.

"There you two are." Coop pulled out a chair and flopped into it.

"Yes, here we are." Eddy yawned. "I think we've looked at every piece of art in this establishment. Some of them twice." She yawned again. "I need to go take a nap."

JT met Coop's eyes. She shrugged. He glanced at Rocky. "Whatcha got there?"

"Coogies ab cream slimb," Rocky answered through a huge spoonful. "Yummy."

"It's a Slime Sundae." Eddy watched Rocky eat, affection radiating from her. "Have to admit it was pretty tootin' good. I 'spose I'll be tootin' too pretty soon. That there's Rocky's second helping."

JT smiled despite herself. "Have you guys seen Shay?"

Eddy glanced at her. "Isn't she in the BOB?"

"We don't think so."

"Ruh roh." Rocky chewed and swallowed a particularly large piece of dirt. "A lost Shay O'Hanlon is not a good thing."

"No, Rocky, it's not." Coop related Shay's mad dash for the restroom and her subsequent disappearance.

"However," JT added, "it's certainly possible—actually quite probable—she inhaled too many coffee fumes and wandered off on a contact caffeine high."

Eddy pulled her cell out of her fanny pack and fired it up. "Lemme see if she texted." She stared at the screen then shook the phone. "This here doodad doesn't seem to be working."

Coop grabbed the cell before Eddy lost her grip on it and sent it sailing. "The phone's fine. Reception in here is iffy at best. I think it's all the concrete. Sometimes one carrier works in places like this better than others."

"Okay." JT drummed her fingers on the table as she scowled. "How about this plan. Let's go back to the motel and Eddy can crash. We'll be able to see if Shay's texted and the messages were hung up because of the reception."

Rocky scraped the last of the edible slime from his cup. "I am ready to go, JT Bordeaux."

Coop stood and pushed in his chair. "Once we're outside, we can check Trip a Go Go too."

Rocky found a garbage can and deposited his cookies and cream slime transporter, as he called the cardboard bowl it'd been served in, and they bid the Stumptown Slime Convention goodbye.

The sunlight felt good on JT's face as they exited the building. The morning began gray, but now the weather was sunny and pleasantly warm, maybe seventy. She pulled her phone out of her pocket and waited for it to recalibrate from searching for a signal to locking on one. Ping, ping, ping, about twenty notifications and reminders came through as the device caught itself back up. One text was her work partner, Ty, asking if they'd made it to the convention okay, but there wasn't a single thing from Shay. "Nada." JT's heart began to beat harder, a human metronome thumping on her rib cage. Her face warmed as her anxiety level rose.

"Pulling up Trip now." Coop stepped aside to let a woman in a motorized scooter pass by.

JT finally appreciated his efforts to install the application on all their phones. Problem was, no one other than Coop was familiar with how the app worked, herself included. She hadn't really paid a whole lot of attention except for a bit of half-assed focus this morning when Coop had made sure everyone was showing up on it.

"All right!" he exclaimed after maybe a minute. "I see her."

"Where?" Eddy asked."

"Old Town Chinatown, kind of by Voodoo Doughnuts."

"Doughnuts," JT muttered, the word soothing the slight churning in her belly. "Should've known."

They hung a left on Couch. JT pulled up favorites and hit Shay's name, put the phone to her ear, and said as it rang, "I know she was looking forward to Voodoo Doughnuts, but why on Earth would she—" She cut herself off as the call kicked into voice mail. "Shay, where the hell are you? We've been looking for you for the last hour. Call me." She hung up and rapidly composed a text to her soon-to-be-dead lover.

Rocky put a hand on JT's shoulder. "Maybe Shay O'Hanlon is buying you Voodoo Doughnuts and is bringing them back as a surprise. That would be very tasty. You do not want to be angry with her then, JT."

She stuffed her phone back in her pocket. "You're right, Rocky. We'll see."

Rocky proceeded to extract his own phone. After a few seconds, he said, "My Tulip's head is kind of near the Upper Macleay Parking Lot. They must be at the evil scary place now. I will not send her a text because I want to be respectful and let her have fun with her friends."

"You're a good man, Rocky." Coop clapped him on the shoulder.

"Well," Eddy said, "the mystery is half solved. If you'll excuse me, I'm going to hightail it back to the room. Those two extra-large pops are ready to make a reappearance."

"I do not like this. My Tulip's head has been at the scary place for two hours and"—Rocky looked at his watch—"seventeen minutes. She has not texted since 11:52 a.m. when she said Scary Mary and Pretty Boy Robbie were at Taco Bell and she ordered two Nacho Cheese Doritos Loco Taco Supremes, one Chili Cheese Burrito with sour cream, and a medium Baja Blast. I knew something bad was going to happen at the scary place." He paced the width of the motel room as JT, Coop, and Eddy watched him, their heads pivoting back and forth as if they were spectators at a tennis match.

"According to the Atlas Obscura," Coop said, "the Witch—er, the scary place—is a half-mile hike into a ravine and can be approached by a different direction as well. Rocky, there's probably a bunch of hiking paths, and the three of them are likely exploring."

"But then why is my beloved Tulip's head not moving?"

Coop glanced at JT, who shrugged in a ball's-in-your-court-now-sucker kind of way. She doubted anything bad had happened to Tulip, but she wasn't about to lead poor Rocky down an unproven bunny hole. Maybe the app had a lag time, and what was supposed to be real time wasn't real at all.

Coop scrubbed his cheek. "Could be reception is as shitty down there as it is in the convention center."

"I do not know about that, Nick Coop." Rocky's voice was tight, and it sounded like he might be on the verge of a full-on meltdown. "I want to see my Tulip."

Eddy sighed. "Rocky, what if we take a Ryde to the Witch's Castle—"

Rocky slammed his hands over his ears. "Stop! Do not say it. It is the Scary Place. With capital letters. And I do not want to take a Ryde or Lyft or an Uber or a taxi to the Scary Place."

Ryde was a lot like Lyft and Uber, but not as structured and without so many rules.

"Rocky, skedoodle your butt over here." Eddy climbed off the bed. Rocky shuffled to her and she pulled him into a hug. "We'll zip over there, and you can see for yourself that Tulip is hunky dory. Okay?"

Rocky's nod into her neck was followed by a muffled, "Okay, Ms. Eddy." He pulled away and dragged his forearm across his face.

JT caught a glint of the old glitter that came into Eddy's eyes when she was on a mission, be it helping in the Rabbit Hole when it got busy or grabbing her Whacker—the Minnesota Twins mini-baseball bat she used to keep people in line when they needed to be kept in line—or breaking into a battered, old bingo barge to prove Coop hadn't murdered someone. Maybe helping Rocky would pull her out of her funk.

One could hope.

CHAPTER FOUR

Shay

The middle-aged thug reminded me of the old cartoon character Dudley Do-Right, coiffed blond hair and a jutting chin with a razor-sharp crease down the center. It would've been funny if I hadn't been so terrified.

With one arm over my shoulder like a close friend he was not, he kept the barrel of his gun pressed into my ribs as he guided me through the masses of single-minded coffee fiends to a freight elevator. Every time I thought I might be able to break away, the bastard read my mind and jabbed the gun harder into my side. He forced me to push the down button as the stench of acrid sweat rolled off him like fog on a spring morning.

The door slid open and in we went.

Duds pushed the P1 button, and the door slid closed. I frantically scanned the banged up, grease-and-sardine-smelling interior for anything potentially lifesaving. Other than the too far away emergency button, I didn't see anything helpful for my current predicament.

Pulleys and cables groaned, and too soon we were regurgitated into a below-ground parking ramp.

Initially, I'd been too stunned to take in the enormity of the situation in which I found myself. The "girl, you're in a shitload of trouble" realization became a whole lot more vivid when Dudley steered me to a dented white panel van. Oh, shit. I didn't want to become a statistic of white panel vans and murder.

"Listen, you, I'm going to let you go, but one wrong move, and bang!" He punctuated his words by trying to shove the gun barrel through my ribs.

"Ow!" I yelped. "Okay. Not moving." I considered my chances of nailing him in the nuts with a swift backward kick before he could shoot me and decided the odds were not in my favor. Sweat rolled down my back as I scanned the ramp for anyone within earshot. But as far as I could tell, I was alone with a sea of cars, tons of dirty gray concrete, and Dastardly Dudley.

He unlocked the passenger door while keeping me between his chest and the vehicle. "Open the door."

I did.

"Crawl over to the driver's seat. Try and escape and I'll introduce your ass to a little ballistic therapy."

I wasn't keen on a buttload of lead, so I clambered over the console and slid my intact behind into my assigned seat.

Fast food wrappers, empty pop bottles, and other garbage was scattered between the seats and on the floorboards. The stink of old car filled my nose along with greasy fries and remnants of cigarette smoke. The one thing missing was the pungent smell of coffee, which was weird since the vehicle belonged to Ochoco Coffee.

Trying not to look obvious, I searched for a way out of this fiasco, running possible escape plans through my head and discarding them faster than I could come up with them.

"Seat belt on." He returned the gun to my gut. "If you don't do what I tell you, when I tell you, I'll pull this trigger and decorate the inside of this crapper with your innards. If you think I'm kidding, give it a try and see what happens." He dangled the keys on a finger, and then snatched the ring away when I attempted to grab them. "One wrong move and you're toast, got it?"

"Got it," I squeaked.

Desperation hovered around the man like the cloud of dust swirling about *Peanuts* Pig Pen, and his body odor grew stronger by the minute. It was starkly obvious the trouble here was deep.

My hand shook as I started the van. He directed me out of the lot, across the Willamette River, and into downtown Portland. We passed a Voodoo Doughnut shop and under different circumstances I would've been delighted.

We rumbled by Stumptown Coffee Roasters, made a right turn at a hotel and then another right. I wondered if he was trying to confuse me, and if so, he was doing a fine job. A couple of blocks later I braked to a stop at a red light. A Chevron gas station occupied one street corner, and a parking lot the other. Bored people waiting in their cars for the gas attendants to fill their tanks were blissfully unaware a kidnapping was occurring before their very eyes. Not a soul was close enough for me to blink SOS to, even if I'd known Morse code.

Dead ahead, an arched, three-tiered, red-and-white Chinese pagoda stretched from one side of the street to the other. Four Chinese characters, probably reading "Welcome to Chinatown," were centered on the topmost tier.

"Keep going straight." He nudged me with the gun.

"Okay."

The light changed. I slowly accelerated and we passed under the pagoda. The sidewalk was lined with bright red, Chinese style streetlamps.

We drove by Charlie's Deli, another place I would've liked to try had I not literally been under the gun. I figured I should probably be working to remember what I was seeing so I could lead law enforcement back to wherever I was being taken. Assuming, of course, I'd still be alive to retrace our path. Jesus, Shay. What a bad thought to think. Keep cataloging landmarks and stop calamitizing.

A long brick, two-story building with huge red pillars—so wide I wouldn't have been able to wrap my arms entirely around them—held up an upper balcony which ran almost the entire block. It appeared the building had been divided into smaller offices or businesses, and several hexagon-shaped windows displayed For Lease signs.

We crossed a side street, and the front window of what appeared to be an ex-Chinese restaurant was blocked with white paper and a four-by-four-foot For Sale sign. Another block and a green-and-white 1950s-era neon sign that probably looked amazing when lit advertised the Republic Café. The Golden Horse Seafood Restaurant bookended one end of the block.

About ten feet before we crossed the next street, Dudley barked, "Take a left."

Around the corner we went into a narrow side street, the wheels only squealing a little bit.

"Now take a right at the end of the block."

We bounced over the rails for the Portland light rail train, and I made an awkward turn to parallel the tracks. Tall buildings lined both sides of the car-train-shared street. I felt squeezed, as if we were in a tube of toothpaste being squashed by a heavy-handed brusher.

"Left at the next intersection."

I complied. This side street was a two-way, between a multistory office complex on the right side and what appeared to be an amalgamation of three very old buildings connected to each other on my left. Five trees with trunks at least three feet in diameter, spaced evenly along the block, grew forty or fifty feet tall. Their thick leaves shaded much of the sidewalk. Someone, or maybe more than one someone, had erected a small camp on the shaded sidewalk, complete with a dome-shaped tent covered with a blue tarp.

My captor prodded my shoulder with the gun barrel. "Make a U-turn and pull over."

Real fear had burned through my initial shock, licking at the hairs on the back of my neck. I tightened my fingers on the steering wheel to stop the shaking and completed the maneuver. Maybe once we were out of the van I could make a break for it.

I jammed the shifter into park next to a squat brick building. Two Harleys were backed up against the curb in front of a viciously abused metal door. A rusted sign above the entrance read The Drunken Tankard. Why had Dudley brought me to a dumpy biker bar?

Duds didn't give three craps about my curiosity. He unceremoniously forced me to exit the van the same way I'd gotten in, by crawling over the console and passenger seat, depriving me of a ripe opportunity to escape.

Jesus Christ. How did I wind up here, backing ass first out of a white panel van in front of a derelict dive bar instead of back at the BOB, ordering coffee for my café and getting high on the aroma of roasted beans?

Stupid curiosity, that's what happened. In my head I heard Eddy, loud and clear. "Girl, you've about used up every one of your nine lives. Practice keeping your nose where it belongs once in a while. Might keep you out of a spot of trouble."

I sure hoped I had a tenth life left in me.

"Come on." Dudley poked the gun into my lower back and clamped my shoulder with clawlike fingers. "Inside."

I took a furtive glance around to see if anyone was close enough to hear my scream of bloody murder, but the area remained devoid of pedestrian traffic. And car traffic. We were in the middle of a major metropolitan city, for Pete's sake. Where was everyone?

"Move it."

We crossed the sidewalk, and I pulled open the Drunken Tankard's front door. The interior was your typical dark-in-the-day tavern, and smelled much like my father's, all stale beer and stale smoke.

Thanks to the bright light outside, until my eyes adjusted, I couldn't make out much of anything except the bar itself, which was backlit by a half-lit string of Christmas lights.

A bald bartender in a black T-shirt and a sleeveless leather vest didn't even bother to look up from whatever he was doing as we made our entrance. Another guy with a baseball hat and a handlebar mustache sat on a stool at the bar, a half-filled mug of beer on the counter and a smoldering cigarette hanging off his lip.

My eyes began to adjust. Eight square tables with sticky-looking tops were surrounded by chairs whose padding had given up the ghost about thirty-eight years ago. Five cavelike booths lined the rear of the pub. The bar's footprint left no room for a dance floor, but I doubted any of the people who frequented this juice joint came to get their boogie on anyway.

The man at the bar glanced at us, took a hard pull of his cigarette, and mashed it out in an ashtray. "What the fuck, Canavaro?"

Canavaro? Holy crap. Was my captor Randy Canavaro, owner of Ochoco Creek Coffee? I'd never seen a picture, but in the last ten years, he'd cemented his reputation as a purveyor of the finest of fine fair-trade coffees. What would a coffee man be doing in a shithole like this?

"We got ourselves a situation, Bender," the man who was apparently Randy Canavaro said. "Tim Burr is on his way here. The idiot diverted the shipment to the goddamn convention center instead of to the plant, and he needs to fix it."

"Are you fucking kidding me?"

"Wish I was."

"Jesus." Bender jerked his head at me. "Who the fuck's she?"

"Grace, here"—Canavaro rammed the gun hard into my kidney, making me grunt—"was listening through the curtain at the back of the booth to my conversation with Burr. She knocked over a stack of the misshipped crates. Earlier I'd pried the lid off a couple of boxes thinking it was coffee for the show. Oh, no. Of course it wasn't. When those goddamn crates hit the floor, ammo scattered everywhere. Couldn't exactly let her go after that."

"Fuck."

Fuck appeared to be Bender's word of choice.

"I didn't know what else to do except bring her here."

"Fuckin' A."

All forms of the word fuck appeared to be the extent of his vocabulary. Bender grabbed his mug and swallowed the last of his beer in two long glugs, then ripped a loud burp.

"We gotta do something with her before Burr gets here."

"She's your problem, Canavaro."

"No, she's our problem."

"My ass she's *our* problem." He leered at me for what felt like fifteen minutes but was probably less than fifteen seconds. "Let's dump her. We'll deal with her after we figure out how to clean up your mess."

"It wasn't my mess, it was Burr's."

I didn't like the sound of being dumped. What did dump mean? Did dump equal dead? I glanced at the bartender to see if he might be sympathetic to my case, which I hadn't even had a chance to make yet, but he'd disappeared.

"What-the-fuck ever," Bender said, and stood on the footrests on the stool to reach over the edge of the bar. "Just do it."

I wanted no part of the "just do it," but before I could mount a defense, Canavaro gave me a shove sideways.

The world dropped out from under my feet. One moment I'd been standing on warped floorboards. The next I was in freefall. A split second later I hit the ground and fell sideways, landing on my side, then skidded cheek-first to a stop.

Holy crap on a saltine, what just happened?

I spit out a mouthful of musty earth, then sucked rapid gulps of equally musty air. The side of my face was road-rashed, and my shoulder felt pulverized. If worst came to worst, I was pretty sure I'd left plenty of my DNA behind to prove I'd been here.

The dim glow from the bar stained a three-by-five-foot rectangle on the lumpy dirt floor. Above, a trapdoor swayed slowly back and forth. Then with a whomp! it somehow snapped up and shut tight, leaving me all alone, deep in the dark.

CHAPTER FIVE

JT

JT and Coop stood on the curb by the motel lobby waiting for a Ryde. According to Go Go, Shay's dot was now at a place called the Drunken Tankard, not far from Voodoo Doughnuts. Why would Shay be at a bar? If she had really wanted a drink, the convention center had a bar right on site. And why wasn't she responding to texts or phone calls? JT wasn't often quick to anger, but she was known to build up a decent head of steam when pushed far enough. Right now, righteous exasperation was winning over curiosity.

Coop gave her a sideways eye. "Deep breath, JT. You know this isn't exactly normal behavior for Shay."

"I'd feel a whole lot better if she'd text or call one of us. Why would she leave you high and dry at the Ochoco booth? Why wouldn't she let you know she was taking off, for whatever reason? Or tell me, for that matter."

He raised a bony shoulder. "She's not middle-aged yet, so it shouldn't be the inevitable midlife crisis."

"Midlife crises aren't inevitable. I don't think, anyway. I'll let you know when I get there. Is Shay's dot still at the bar?"

JT would've checked it out herself, but the Ryde app was open on her phone, and she studiously scanned traffic for a black Honda CRV. For Christ's sake, how many black Honda CRVs could there be on the road? Three had already passed them by.

"Hasn't moved."

"I have to admit, Coop, your idea to download the Trip a Go Go app was genius. If we didn't have the ability to track Shay, I'd be on the phone to the cops right now. At least we know where she is."

"You're welcome."

"Smart to the ass." JT cracked a smile as she saw a black CRV pull up to the curb. "There's our ride. Come on."

Fifteen seconds later they were strapping seat belts on in the back seat of the SUV. The driver introduced herself as Allison Mugnier, but they were told, ever so politely, to please call her Mugs. Mugs had a salt-and-pepper bob and an oval face with friendly eyes. "So, we're headed to the Drunken Tankard," Mugs said as she merged into traffic. "What are two nice kids like yourselves doing going to hog heaven?"

"It's a biker bar?" JT barked a laugh. Any other time, she would've thought the woman kind of nosy, but right now she was simply happy to have the information.

"Should've known by the name," Coop said. "We think a friend's there, and we need to get her back."

"Well, sounds like a good quest. We'll be over the Burnside Bridge into Old Town Chinatown in no time. Where y'all from? I'm a transplant from Galveston."

"Minnesota," Coop told her. "Minneapolis."

"Ah, yes. Home of the killer mosquito, ten-foot snow drifts, the Twins, and a cherry in a spoon. I was there one year for a book convention. The Golden Crown Literary Society. Ever heard of it?"

"No," Coop said. "What kind of book convention is it?"

JT tuned out while Coop and the driver talked books and conventions and awards. What was going on with her lover? Coop was right when he said it was out of character for Shay to disappear. Maybe she had a good reason. But was there really any good reason for Shay to leave her bestie hanging high and dry at the Ochoco booth? JT clenched her teeth as she ran potential scenarios through her head which might explain what the hell was going on.

In less than six minutes, they pulled up behind a white Ochoco Creek Coffee van parked in front of the Drunken Tankard. That must have been Shay's ride. Relief flooded JT's veins.

"Here you go." Mugs peered at them through the rearview, her eyes clouded with concern. "You want me to wait while you see if your friend is there?"

JT glanced at Coop, who gave her a thumbs-up. "That'd be great, if you don't mind."

"No problem at all. Give me a chance to do a little reading. Go find your wayward pal." Allison settled back in the seat and pulled a book out from the side of the door. The red cover with a double-barrel shotgun and fluttering money caught JT's eye. "What's it about?"

"It's a caper series. The main character and her quirky crew always wind up with a little murder and a lot of big trouble."

JT laughed. "Sounds like my life." She elbowed Coop. "Out. Let's go fetch Miss Sassy Pants."

They extracted themselves from the SUV. JT did a quick perusal of the area. Not much going on outside of the bar. Down at the far end of the block, a couple of Caucasian bangers loitered at the intersection, all baggy white T-shirts, low-riding, oversized jeans, and red, flat-brimmed, snapback hats. She caught the tail end of a lightning-fast transaction between one of them and a passerby, a transaction she'd have missed had she not been a cop. She wondered what the current drug du jour was out here. Probably heroin, fentanyl, oxy. Pervasive and deadly.

Down on the other end of the block, a homeless person had pitched a tent on the boulevard and part of the sidewalk, and three people hustled past on the opposite side of the street.

That ingrained situational awareness took less than the ten seconds it took to follow Coop into the seedy interior of the bar. The door swung shut with a hollow thud and JT almost ran Coop over when he stopped, probably to let his eyes adapt to the dim interior. The familiar, every-bar scent enveloped her like tendrils of steam escaping from behind a shower curtain.

Most of the ambient light came from a partially lit set of holiday lights strung up around the liquor shelves behind the bar. A bartender slouched between the booze and the bar, eyes on his phone. He glanced up at their arrival, then back at whatever app had his attention.

A couple of men, one in a T-shirt, jeans and a baseball hat; the other in a suit—a little odd, JT thought, for a dump like this—sat at the far end of the bar in quiet, intense conversation. Intense conversation in bars, especially dive bars, always put JT on edge. Probably from all the time she'd spent in uniform responding to countless Minneapolis bar fights before she made her detective's badge.

Baseball yanked the hat off his head and swatted it against the edge of the bar.

JT stiffened.

Suit held up both hands and said something that appeared to calm the other man. Baseball ran a hand through stringy dark hair, slammed the hat back on top of his head, and the conversation continued.

"I don't see Shay," Coop whispered.

She pried her attention from the two men. "Me either." JT expected her wayward girl to be sitting at the bar or maybe chilling at one of the tables. She blew out an irked breath. "Come on." She took the lead and crossed the floor, Coop in her wake. The anxious buzz at the base of her skull that'd begun when Coop found her at the Slime convention buzzed harder.

"Hey," she said to the liquor slinger, "I'm looking for a friend. She's about five-eight, spiky black hair, midthirties. She was at the coffee convention and the Ochoco Creek Coffee van is parked right outside."

The bartender peered up at JT from under heavy brows. "Coffee convention? Ain't no coffee here. Look like I got a drop of coffee here? And I ain't seen no one fitting that description."

"So weird," Coop said. "Mind if we check the restrooms?"

"Knock yourself out."

Coop and JT made their way toward the rear of the bar, past Baseball and Suit, into the only hallway in the place. "If she's not in the women's, Coop, you can check the men's."

"I gotta drain the main vein, anyway. I'll take a gander right now."

"Some manners you got there, stud."

He gave her a friendly flip-off and headed for the john.

JT followed him down the corridor, which was appropriately dark for a dumpy watering hole. The walls were painted black like the rest of the of the establishment's vertical surfaces. One way to keep the grime from showing.

A door on the left was closed. Two doors on the right had sign plates attached, one for DICKS and one for CHICKS.

Coop paused in front of DICKS and groaned. "Seriously?"

"Looks like that's where dicks drain their main veins. Meet you back here in two and two." She pushed open the Chicks and grimaced. The three-hole restroom smelled like fifty years of inebriated patrons, poor aim, and not enough cleaning product. She knocked the stall doors open with a foot. No Shay, only toilets begging for a good scouring. "Goddamn it," JT muttered and made a fast retreat. No sense in staying when the struggle to breathe was real.

A minute later, Coop emerged. He took one look at JT and said, "Zero sum game. What now?"

"I want to take a quick look in there." She jerked her thumb toward the end of the hall where a set of chest-high saloon doors blocked the view into another room. "Cover me?"

"Got it."

JT scooted to the chin-level doors and cautiously peered over, not wanting an awkward conversation with anyone who might be within. Didn't matter because no one was in the twenty-by-twenty-foot space, which was the bar's kitchen/ storage area.

In she went.

A triple sink with grimy stainless counters on both sides occupied one wall. An ancient cage elevator took up half of another. The metal making up the cage of the mechanized conveyor was rusty, and the entire thing looked like a very bad idea. The rest of the kitchen held two microwaves, an AutoFry machine, an oversized toaster oven, two big white commercial fridge/freezers, and a four-shelf metal rack loaded with liquor bottles. Behind the rack was a door that probably led to an alley.

A panicky ache settled into JT's chest as she hustled out. Where on Mother Earth was Shay? Maybe Coop's fancy app wasn't working right, and she was really back at the coffee convention wondering where the rest of her tribe had gone.

She gave her head a shake at the question expressed by his raised brow. "Let's go. She's not here. Maybe Go Go isn't working right."

The bright light was stunning after the drear they left behind. The heat of the sun felt like walking into heaven. JT was relieved to see Mugs and her CRV still idling at the curb.

"Hang on," Coop said, "before we go, I wanna check the app one more time. The people I know who've used it and the reviews I researched had nothing but good things to say." He thumbed the screen open. "No talk about glitches. But then again, you never know."

JT shaded her eyes as she watched the app open. The dots representing each of them popped up on the screen as GPS locked onto their locations. Rocky's and Eddy's were in the area of the Witch's Castle. JT's and Coop's appeared right where they stood.

"That's odd." Coop tapped the screen. "Where'd Shay go?"

JT leaned closer. Nowhere on the three-by-six screen was a dot representing Shay. "And where's Lisa?" She hadn't thought about Lisa all day, probably because she'd gone off on her own so early before the rest of them got up. But now, the Lisa dot was as absent as Shay's. "Maybe it's a problem with their phones?"

"Who knows."

"Come on, let's go back to the motel." She took a step toward their ride.

"Guess I should've done more field testing before—wait!" Coop's voice rose. "Look. There's Shay's dot."

About-face. Sure enough, no more than a block away. "Jesus

Christ." Irritation overran the anxiousness swamping her head. Shay was going to have some fast talking to do when they caught up with her. She stomped over to the passenger side of the SUV.

Mugs lowered the window.

"It looks like we're on a bit of a wild Shay chase. She's down the block, and we might as well hike it and not keep you tied up."

"No problem." Mugs handed JT a business card. "If you need a ride, give me a buzz or shoot me a text. If I'm free I can swing by and grab you guys."

JT tapped the card twice on the doorframe in appreciation. "We'll do that." She stepped away from the vehicle. Mugs pulled out and cruised down the block.

"Come on, Coop. Let's go find your best bud and my wayward girlfriend."

CHAPTER SIX

Eddy

"Thank you, Niccolo, for the ride."

"You are most welcome, Miss Quartermaine. Are you sure you would not like me to stay and wait for you? I am not fond of leaving you here." The driver waved his arm over the dash. "So far away from the city."

"I got my phone and can call another Ryde when we're done. There's no sense in you wasting your time and not making money when we don't even know how long we're going to be. 'Sides, we're only ten minutes from town."

Niccolo's expression was downright crestfallen. "If you say so, my dear." Then he brightened. "Please do not forget to stop by my cousin's restaurant, the Mad Greek Deli, on Burnside. Tell him Niccolo sent you. He will take very good care of you."

"Darn tootin' I will." Eddy scrambled out of the back seat after Rocky. "You be safe out there, okay?"

"Yes, ma'am, I certainly will."

Niccolo turned his car around and waved as he left. Four other vehicles occupied the narrow dirt lot, but no one was around. Eddy opened the Ryde app and tipped their very Greek, very concerned, chauffeur.

"Oh! Ms. Eddy, look!" Rocky grabbed her hand, hauling her beyond the lot to an eight-foot-wide, well-tended trailhead. A weathered, split-log fence corralled absent-minded hikers and kept them from toppling over the edge of the ravine. A waist-high post next to the trail held rectangular, olive-green directional signs. The top one read Forest Park. Wildwood Trail was listed below it, with arrows pointing in either direction. Then, underneath Wildwood in smaller letters, another sign indicated the Stone House, better known as the Witch's Castle, was to the left. Under that, Pittock Mansion was somewhere off to the right. The bottom sign indicated the direction to the Portland Audubon Society.

Eddy pivoted from the signage and studied the trail. "Well, doesn't look too bad for these old legs to navigate."

"No, Ms. Eddy, it does not look too bad. The path is only one half mile into the gorge. And to my Tulip. We must go now." And off he went.

"I sure hope it's a nice gentle half mile," she mumbled, relieved to see Rocky seemed to have put his fear of the Witch's Castle on the back burner in his quest to find his mate. "Hey, wait for me."

Eddy caught up to him as the dirt-mixed gravel trail descended at a reasonable decline, disappearing as it curved to the right. She was stunned by the incredible variety of greens and endless shades of brown. Leaves, ferns, and multitudes of mosses ran the verdant spectrum. Tree trunks so dark they appeared black contrasted with washed-out lumber used for safety railings and shoring where winter rain had washed out the trail.

Lichen grew like an invasive species on almost everything. It covered rocks and exposed roots, flourished on the bark of trees so tall they made Eddy dizzy. Three-foot-tall ferns sprouted out of the steep hillside like strangely shaped hair combs. The nearly impenetrable leaf canopy did a good job of shielding the sun, although Eddy could feel the humidity rise the deeper they descended.

"Ms. Eddy, it is like we are entering Jurassic Park. Maybe we will find a dinosaur along with my beloved Tulip."

"You never know, Rocky. You just never know."

The path grew steeper and more uneven as they navigated a couple of switchbacks. Eddy's chest burned with each rapid inhale, and Rocky breathed heavily even though they were headed downhill. The steepish grade was more of a workout than Eddy had anticipated. Tree roots jutted up through the hardpacked soil, and rocks of various sizes made walking a real effort. Eddy took care to watch her footing, and she kept a sharp eye on Rocky. It'd be a heck of a note to take a header on a rescue mission.

"Ms. Eddy?" Rocky sucked air. "Did you know there's at least"—pant—"thirty invasive plant species causing very"—pant—"great concern in Forest Park? That is where we are now."

"No, child." Good Lord, when did he look up invasive plants?

"Most dangerous, poison hemlock." Rocky continued to pause every few words to refresh his oxygen levels, then he stopped his forward movement altogether. They caught their breath, and then he said, "Did you know back in the ancient days of Greece and the Roman Empire, when someone was sentenced to death, they could be forced to drink a potion made of hemlock? Socrates did. Do you know who Socrates is, Ms. Eddy?"

"Some ancient smart guy, I think."

"Yes, he was a very smart ancient guy. He was a philosopher."

"Gotta think too much for that job."

As they continued downward, the oppressive air and the feeling of almost complete envelopment by all things overgrown ratcheted up Eddy's already heightened sense of unease. Sure, Minnesota had plenty of forests, and there had to be a million trees in Minneapolis itself. But anything back home paled in comparison to the height and breadth of the behemoths here. Trees with trunks a mile in diameter grew ten miles high. Probably, Eddy figured, because of all the rain the Pacific Northwest was subject to.

Snatches of blue sky peeked through layers of branches and leaves, and the sight made her feel fractionally better.

Then there was the damn moss. She couldn't get over the moss. It lived on everything and frankly, the feathery and sometimes slimy stuff freaked her out. Calm down, old woman. Hold it together for Rocky.

A few steps ahead of her, his eyes were glued to the ground, his face set in that stubborn expression which meant he was all business.

The steepness of the gorge walls varied from mild to a sheer cliff. In places, the trail narrowed to only a few feet across, and that fired her heart right up until the trail widened again. Occasionally, branches and leaves from nearby trees and brush created what amounted to a tunnel over the path itself, dimming the ambient light even more as they passed through. Good thing neither she nor Rocky had claustrophobia or a major fear of heights.

Rocky remained silent, intent on getting to the destination. As long as he was calm, Eddy could live with his unusual absence of chatter. Other than the crunch of gravel under their shoes, all she heard were their sharp inhales and exhales, and chirping birds. No breeze, just hellish, soggy air. Sweat beaded on her forehead.

Far below, she glimpsed a creek at the bottom of the ravine. It wasn't large by any measure, varying from six to maybe twenty feet across. Dirty water flowed at a leisurely pace, but they were still too far away from its gurgle to reach them.

Approximately twenty-three thousand switchbacks later, they arrived safely at the bottom. Eddy refrained from dropping to her knees and kissing the dirt only because she figured she wouldn't be able to get up again.

Once they caught their breaths, Rocky said, "We made it, Ms. Eddy!"

"That we did, child. I wonder how much farther this gosh darned castle is."

"It cannot be too far, Ms. Eddy. We must go over the bridge up there to the other side and keep following the trail."

The only way to ford the stream was via a newish bridge about thirty feet dead ahead. Newish because moss hadn't engulfed it.

Yet.

The burble of the creek was now much louder. Access to the stream itself was an iffy proposition, which, Eddy thought, might not be a bad thing. In some places, footpaths from the main trail led to the water, and she wondered what people did that close to the murky liquid. No way did she want to get anywhere near it.

The damp clung to her skin and her clothes, chilly and clammy. Gloom saturated her neurons, and she was sure she'd never see the sun again. She shook herself back into the moment and concentrated on keeping up with Rocky. He usually traipsed along slowly, enjoying the experience of the journey, but now that they were on level-ish ground, he was full steam ahead, intent on finding his wife.

They passed fallen timber in various states of decomposition. Ashes to ashes, dust to dust and all that jazz. Eddy couldn't get over the circumference of the logs. At one point a fallen tree, wider in diameter than she was tall and so long she couldn't see where it began or ended had blocked the path. To allow hikers passage, someone had chainsawed a chunk out of the trunk the width of the trail. Paul Bunyan, the Popeye of Lumberjacks, and his colossal blue ox, Babe, must've been called in to lend a hand.

The air was heavy. Each breath felt like inhaled glue tinged with the taste of musty earth. Eddy wondered when she would ever fully catch her breath again.

The trail continued to parallel the creek, rolling gently up and down like a kiddie coaster. Multitudes of trees had fallen, all in various states of decomposition. So much timber. So much kindling if things ever dried out down here. Some of the logs rested in the creek bed itself, and others were so enormous they bridged the entire width of the stream, bare of bark and worn shiny from adventurous feet.

Eddy wondered what would bring down so much of the forest in a land without tornados. She passed by yet another woody victim. The trunk, near the roots, was full of holes. Either a woodpecker the size of a small child or something far more sinister was going on from within. Maybe that was part of the problem.

They trekked upward once again, but this time, appearing between the trees, the ferns, the brush, and the undergrowth, was a corner of a moss-coated, man-made structure. If she hadn't known what she was looking for, she might have missed it entirely, because, at least at the angle from which they approached, it blended right in with the landscape.

"Look, Ms. Eddy!" Rocky pointed in the building's general direction. "We have made it!"

Twenty feet ahead, the trail narrowed. Exposed tree roots became a makeshift stairway leading to what could only be the infamous Witch's Castle.

CHAPTER SEVEN

Shay

I tried to shut out the almost immediate grip of holy-shit-I-can't-see-a-damn-thing-in-the-dark claustrophobia and groped in my pocket for my cell phone. My thumb found the circular button on the bottom, and it lit up. For a tenth of a second, relief slithered through me until I realized the light was shining through a completely shattered screen. I'd seen cracks before, but this looked like a mini windshield some aggressive woodland sprite had used as a trampoline. I jabbed the home button, tried to swipe around, but the glow behind the cobwebbed glass didn't even flicker. On the bright side, pun intended, the phone did emit enough light I could see about a foot in front of my nose, which was better than drowning in inky nothingness.

Up above, Canavaro and Bender's loud, furious voices seeped through the floor, but I couldn't make out much of what was being said. I pulled my wits together, got my feet under me, and stood. The adrenaline drop after the adrenaline dump made me feel like a wobbly bobblehead.

As I strained to catch even some of the argument, I rotated my sore shoulder a few times. Nothing broken or dislocated. Here and there a "Fuck you" was flung, and a "You fix it, dumbass" was returned, but I couldn't follow the convo close enough to clue me in on how I ended up, scuffed and traumatized, in the Drunken Tankard's basement.

I moved closer to the trapdoor that had done me wrong and tried to recall exactly what had occurred at BOB. What had I seen before my eyes crossed as I tried to focus on the sudden application of a gun barrel to my forehead?

Stacks of coffee crates with Flying High Coffee logos when I'd expected to see the Ochoco Creek brand. The flood of ammo spilling out in the back room of the Ochoco booth, rolling every which way across the floor after my spectacular header. And Randy Canavaro. The face of Ochoco Coffee as apparently seen on TV channels up and down the West Coast, between afternoon soaps and the nightly news, hawking his incredibly fair-trade java.

The ammunition had to be the issue. It was packed in Flying High containers, and Canavaro had mentioned a shipment of some sort had been diverted accidentally. All of this had to be connected to Canavaro, or I wouldn't have landed headfirst in the dungeon. Someone, or maybe someones, was supplementing their paychecks by smuggling ammunition. And what? Selling it? To whom? No one with a reputable track record. How did they get a hold of that much ammo? Too many questions with no answers.

A sudden lack of arguing brought me back to my new, dark, and very stark reality. I didn't know how long I'd been contemplating the uncontemplatable. I strained for long minutes to pick up any additional conversation over the roar of nothingness. Amazing how loud nothing could be.

Eventually, the floorboards overhead groaned, and faint footsteps grew louder. Bender's gruff speech sliced the silence like a blade. An unfamiliar voice rambled for some seconds and then Canavaro cut them off, his tone decidedly unfriendly.

Probably the guy who'd screwed up the coffee delivery. I sure wouldn't want to be him. The garbled sound of their exchange was like listening to the "wha wha wha" of adults talking in a *Peanuts* television special.

Round and round they went, until two sharp explosions made me reflexively duck. Then I scuttled backward until I banged into something unmovable and could go no further. Shouting of a more intense nature commenced, and the trapdoor fell again.

"Timberrrrrr, you asshole!" Bender hollered.

A body dropped through the opening and landed with a dampened thud in the space I'd occupied only moments before. Holy shit, I could've been a smashed potato.

"Canavaro," Bender bellowed, "this fuck-up is going to end everything. Jesus fucking Christ. Go back to the convention center and get the ammo out of there."

Canavaro said something I couldn't make out.

"And hurry the fuck up. We have to take care of that girl and now, Burr. Goddamn collateral damage."

It was surprising what my mind processed in a fraction of a second. Those assholes planned on taking care of me. What did that mean? Haul me somewhere far away and release me in the wilderness like a no-longer-wanted four-legged creature? That scenario beat their other, more probable choice: silence me like they silenced Mr. Burr. But, before anything would happen, Canavaro needed to take care of the mess I caused, theoretically buying me some time to figure out how to get myself out of this. For once it was a good thing I was proficient at making messes.

The dim light shining through the opening cast a casket-shaped spotlight on my fellow captive, who lay crumpled, the upper half of his body face up, hips and legs twisted awkwardly sideways. He was probably nudging forty, with sandy hair and a scruffy beard, clad in a gray T-shirt, blue jeans, and dusty, worn-at-the-heel work boots. The front of his shirt had two dark, not-quite-circular holes at chest level. I didn't want to think about what the other side might look like.

Oh, my god. Bullet holes? They could be deadly. Was this really happening? I scrubbed my eyes and when I opened them, Burr still lay splatted on the ground. I tried not to hyperventilate.

The assessment of my lack of air, and the unfortunate man before me, was cut short as the trapdoor reversed course and banged shut. The abrupt change from light to dark once again left me with nothing but a rectangular afterimage flickering on the back of my eyelids.

The phone was still clenched in my hand, and I lit up the screen again. In its weak glow, I was able to ascertain my new captive buddy hadn't budged.

At all.

Well, crapola. No one else was down here to help Sir Scruffs-A-Lot except me. As JT could attest, I was no nurse. But any first aid I could offer was better than none. Unless he was already dead.

I resolutely dropped to my knees beside him. "Hey." I gingerly laid a hand on his shoulder and gave him a shake. "You okay?"

Scruff didn't twitch, so I did what I saw the cops do on Eddy's crime shows and laid two fingers on the side of his neck. His skin was surprisingly warm. After a couple of seconds of not feeling any thumping, I readjusted, then checked a couple more spots. This dude might actually be of the no longer living.

A list of all-too-descriptive words spun through my horrified brain. Expired. Croaked. Bought the farm. Cashed it in. Soon to be a real stiff.

I yanked my hand away faster than a crab trying to escape a boiling pot of water at Red Lobster.

Now I was in really, honestly, truly a shit-ton of trouble. I'd witnessed a murder. Or heard it, anyway. Hearing a homicide probably trumped seeing ammunition scattered all over the convention floor. Canavaro and Bender knew I was down here and knew I was now hanging out with a body. A body one of them had made dead. The knowledge made me even more expendable than I'd been before.

As much as every fiber of my being yowled to get the freak out, I remained crouched at my new, albeit lifeless, buddy's side. My barely there light bathed the upper part of Scruff as panic squeezed my intestines. I thought Bender had yelled, "Timber, you asshole," but now that I could actually form half a solid thought, I realized he was referring to Tim Burr, the guy he'd mentioned earlier. Tim's screw-up called for capital punishment.

What the flying fuck-a-roo did I manage to get myself caught up in this time? I dragged a forearm across my eyes and winced when I hit the dirt-burn on my face. Get your shit shipshape, Shay. Stay in the moment. How long did I have before they came to gather me up? Panic welled, burbling from my stomach into my throat.

Since Scotty wasn't about to beam me up and transport me to a distant galaxy, I was on my own. What next steps could I take to insure longevity in my life?

I needed a light. And a weapon. A place to hide and figure out how to extract myself from whatever this was without getting killed.

These days most people carried cell phones. Most of those cell phones had a flashlight. Odds were, Timmy boy had a cell on him right now. Unless those two carbuncles on a mule's derriere relieved him of it before delivering him to me.

No way to know without looking. That meant touching him again. I swallowed with difficulty and laid my phone with its dim glow on the hard-packed earth—some light was unequivocally better than none down here in the dungeon—and gingerly patted the three easily available pockets on his jeans. Nothing in his right hip pocket or back pockets. Last hope was his other front pocket.

I studied the situation and realized I needed to rearrange him to access my last hope, something I really didn't want to do. But if he had a cell, I needed it way more than he did. Then another thought gave me pause. What were the odds the device wasn't passcoded? Not good. But it probably had a flashlight I could get to. Even if I couldn't access the flashlight, I was pretty sure I'd be able to call 911 without having to unlock it. Wouldn't that be one hell of a conversation?

"9-1-1, what is your emergency?"

"I've been kidnapped."

"Where are you?"

"I have no idea. Well, in the basement of a bar, actually."

"What's the name of the bar?"

"The Drunken something."

"Are you injured?"

"No. Well, I have facial road rash. And I think my shoulder is out of whack. Oh, and there's a dead body down here with me."

"How much have you had to drink today at the Drunken bar, ma'am?"

Jesus. Bottom line? If he indeed had a cell and it hadn't broken like mine when he hit the dirt, I'd guard it with my life like Gollum guarded his Precious.

I gazed grimly at Sir Tim Scruffs-A-Lot, sent an apology into the ether, and tried to push his hip toward the ground. Holy mac and cheese, this guy's legs were the definition of dead weight. I wondered what the charge was for messing with a corpse. It wasn't like I was desecrating or damaging his person, only borrowing something he was no longer going to use. I'd be happy to confess all my sins—well, most of them, anyway—as soon I was out of here and miles away from the murderous duo above.

After a couple of go-rounds, I managed to wrestle Tim Burr's legs straight and he flopped onto his back. I whispered apologies and tried not to look at his face, but my eyes were drawn to it. Poor sod had a surprised, wide-eyed, slack-mouthed expression. I imagined being shot by your evil business partners would certainly come as quite a shock. Before I got carried away thinking about what good ole Tim's last moments might've been like, I retrieved my phone and zeroed its glow on his left front pocket. A rectangular object about the correct size and shape pushed up the denim.

Jackpot.

Unless it was a pack of smokes. Christ, that'd be just my luck. Gingerly, I dove in and withdrew a battered but bullet-hole-free iPhone. "Oh god, yes," I muttered, relieved the item—still warm from Tim Burr's now-cooling body—was a cell phone I was familiar with.

"Sorry to manhandle you." I gingerly gave Tim's knee a pat. "Thanks for the help."

I pocketed my phone and turned my attention to Tim's. With a touch of the home button, the screen blazed to life, asking for a passcode. Well, that wasn't nice.

The time was 1:32 p.m., the cell was at seventy-six percent battery life, and, of course, since nothing was going to be easy, it had no service. Just in case, I held it up to Tim's stunned face. Ziporola. Too old for facial recognition.

"Of course," I muttered, then tried swiping down. That didn't work. Up then. The utility screen slid into view, and the knot in my stomach eased the tiniest bit. I could now turn the Wi-Fi and Bluetooth off and on, raise and lower the volume, pull up the calculator if I cared to calculate my chances of escape. And there, on the bottom right corner was exactly what I was searching for. The flashlight icon.

I lit it up and got my first real glimpse of my surroundings. It was the weirdest basement I'd ever seen. Tim and I were alone in what was basically a room with three walls, maybe twelve feet across by twenty deep. Two of the three walls were made of rough-hewn, concrete-block-sized stones oozing ancient, crumbling mortar. The back wall was comprised of what looked like mud, and dead in the center of the mud wall was a vertically barred window. What? I sidled over and inspected the window. Yup. Bars. Like prison bars? They were square, set so closely together I could hardly squeeze the end of my pinkie through them. Thankfully the room only had three walls.

The missing side of the room was entirely open, no crumbled bits of the wall scattered on the ground, at least as far as I could see, which wasn't much. My light wasn't powerful enough to penetrate more than four feet into the black nothingness.

This whole basement was weird. No weirder, I supposed, than two people unexpectedly dropped through the floor of a bar. Doofus and Roofus were doing a good job of keeping Portland weird.

I shined the light at the ceiling. From where I stood, it was about four feet above my head, made up of planks and cross-timbers darkened by years of dry, stale air. Pretty much looked like any unfinished basement from 1792.

Dust-coated wires and cobweb-covered metal pipes of various diameters snaked overhead. Some of the tangle was fed through holes drilled in load-bearing beams. Below the ancient, interwoven mess, newer ductwork, shinier pipes, and more modern wiring had been installed.

I aimed the light at the trapdoor above Tim. The door was framed with battered two-by-fours so dark they were nearly black. I wondered if the tricky trapdoor was used to access the basement to store booze or other tavern necessities. Or maybe it was a way to get drunks out of the bar and into a place they could sober up without bothering the rest of the patrons. I shuddered. That was a creepy thought. Could explain the barred window, though. But not the entirely missing fourth wall.

Well, if that trapdoor was the way down, there obviously had to be a way up and out of this dungeon. Just needed to find it.

Dust or something less benign floated in the beam of Tim's light. If I didn't die at the hands of Bender and Canavaro, lung cancer from whatever toxins were flying around would probably take me out. I ignored whatever I was inhaling and concentrated on the other side of the prison window.

I wandered back to the window and aimed the flashlight through the bars. I could barely make out a room, almost completely trashed, no more than eight feet by ten. A floor-to-ceiling, three-level bunk had been constructed against one wall. A plank floor at one time covered the dirt, but years or vandals had pried up much of it. Either that or the earth directly below the suffocatingly small room had somehow undulated like a mini tidal wave, heaving up the floorboards and somehow splitting them into dangerous-looking shards. Some of the jagged splinters were as long as my arm. If nothing else, I could use one as a giant needle and jab it through my captors, like a friend who made a hobby of skewering wood ticks with a safety pin. When the pin was full up, she'd brandish her carcass keepsakes as if they were crucifixes to keep evil spirits at bay.

My light reflected off a rusting milk can and then caught the remnants of a chair. Other than decades of thick dust on every surface, and strings of cobwebs floating on periodic currents of swirling air, there wasn't much to see. At least the air was circulating even if I couldn't feel it.

Wait a minute. I flashed the light around one more time. Other than the barred window I'd peered through, none of the room's three walls had a door. When the fourth wall had existed, it hopefully held a door out of there. Or maybe people were left in there to die. Goosebumps hovering below the surface of my skin came to full attention. As intriguing as it might be in the moment, this bit of weirdness was a puzzle for another day. I needed to hunt down an escape route and get the hell out of the past.

I cautiously skirted the newly departed. "Hey, Tim, sorry to leave you here all by yourself, but, somehow I don't think you'll mind."

Tim didn't answer, which brought the reality of the situation full circle. The basement felt like a haunted house. On one hand, in light of this potential jail cell, plenty of other ghosts probably hung out down here—a thought which doubled my goosebumps—so I doubted good old Tim would be lonely. On the other hand, I wanted to remain alive and kicking, which meant I better figure shit out so I didn't wind up a lonely, murdered phantom aimlessly wandering subterranean Portland for all eternity.

CHAPTER EIGHT

Eddy

"We have indeed arrived." Eddy paused at the base of the makeshift root steps to catch her breath. The closer they'd come to their destination, the more foreboding the whole thing felt. She shoved her worry away. Here and now, Eddy, here and now.

"I must find my Tulip, Ms. Eddy." Rocky scrambled up the incline and disappeared.

Eddy blew out a heavy breath and rubbed her aching back. She was getting too old for traipsing around the countryside, and she needed a drink. For once Coke or Red Bull wasn't top of mind. Plain old water sounded like nectar of the gods. Preferably with ice. She felt wide awake for the first time in a long time, and by god, she didn't have to pee. She marched over to the steps nature had created and made her way upward.

Once she cleared the stairs, she entered a thirty-by-fifty-foot clearing. From her initial vantage, what had looked like a mirage was instead a crumbling two-story, hand-chiseled stone edifice. The building appeared to be on its last foundational leg, yet was alive with moss, lichen, plant life, and people.

The location would be a perfect setting for a horror movie. What was left of the decaying mess did look like a roofless mini castle, complete with a walkout patio which could double as a stage. To the right of the open patio, a shedlike appendage was set back about five feet from the front of the main structure, and a door-sized portal led into an inky black beyond. Reddish fog billowed out of the opening and the acrid odor of a smoke bomb wafted lazily in the heavy air.

A staircase to the second floor spanned the top of the shed and served as its angled roof. Stone steps were worn in the center from countless feet traipsing up to an arched doorway on the second level. The door itself had long ago been consumed by nature. From the number of hikers taking their lives into their own hands and wandering around up there, the floor itself must be intact.

Another staircase—a switchback—was located on the left-hand side of the castle. It led to another arched doorway which also accessed the second floor.

A modern-ish double railing made of two-inch metal pipes kept star-struck adventurers from taking a header onto the patio below. With the steeply pitched roof missing and only half the back wall left, the rest of the second story was comprised of two parallel, triangular walls jutting skyward as if in supplication to the heavens.

Back on the ground, the centralized, fifteen-foot-wide patio extended maybe eight feet into the building. Graffiti filled the interior.

The entire edifice was maybe the size of three rooms back at the Eastside Lodge. The green ivy encasing much of the building softened its hard edges and gave the whole shebang an ethereal feeling. Which fit right in with the shenanigans of two almost identical-appearing girls—neither Tulip nor Mary—who were in the middle of some kind of photo shoot. They matched all the way from mid-length, platinum blond hair to their black blouses, black miniskirts, and the black Doc Martens on their feet. The only difference Eddy could see between the two were the fishnet stockings encasing one set of legs. They'd covered much of their ensembles with long black capes. A couple of modern-day witch wannabes.

A man wearing a photographer's vest hefted a dinner-plate-sized camera and snapped pictures so fast it sounded like machine gun fire. The girls sat cross-legged inside the stage, holding between them a crystal ball, much like the one the Wicked Witch of the West used to track Dorothy.

Eddy caught another snootful of the acrid smoke and wrinkled her nose. She wasn't fond of the stench a smoke bomb gave off. But it did pep up the supernatural ambiance. On the ground behind her, a couple of two-foot-wide, fallen trees were arranged in an L-shape to hem in the area and keep the bewitched from tumbling down the embankment into the stream ten feet below.

The trail she and Rocky had been following resumed on the other side of the clearing and disappeared into the forest.

"Ms. Eddy, come up here!" Rocky sounded positively panicky as he leaned over the railing on the second story and frantically waved. "Hurry!"

Eddy's heart tripped. "I'll be right there." She envisioned Tulip, knocked unconscious thanks to a dislodged rock from the steep slope, or maybe taken down by some other unfortunate, grievous mishap. Eddy tore herself away from the *Blair Witch Project* redux and made her way up the set of switchback stairs. Black moss had taken up residence in the cracks and crevices of the three-foot walls on either side of the steps, and she stuffed her hands in her pockets so she wouldn't accidentally catch something from the fungi or whatever made up the black menace.

At the top, she crossed through the arched opening onto a dirt-and-rubble-covered floor.

Rocky nearly tackled her. "Look, Ms. Eddy, look," he screeched, waving his phone in her face. His eyes were wide and his face a strange shade of red.

"I can't see a thing if you don't stop octopussing." She grabbed the trembling hand holding the phone and stilled it. "What's the fire?"

"This!" He jabbed a finger from his free hand at the screen.

"Rocky." Eddy put her palms on his shoulders. "Take a deep breath, like we practiced."

He pressed his lips together and sucked air through his nose. The more he inhaled the wider his eyes grew. Then he huffed out and his shoulders dropped.

"That's better. Now tell me what's going on."

"Ms. Eddy, Tulip is not here. She is not down there. She is not in the tiny scary room full of smoke. I looked." He bounced up and down on his toes.

"Rocky, you gotta stop flopping around. I'm getting seasick." She grabbed the cell and tried to pry it out of his grasp, afraid he might accidentally clobber her smack-dab in the face in his fear-based frenzy. After a brief tug-of-war, Eddy persevered, and glimpsed the screen. The Trip a Go Go app was up, and Tulip's dot blinked, unmoving, not far from the steady dot pinpointing the location where she and Rocky stood. At least it appeared as if they could reach out and touch her. But, in this junglelike maze of a forest, who knew how far away she might actually be?

"Ms. Eddy, I thought she was"—Rocky stomped a foot—"right here. Her dot is not right here. I knew those two friends of hers were no good, very bad people." His eyes welled up, and his lower lip trembled. When he got an idea in his head, his stubborn side emerged like a pissed-off grizzly awakened before his hibernation alarm clock rang. Trying to reason with him while he was in bear mode was a difficult prospect.

"You don't know anything's happened to Tulip. Those kids are probably all right where her dot is, and she's busy appreciating the insect population or something. Let's check again."

She shifted to stand beside him so they could both see the screen. From the look of it, Rocky's dot and her own appeared, as expected, exactly where they were standing. Tulip's flashing dot hadn't moved, which was a comforting thing. The last thing she wanted was to try and chase three much younger sets of legs around the steep slope.

"Here's what we're going to do, Rocky. We'll head that way"—she pivoted to face the ruinous back wall—"up there, which should bring us to Tulip. She can't be too far away."

Hopefully in a few minutes they'd hunt down those three honyockers and poor Rocky could stop panicking.

"Okay, Ms. Eddy." Rocky rubbed his eyes with his fists. "I like the plan." He held his hand out and Eddy returned his phone. He peered at it a moment. "We must go now." With that, he hustled out the opposite door and down the short stairway faster than she could get her own keister in gear.

CHAPTER NINE

Shay

I exited the Drop Room, as I'd begun to think of it. The pitch black surrounded me like slime, oozy and fully encapsulating. The ooze made me think of JT and her newfound slime interest, and Eddy, my dad, and the rest of my friends, friends who were my family too. What if I never saw them again? What if I died a lonely, dusty, dastardly death down here in the dungeon? Stop it, I ordered myself. The only reason they aren't going to see you again is if you allow yourself to panic and—stop it, Shay. Stop and concentrate on finding a way out of here. I exhaled a shuddery breath.

Go.

Tim's flashlight reached maybe ten feet ahead before the beam was swallowed by the crushing absence of light. I was in what felt like a huge room, three times the size of the three-quarter room I'd left. The dirt floor was higher by the walls and lower in the center, where the earth was compacted as hard as dusty concrete.

Running down the center of the space and out of sight were roughly cut, twelve-by-twelve-inch pillars at perhaps ten-foot intervals.

A rusty ceiling-to-floor mesh barrier pinned discarded furniture, tools, chains, and other household detritus against the walls on either side of me. The junk had been piled from ground to ceiling timbers. Why would someone do that?

Too weird.

Also pinned behind the barrier was a mishmash of ancient rubbish of indistinct origin. Over time, subterranean explorers or other unknown persons had cut away pieces of the barricade, presumably to hijack anything left of value, leaving behind remnants of the past scattered all over the floor. Upon closer inspection, the trash evolved into various lengths of filthy gray lumber, once-white metal cups, a couple of rusting coil spring mattresses possibly from the heyday of the Gold Rush, broken chairs, and other castaway items of a time long past. I wondered if the basement had become the garbage dump of the businesses overhead.

I tried to hurry but was wary of overshooting the very insufficient light of the phone. No way did I want to run headlong into something which might end my escape attempt.

Ahead, the light reflected off something shiny protruding from the wall between a break in the mesh. As I approached, like an otherworldly gift, there appeared a wood slab door with a newish-looking knob. For a moment my heart skipped, and hope flared as I scrambled to open it.

Of course, it was locked. So much for an easy answer. The thought flicked across my mind that maybe I could kick the door open like TV cops did on the boob tube. I rattled the door but it was too tightly seated in its rebuilt-sometime-this-century frame to make that choice a reality. The likely outcome would be a broken foot instead of a broken door.

Maybe I should pound the crap out of it and hope someone would hear me. I discarded that idea since I couldn't be sure whoever might be on the other side wouldn't be Canavaro or Bender. Or Canavaro *and* Bender.

The thought of those thugs, guns in hand, hunting the deep-in-the-dark for their one living witness, propelled me to move deeper into the abyss. I'd traversed maybe fifty more feet when my stolen phone's flashlight hit the brick of a wall dead ahead. I'd run out of running room.

Dammit.

If I were a praying person, I'd be sending emergency smoke signals to the bigwig upstairs. I hurriedly flashed the light around and almost missed a shoulder-width, four-foot high, sort of arch-shaped opening on the left, an arm span away from the end of the road. It looked as if a very pissed-off somebody had taken a sledgehammer and had their way with the brick and stone, or maybe placed a small charge of dynamite—flashback to the Gold Rush again—and blown the hole out. Rubble lay in a heap at the foot of the opening.

Not usually claustrophobic, I had to admit, as I approached the even inkier inkwell blackness beckoning beyond the breach, a bit of tightly-held-in-check terror leaked down the back of my neck.

I shuddered. My choices were simple. Either see where this went or remain a sitting duck. I felt bad for those poor ducks, always sitting and waiting for something horrible to happen. Luckily, inertia wasn't in my nature.

So, come on, Shay, move your ass.

I held my breath, listened hard. The only sound came from the blood pounding in my ears in tandem with the beating of my heart, which was much better than it not pounding at all.

Jesus. How did I manage to get myself into this? I was supposed to be buying coffee right now. Why couldn't I get cell service and text JT? I wanted Apple's tagline, "It just works," to work right here, right now. She'd be able to contact the cops and they'd take her seriously. Too bad that option wasn't in the cards.

I whooshed a frustrated but determined sigh and shined the light inside the opening. A wall of rounded stones lay an arm's reach ahead. A brick wall was on the right, and to the left was nothing but a great big void. So either a cavern or a tunnel. The thought gave me both hope and freaked me the hell out.

Across from where I stood, a finger-wide vertical crack ran diagonally through the grout between the stones from top to bottom. The two halves were slightly offset, like miniature tectonic plates which had shifted apart. Not sure if the structure was stable, I reached in, across the three-foot width, and gave the wall a solid push, ready to jump backward at the first sign of impending collapse. Nothing budged, so I gingerly maneuvered over chunks of brick and pulverized mortar and wedged myself through the opening.

As I stepped inside, my foot hit the earth at a higher point than I'd anticipated, throwing me off balance. Tim's phone skittered out of my hand as I grabbed for the nubby wall to steady myself. It bounced off broken bricks and landed screen-down in the rubble. For a fraction, my beating heart ceased to function, but the flashlight beam didn't waver.

The glow illuminated a low, age-blackened wood ceiling with four-inch joists holding up, or maybe back, whatever was above. I snatched the phone up and realized why I'd stumbled. The ground sloped downward on each side, creating a U-shaped floor.

Everything down here was U-shaped.

"Jesus," I whispered, and scoped my surroundings. The hole appeared to be a tunnel access point, a creepy, cobwebbed, cracked tunnel with chunks of fallen mortar and rock scattered on the compacted dirt. But a tunnel meant options, which I desperately needed. I tried to straighten and nearly knocked myself out on one of the ceiling joists.

I swore some more and rubbed my head as the stars shooting through my brain receded. Now, I probably had a concussion. Oh, hell, what was one more injury?

The walls were weirdly dark and light, kind of like the walls of Spring Valley, Wisconsin's Crystal Caves, without the ropy, wavy, whatever-the-stuff-was leaching down its sides like melted marshmallow. A blackened pipe the thickness of my fist hung from the ceiling by looped steel wire and ran along one side of the tunnel. It disappeared through a hole that'd been chipped out of the wall at the end, or maybe, the beginning, of the tunnel. The hole was twice the size of the pipe itself. I wondered what used to, or maybe still did, run through it.

Get moving, O'Hanlon.

I pressed forward into the unknown, schlepping along like a female hunchback of Notre Dame. Eventually the tunnel made a hairpin turn, and when I began to wonder if it was ever going to end, my light caught another raggedly punched-out hole in the wall similar to the one I'd entered. More of the same kind of debris was scattered on the ground, but this time most of the large chunks were cleared off to one side.

As I approached the breach, I gave myself a mental pat on the back for thinking ahead enough to get close to, but not in front of, the exit—or entrance—depending on which way one might be going, just in case someone was waiting with a shotgun on the other side. I doused the light and strained to listen for human activity. The silence quickly became as menacing as the complete lack of light, but I held the line and didn't move.

One long, quiet minute became two, and then two became three. It didn't feel like anyone was out there, and if someone lurked nearby, they were quiet as sin.

For chrissake, rip the Band-Aid off, Shay. With a fortifying breath, I toggled the flashlight back on, leaned through the break and lit up uncharted territory. The coast was clear as far as my eye could see, which wasn't exactly a whole lot. I clambered from the tunnel and slowly unfurled to full height and stretched my cramped muscles.

The space into which I'd emerged was maybe a quarter as wide as the Pillar Room I'd left behind. A stone's throw to my right was a massive, shiny-silver air conditioner or furnace or some other kind of not-so-ancient HVAC appliance. Ductwork sprouted from the top of the beast like Medusa's hair to disappear through the ceiling.

To my left, a grimy, gray-planked wall jutted straight out into the open space and ended before reaching the opposite wall, allowing room for a passage to somewhere.

So. Left, or right? Right won my mental coin toss. I headed for the air conditioner/heater/mutant machine to see if I could discern what it was and if it might help me in any way. As I neared it, the ground sloped upward enough I had to stoop once again to avoid hitting my head on the ceiling. Low overheads were becoming a painful problem.

A sudden creaking above made me duck quick.

I grabbed onto the huge device and hugged the hell out of it, trying to regulate my breathing. No one can see you here, I lectured myself, but my anxiety had shot from a simmer to a near boil. Maybe I could pound on the smooth metal under my hands and alert whoever was up there. But wait. What if…what fucking if?

Stop and think this through before you make any un-take-back-able moves, O'Hanlon. Pretend you're in that awful meditation class JT insisted we take a few months ago. I pictured our teacher, a very patient Black woman with white cornrows who was hilarious when she wasn't trying to help her students become one with the planet, leading us into a grounding meditation. I drew a deep breath in through my nose as she'd taught us, slowly blew it out of my mouth, and tried to clear my mind.

CHAPTER TEN

Eddy

"Rocky, wait up," Eddy called as she hustled after him around the rear of the Castle. Years of trampling feet had created a dirt path along the back wall, and even here spray paint rascals had tagged the stacked stones. Sad. No place was safe from vandals these days.

Vegetation so thick it was almost impenetrable grew an arm-span from the stone house, a combination of brush, deadfall, baby trees, plant growth.

Rocky paused and faced the tangled growth, craning his neck as he studied the challenge. "Ms. Eddy, my lovely bride, Tulip, should be right up there." He pointed vaguely uphill and yelled, "Tulip! I am coming, my darling." Before Eddy could utter a word, he dove into the greenery and scrambled skyward. Holy snoots, he moved with the ease of a mountain goat for an adorably rotund guy who was almost as short as her own four-foot-something.

Eddy huffed, grabbed a handful of ferns, and pulled herself upward. Dirty-brown dead leaves and awful, insidious moss carpeted the slope. To her surprise, so did broken branches and rotted timber, creating natural footholds along the way. Regardless, a crystal-clear vision of herself toppling backward, head over derriere, scared the patootie out of her. She did what she could to push the negative away and concentrated on how happy she was they hadn't come to Oregon during Portland's rainy season.

Rocky halted about fifteen feet above her. "TULIP!" he bellowed. "Ms. Eddy! Where are you?"

Eddy's breath came in fast pants. "Not far. Behind. You." Dang it, she should've followed Shay's advice the last few months and gotten off the recliner and moved around once in a while. It was a good idea, but she'd always been so darn tired she could barely make it to the bathroom in time. Now, the fact she might be out of breath but wasn't feeling like she couldn't take another step had to be a good sign. Maybe whatever had wriggled into her very being and proceeded to suck the life out of her was loosening its stranglehold.

About three thousand laborious steps later, she arrived at the narrow ledge on which Rocky stood, cell in hand. She needed to inhale oxygen more slowly or she was going to wind up hyperventilating.

He glanced at her as the air whistled in and out of her lungs. "Ms. Eddy, are you okay?"

She nodded and rolled her hand for him to speak.

"TAGG indicates my Tulip should be right over there."

Eddy followed the line of his jabbing finger. More climbing was about to commence, at a diagonal now.

He cupped his hands around his mouth. "TULIP!" Seconds ticked by without a response. "Ms. Eddy, why is my beloved not answering me?"

"I don't know."

She was beginning to feel truly uneasy. She'd initially expected to find Tulip and her friends easily, but their search wasn't panning out the way she'd expected. The last thing she needed was a completely freaked Rocky in meltdown mode, so she'd better come up with something fast. "There's a whole lot of greenery around here. Maybe it acts as insulation and sound doesn't travel well."

Rocky chewed his lip and squinted as he processed her words. Then his eyebrows popped up. "You might be right, Ms. Eddy. Let us go now."

Implosion avoided, they continued their ascent, crab-walking sideways and upward. Twice Rocky paused to double-check the proper location.

"Ms. Eddy," he called after the second recalculation. "She should be straight up maybe thirty feet ahead! TULIP!" Without waiting for an answer, he clambered upward as fast as his legs would go.

It didn't take him long to reach the point in question. Repeated shouts of "TULIP!" would've echoed through the trees, but the vegetation soaked up so much sound anyone over fifteen feet away wouldn't hear much if anything at all.

She cautiously climbed over a rotting tree and caught up to him.

"Ms. Eddy, she should be right here!" His voice shook. "Look." He thrust his cell at her. Rocky's dot had merged with Tulip's, and it appeared as if they were, indeed, standing on top of her.

Her thudding heart thudded harder. Now she was on the verge of her own breakdown. Don't you do it, old woman, she chided herself. If she lost it, who knew what Rocky might do. Nothing rational, that was a certainty. "I wonder if Tulip might've lost her phone. It's got to be around here somewhere. And I'm sure she is too." Eddy really wasn't sure at all, but desperate to put a positive spin on what was becoming their very own *Twilight Zone* episode.

The next five minutes were spent trying not to accidentlly make a painfully rapid return to the Witch's Castle as they commenced the search. Eddy imagined their bodies ricocheting off tree trunks like human marbles in a life-size pachinko game. The castle below was no longer visible. It appeared as if they'd fall into an endless abyss, never to be seen again.

In their quest, leaves were kicked, brush and ferns and whatever else grew wildly out of control was examined. Rocky chattered to himself, his tone growing sharper as the seconds passed. The forest's humidity was suffocating, like the evil clematis Eddy had once planted next to the back door. In two days, tendrils were birthed through the black soil and proceeded to latch onto the brick of the house faster than she could say, "Screw knitting and get the poker cards." The creepy creeper soon crept up the wall and decided the porch light fixture was the perfect place for taking up residence. Before she knew it, vine after vine sprouted out of thin air and made for that poor light until the weight and tension of the six-inch thick, ropelike perennial-gone-crazy snapped the entire fixture clear off the house. Eddy found the shears and a trowel and went after the clematis like a serial killer on amphetamines and didn't stop until the many-rooted corpse lay in pieces on her lawn.

Now, she reflected, that incident was nothing compared to this mess.

"Ms. Eddy! I found her Oracle!" Rocky's shout was muffled.

"What? Where are you, child?"

"Over here."

"Over where?"

"Wherever I am. I am not sure. I am stuck."

"What on Earth do you mean?"

"You will see."

Then Eddy spotted Rocky's Levi-clad butt half-mooning the sky on the far side of a thick stand of ferns. "What on Earth?" she muttered as she fought her way through the overgrowth. And then there he was, sprawled kit over kaboodle atop a fallen tree. His feet hung six inches off the ground.

"Rocky, what did you do?"

"Ms. Eddy, please help!"

She wrapped her fingers around his waistband and dug in her heels. "Young man, how did you manage to beach yourself on a tree trunk?"

"I called Tulip's cellular phone again." Rocky wiggled as he tried to work himself backward with Eddy's assistance. "The tree was wider than I calculated." With a grunt he landed on the forest floor, Tulip's cell in his hand. "It is all okay now, Ms. Eddy. My darling Tulip lost her Oracle. Which is why she did not answer every time I called her."

A tsunami-sized wave of relief saturated her system, much like the way an ice-cold shot of Fireball saturated her veins. She felt the rush of victory so viscerally she suddenly understood why football players treated their coach to a Gatorade shower. Hot, cold, and totally elated.

"All right, Rocky. Now you know what's happened. Tulip might not even know she's lost it yet. When she does, she'll use one of her friend's phones to call us."

"You are right, Ms. Eddy. I want to go back to the room. I am very, very, very tired."

"You and me both." The adrenaline rush was receding. Her knees were rubbery, and she was jonesing hard for a Red Bull or three. "Ready?"

"Yes, I am, Ms. Eddy. Did you know when you walk uphill, your body uses lots of muscles and energy and calories? We are going to lose weight by the time we arrive at the parking lot. It is because gravity…"

Eddy half-listened to Rocky explain the wonders of exertion on the human body. She couldn't ignore the unease settling like a rock between her ribs and her belly. The entire situation with those friends of Tulip's was very, very odd, but at present there was nothing more they could do but wait, and in all likelihood, everything was just fine.

CHAPTER ELEVEN

JT

JT cast a last glance at the door to the Drunken Tankard and hustled to catch up with Coop as he rounded the side of the building, hot on Shay's tail. She stayed within arm's reach so she could grab him before he ran into a signpost or fell off the curb in his haste. He was a human bloodhound, except his nose was glued to the TAGG map instead of six inches above the sidewalk.

They passed one plywood-covered storefront after another. For the most part, even the graffiti artists found better canvases in more favorable parts of the city to leave their marks on. Homeless folks huddled in the indented front entries of the closed businesses, their worldly belongings stowed in carts, duffels, and sometimes plastic garbage bags. This block was in that suspended moment in time where either the city would decide to step up and make changes so businesses could again become viable, or decay would overtake all and the only solution would be to let it go or bulldoze everything and start over.

"She's around the corner of the block." Coop kicked into a jog.

"She better be." At this point, JT's line between fury and concern was so blurry she didn't know which would win the battle when she finally laid eyes on Shay.

They took the corner at a good clip. JT tailgated Coop, and nearly ran him over when he abruptly stopped a quarter of the way down the block. Where they expected to see her mulish girlfriend, the sidewalk was empty. On the other side of the street, someone slept in the partial shade of three colorful plastic, damaged-beyond-repair, newspaper boxes. Whoever they were, they definitely weren't Shay.

"What's happening with this stupid app? It says she's right here. Like literally under our feet."

JT looked over his shoulder at the phone. Sure as shit, Shay's dot pulsed on the screen exactly where they were standing.

Coop wiped sweat off his forehead. "I don't get this. At all."

"Has to be a malfunction of some kind." JT blew air out of her nose like an enraged bull and planted her hands on her hips. "What now?"

"I dunno." Coop pivoted in a slow circle, scanning the street. "I'm going to make a call. I think a friend of a friend knows one of the app developers. Maybe I can find out what's going on." After three phone calls, Coop disconnected.

"Well?"

"According to the last person I talked to no one has reported any issues with the app. Let me refresh it." He paused as they waited for the reload. "Now look." He squinted in the sun. "Now she's back around the corner by the bar."

"I see." JT spun and took off the way they'd come.

The Harleys that had been backed to the curb near the entrance to the Tankard now had riders, and they were readying to pull out. The only other difference was the van that'd been parked in front of the bar was now gone.

Coop said, "You don't think she would've taken off in that van, do you?"

"I can't imagine a scenario where she'd be doing any of this. But then she's done things in the past that make no sense to anyone but her. I'm caught between wanting to throttle her and the nagging feeling something's really wrong. Does TAGG still show her here?"

"Hang on."

JT watched the two bikers pull away and disappear down a side street. She wracked her mind for any reason Shay might play the cold-footed bride-to-be. This was too insane to be happening. She dragged her gaze back to Coop and his flying fingers as he worked the phone.

After a minute, he said, "Okay. I deleted the app and reinstalled it." Once it finished loading, he opened the app again and they both watched the screen repopulate. "Nope. She's gone." He huffed and hit refresh again.

Eddy and Rocky were at the motel, but Lisa's avatar wasn't visible.

"Wait, there she is." JT pointed at Shay's face, which was now floating in the middle of the block. "I don't know what kind of joke she's trying to pull, but she's gonna be one sorry barista. Come on."

She took off. Coop charged along behind her, their feet pounding the eroding walkway as they retraced their steps past the point they'd previously reached. The block was cut in half by an alley running between buildings, and JT veered into its mouth. Dumpsters belonging to the few functioning establishments and trash that hadn't made it into the dumpsters occupied the alley. The smell of sour garbage was stirred by a light breeze.

"God, this stinks." Coop covered his face with his hand. "She's somewhere around here."

Five minutes and one heart attack later—a partial leg, from the knee to foot, was visible between bags of trash in one of the big green garbage bins. Coop had hollered like a madman until JT was able to verify the appendage belonged to a store mannequin—they affirmed, once again, Shay was not where her dot claimed she was.

JT attempted to stifle semi-hysterical laughter over Coop's leg misadventure without much success. At least laughing was better than letting frustration boil into blind fury. Safer and less painful for all involved.

"Come on," Coop said, "if you thought you saw Shay's leg, you'd be freaking out too, probably worse than me."

She opened her mouth to refute him when her phone rang. She fished it out of her pocket. "Eddy, hey. What's up? You guys find Tulip?"

"Well, not exactly." Eddy's tone was off, and the small hairs at the back of her neck stood on end.

"What happened?" She glanced at Coop, who was watching her, a wary look on his face.

"We made it to the Witch's Castle in one piece. Let me tell you, that walk nearly killed this old fart. But that's neither here nor there." Eddy went on to detail their search and how they eventually located Tulip's phone. Then she said, "Hang on a second. Rocky's sound asleep, and I don't want to wake him."

JT heard rustling, then a familiar metallic snick. Sounded like the motel door closing. Eddy must have stepped outside.

"'K, now. I tell you, child, I have a bad feeling about Tulip's two friends. Scary Mary and Pretty Boy Robbie. Rocky might've been right to be worried. But I sure as shootin' don't want him to hear me say that. He was beside himself until he found her phone, and now he thinks she simply lost it and is out having a good old time. But where we found it, so far off any path, beaten or unbeaten, it doesn't make a lick of sense."

JT glanced at her watch. "It's ten after two. Tulip's not supposed to be back till seven, right?"

"That's what she said." Air whistled through the receiver as Eddy exhaled. "Not much more to do till then, I s'pose. Did you find Shay?"

"Not yet. I'm not sure what she's doing, but I'm going to dismember her one body part at a time when she shows up, and then I'll deposit the remains in a dumpster." She glanced at Coop, who gave her the finger. "I think we're ready to head back to the motel too." Screw it. At this point Shay could finish playing her games and find her own way home.

"See you soon." Eddy hung up.

Coop summoned a Ryde as JT tucked her phone away. She threw her head back, eyes on the puffy white clouds suspended in the sky. "Why is nothing ever simple?" When Shay came back, they were going sit down and have a nice long talk whether her recalcitrant lover wanted to or not.

CHAPTER TWELVE

Shay

Stilling the mind was galaxies beyond reach but the breathing helped some. The fuzzies at the edge of my vision came back into focus. Back to my conundrum. One person was dead. Who knew what those two murderous bozos planned on doing to me? If the creaking I heard was them and I went bang, bang, bang, they'd know exactly where I was. And that could be deadly.

I attempted to mind map the location where I'd been dropped into this whatever-the-hell-it-was-world to where I now hugged my cool new friend. I doubted I was still beneath the Drunken Tankard, unless the bar was a whole lot bigger than it appeared topside. The big but: what if I was wrong? This maze-like basement could extend for blocks. It reminded me of pictures I'd seen of the catacombs below Paris, but without the walls of bones.

Bones.

The hair on my arms popped up. I wouldn't be at all surprised if I stumbled across the mummified corpse of some sad sack who'd been banished here for reasons unknown and had no idea they'd never see the light of day again.

For Pete's sake, Shay, turn off that nasty little voice in your head.

Right.

Now.

I released the metal beast with a resigned sigh. Allowing the light from my pilfered phone to lead the way, I followed the passage away from the tunnel and the great metal monster as it turned left and narrowed drastically. I could reach out and touch the jagged rock walls on either side. Fifteen more feet and the corridor hung another left.

It was such a good thing I wasn't afraid of tight spaces. Beyond the ten-foot, dust speck-filled area the phone's flash illuminated, the utter blackness pressed in so hard it felt like nothing existed outside of my itty-bitty circle of light.

Shay, I ordered myself, crumple up your shitty thoughts and toss them in your mind's garbage can. Twenty-five or so steps later, I came across a chest-high door. The charge of adrenaline was instantaneous, turning my insides to Jello and making my limbs tremble. I took a couple more of those calming breaths, which didn't help an iota this time, and decided meditation wasn't for anyone whose life was in danger.

A crusty doorknob protruded from what appeared to be a hastily cobbled together chest-high door. Whoever constructed it was either in one big-ass hurry or flat-out drunk. Some of the nails jutted out a half inch or more, while others were bent in half, the product of a misplaced swing of a hammer, their heads embedded sideways in the wood.

Heart lodged firmly near my thyroid, I took hold of the knob. Please let this be my ticket to freedom. I needed to get the hell out of this stank.

The potential for hope lasted until I attempted to turn the handle. The mechanism was frozen in place, too stiff to move beyond an inch either way.

I needed both hands. I propped Tim's phone on the ground against the far wall. Illuminated from behind, my body became an oversized silhouette against the door. I wrapped my fingers around the knob and twisted one way, and then the other, as thoughts roared through my brain. What was on the other side? *Who* might be on the other side?

The knob moved a little more with each twist until it felt like it could go no further. I tugged on the knob. The door refused to behave.

"Oh, no you don't." I planted a foot on the jamb. No way was this fucking door going to defeat me. With a mighty twist and heave, the door sprang open and I slammed into the opposite wall. I slithered down the stones and my ass hit the dirt.

For a split second, elation flooded my system. Then I realized the opening was bricked shut. The bricks were a brighter reddish-brown than any of the ones I'd run across to this point, so the opening hadn't been sealed very long ago.

"Oh, goddammit, no!" I bounced my head off the wall behind me and winced. I was in one of those run-for-your-life-through-the-maze nightmares. Nothing else would explain this insanity.

Then I sneezed once, and again. This place was a dust fuckpalooza.

I staggered to my feet, dusted my butt off, then inspected the brickwork. The craftsmanship was, unfortunately, very solid.

Letting loose a string of disgusted oaths, I grabbed Tim's phone and stomped on. The passage opened into a near mirror image of the first area I'd navigated when I'd left the Drop-A-Drunk Room and Mr. Burr behind. It was about the same width, with another line of twelve-by-twelve pillars running down the center of the space and disappearing into the dark.

But here no junk lined either side. With a renewed sense of urgency, I hustled what had to be another hundred feet before the end of the road forced me left again, this time into a six-foot wide corridor.

The cobwebbed joists here were lower, and once again I had to duck to avoid shearing off the top of my skull. Before long, my light reflected off something in the distance. After scuttling along a bit farther, I realized the reflection was the shiny mechanical beast I'd inspected earlier. Damn it. In my rush to anywhere but here, I almost whipped past yet another doorway.

I slammed on the brakes and backed the buggy up.

CHAPTER THIRTEEN

Eddy

Eddy had no sooner disconnected from JT when she heard
Rocky's phone ring through the door. The knot in her stomach
eased. It had to be Tulip. She was making a bigger deal out of
things than she needed to. Damn imagination and one too many
murder shows on the boob tube. Did televisions even have tubes
anymore? Who knew.

She let herself in.

"My lovely Tulip!" Rocky perched on the edge of the bed,
bouncing up and down with excitement. "I have been so worried
about you. You are on speaker so Ms. Eddy can hear your most
beautiful voice."

"Rocky, I need you to listen to me."

Eddy felt the cleft between her eyes deepen as she frowned.

"I will listen to you always and forev—"

"Rocky." Tulip's tone was uncharacteristically sharp.

Taken aback, he froze, and his face scrunched. "Yes, my
darling?"

"I need you to gather all of our riches and meet me at Portland's Freakybuttrue Peculiarium at six this evening."

"But our riches are our love. And our friends who are now our family. Should I bring them all?"

"Maybe one person, and, um, four thousand nine hundred thirty-seven dollars and ninety-four cents." Her voice sounded strained, breathy, off pitch.

Eddy stared at the phone in shock. What was going on here?

A cross between a hiss and a growl came across the line and then a snippy voice whispered, "Hurry it up, Balloon Girl."

"Fine," Tulip muttered, presumably to the pissy hisser. Louder, "Okay. I borrowed five thousand dollars from Scary Mary and Pretty Boy Robbie when I lived in New Orleans. Now it's pay up time. I already gave them sixty-two dollars and six cents. Gotta run. Love you, bye." She spoke so fast it was hard to keep up, and she disconnected before either of them could respond.

Rocky stared at his phone for a long moment, then looked up at Eddy with wide eyes. "Where are we going to get four thousand nine hundred thirty-seven dollars and ninety-four cents? We are supposed to meet Tulip and her friends, who I still think are not very nice people, at some place called the Freakybuttrue Peculiarium in Portland at six o'clock."

"Yes, Rocky, I heard." What had that girl gotten into? To her recollection, Tulip rarely borrowed more than ten bucks from any of them, never large amounts, and she always paid it back. Maybe it was a good idea to go back to bed and restart this entire day. Then she'd know where Shay was, and Tulip could make a different choice when Scary Mary and Pretty Boy whatshisname showed up. Where was the rewind button when you needed it? "Tell you what. You look up the Peculiwhatever and see where it is, and I'll count up my dough."

He hunched over his phone. "It is the Peculiarium, Ms. Eddy. Not the Peculiwhatever."

"Peculiarium," she repeated absently. Caffeinated pick-me-ups remained the furthest thing from her mind. Her nerves were sizzling, and she was more alive than she'd felt in months.

"Here it is, Ms. Eddy. I have found the location where my lovely Tulip will be in three hours and twenty-seven minutes. I will now count all the money I have." He dug into his pockets and emptied the contents onto the bed.

This was crazy. But until JT and Coop arrived, she'd go along with whatever this was without argument to keep Rocky even-keeled. He'd been right to worry about those so-called friends after all. Did Tulip really owe those two good-for-nothing twerps five thousand bucks? It would be so very out of character, but who knew what went on down in the land of beignets and Bourbon Street before she and Rocky and the rest of the crew had come into Tulip's life.

Eddy sat at the desk and pulled out her wallet. She removed every bill she had, counted them, and put the pile aside. Then she emptied the purse and tipped it upside down. Three quarters, two dimes and a nickel fell out. Three hundred fifty-seven bucks including the change.

"I have twenty-three dollars and forty cents, Ms. Eddy."

$380.40. Plus Tulip's donation of $62.06, for a total of $442.46. Didn't make much of a dent in the five grand Tulip had requested.

Ten minutes later, a knock on the door made Eddy jump. "I'll get it, child." She gave Rocky's knee a pat, stood stiffly, and shuffled to the door. She'd had more exercise today than she'd had in weeks, and dang it all if she didn't feel better than she had in a long time.

The peephole was high enough she had to stand on her tippy toes to get a gander outside. Too many strange things happening not to be careful. She squinted through the fish-eyed lens and saw a distorted Lisa outside, blond hair shining in the sunlight.

Eddy unchained the door, opened it, stuck her head out, and furtively glanced in both directions before grabbing Lisa's arm and dragging her inside. Once Lisa had cleared the threshold, she slammed the door, chained it, and threw the deadbolt for good measure.

Lisa cut a look from Eddy to Rocky and back again. "Is there something I need to be worried about?"

"Oh yes, Miss Lisa," Rocky said, his voice solemn. "Shay has gone on walkabout and Tulip needs exactly four thousand five hundred fifty-seven dollars and fifty-four cents by six o'clock Pacific time."

Lisa's face morphed from confusion to surprise to suspicion. "Why?"

"It appears," Eddy said with a sigh, "she owes Scary Mary and Pretty Boy Robbie five grand, and they want her to pay up."

"Are those her two friends? Maybe I better sit down." She lowered herself into a chair near the window.

Rocky and Eddy took turns explaining Shay's disappearance, finding Tulip's phone at the Witch's Castle, and the phone call that'd come through minutes before.

"I'm gone less than half a day and look what happens." From her back pocket Lisa produced a worn black leather wallet secured to chain attached to her belt. She opened it and counted. "A hundred and twenty-three bucks." She checked her pockets and added twenty-two cents. "Taps my cash out, but you can have it."

"Thank you for donating to the Save Tulip Fund, Miss Lisa." Rocky thrust his hand at her, and she shook it. "Now we only need four thousand four hundred thirty-four dollars and thirty-two cents. That is still a lot of money."

"I didn't think to bring a debit card or I could've—" Lisa's cell rang. "I'm sorry, I need to grab this." She turned toward the window and pressed her phone to her ear. "Hey, yes, this is she." She paused. "Yeah, I can do that. Can you hang on a second?" She headed to the door. "Sorry to run, but I have to meet someone in fifteen." She undid the chain, twisted the dead bolt open, put the phone back to her ear, and was gone.

The door had no sooner clicked shut when the sound of the access card in the card reader gave Eddy another heart attack. She jumped up as if she'd been electrocuted, grabbed her Whacker from her suitcase, and took up a position of defense next to the door, the bat cocked at the ready over her head.

The handle turned.

The door opened.

JT and Coop walked in.

"Where's Lisa going in such a—" JT spotted Eddy on the brink of bopping her in the belfry. "Hey! Ease up, Babe Ruth. What're you doing?"

Eddy dropped the bat to her side. "Am I ever glad to see the two of you."

Rocky crawled to the edge of the bed. "Nick Coop and JT, I am very happy to see you too. We have another very big, very bad problem."

This time it only took three minutes to run down the last twenty.

JT collapsed into the chair Lisa had vacated and rubbed her face. "I think we've been transported into an alternate universe, and I have no idea how to navigate it. Coop, can you please grab me a bottle of water?"

"Sure." He opened the mini-fridge. "Eddy, you want anything? Rocky?"

"Water, thanks," Eddy said. "For once I think I'm plenty wired up." It felt good to say that, and better to feel it. Maybe the malaise she'd been living with really was lifting. Strange time for this to be happening what with all this craziness going on.

Coop glanced at Rocky and held out a bottle.

"No thank you, Nick Coop."

"Okay." He distributed the water, unscrewed the top off his and sucked the entire contents down without stopping for air. "Ah, god. Needed that." He wiped his mouth on his sleeve. "What happens if we don't bring the requested amount?" He crushed the bottle and deposited it in the bag Eddy had left out for recycling.

"My most dearest flower did not say, Nick Coop." Rocky sat poised on the edge of the bed, his aviator hat askew. His hands twisted the bedspread and he nervously bounced both knees up and down. "We need exactly four thousand four hundred thirty-four dollars in greenbacks and thirty-two pennies. Or a quarter, a nickel and then two pennies. Or—"

"We've got the picture, Rocky," Eddy gently interrupted. "Lisa donated all the cash she had on her before she skedaddled. And to answer your question, she got a phone call, said she had to go, and hot hoofed it right on out of here. Seemed kind of odd to me, but then, about now I'd probably think anything and everything normal wasn't. Anyway, JT, is this something we should bring the police in on?"

"I'm not sure. From the sound of it, they haven't directly threatened her, and she didn't indicate she was being held against her will. She told you where and when to meet." She raised a hand at the expression on Eddy's face. "I'm not saying this whole thing doesn't sound hinky as hell. But I think we need more before I'd be able to convince the police we have at the very least a missing person. Speaking of missing persons, let's talk about Shay."

She and Coop ran down their efforts of the last couple of hours.

"Sounds nothing like the Shay we know and love," Eddy said. "That girl was itching to get to her coffee convention. I can't see her voluntarily pulling something like that. And to leave Coop high and dry? Makes no sense. Can't you call in the po-po for Shay, if not Tulip? And Nicholas Cooper, you need to sit up straight."

"Yes, Coop." Rocky flung himself facedown across Eddy's bed, his head hanging off the edge, staring bleakly at the carpet. "Harvard Medical School says poor posture contributes not only to head and neck problems, but also incontinence, which is when you pee if you sneeze or laugh too hard, heartburn, and constipation, which is—"

"Thanks, buddy, we all know what that is." Coop straightened, gaining about two feet.

Weariness and stress pinched JT's face, making Eddy worry even more. "I don't think we have any reason the cops would buy Shay's absence as anything more than someone who wandered off on her own volition. She's of sound mind and makes her own decisions. At least she does until she comes home. Then I'm buying one of those Tile Tracker things and permanently attaching it to her wrist." She fiddled with her phone and put it to her ear and waited long seconds. "Still not answering. I'm gonna kill her. Anyway, let's see what Coop and I can contribute to the Tulip cause."

After they both pillaged pockets, backpacks—Shay's included—and everybody's suitcases, they came up with a grand total of $746.98.

Rocky woefully said, "We are three thousand six hundred eighty-seven dollars and thirty-four cents short of five thousand dollars for my Tulip."

Coop sat down and slung an arm over his shoulders. "Don't worry, buddy. We'll figure something out. We always do."

"Can either of you pull any cash out of an ATM?" Eddy asked. She had no use for one of those fancy debit card jobbies but figured the young'uns did. Well, except for Lisa.

"I would," Coop said. "But I maxed my card out at the Ochoco Creek Coffee booth. It was so packed and I didn't want Shay to miss out on the deals they were offering. I wasn't sure what she wanted for the café but figured if I got some of all of it, that would be better than nothing."

"You're a good friend." JT returned to her chair. "We brought a cash card. Of course, my missing girlfriend has it with her." She slid her phone out of her pocket and opened the TAGG app.

"Do you see her?" Eddy asked.

"Not right now."

"Hang on," Coop said. "Let me pull up her history."

JT put her phone on speaker and hit Shay's number for the millionth time while Coop did his thing.

"Looks like she's been moving around the same area," he said. "Her battery's at forty percent. I don't like it."

Shay's voicemail kicked in. "Call me," JT ordered. She disconnected with a huff and tossed the phone on the desk. "Her mailbox has to be close to full with all the messages I've left."

"When things are too confusing to move forward," Eddy said, "I think it's tummy time. Let's order up some pizza and see what life looks like on a full stomach."

CHAPTER FOURTEEN

Shay

I raked Tim Burr's cell light over the door, my heart rate increasing only a little this time. The planks were still light brown, the wood not yet aged. The doorknob reflected nice and shiny in the light. It had to have been built in the last few years. What were the odds this one would be unlocked?

Less than zero.

The metal knob was cool against my palm. I gave it a twist, and holy balls on fire, the door swung inward on silent hinges. My first impulse was to charge headlong inside, but then JT's calm, rational voice shouted, "Stop!" She'd once told me a doorway was nothing more than a vertical coffin, and then you had to tread with utmost caution. A shooter could be waiting inside, and faster than the snap of the fingers, ding dong dead.

I dropped, banged my funny bone against something, and repressed a yelp as I hit the deck, slamming the phone against my chest to douse the light. Then I scrabbled backward like a one-armed crab.

Dead silence. No one hollered, no shuffling footsteps coming to do me in. No "there's a person near me" feeling.

After long, drawn-out seconds, my body decided it was okay to breathe again. I whooshed great gusts of particle-laden air like an out-of-control bellows.

Once I regained control of my bodily functions, I held still and listened some more. The silence remained deep and pure. I reversed my crabwalk and craned my neck around the edge of the jam for a gander inside. As dark within as without.

I checked the battery on Tim's phone. Fifty-three percent. The time was now 2:40. I'd been wandering this cavernous whatever for forty-five minutes.

Forty-five minutes too long.

Once again, I hauled myself up, shined the light through the door. As I crossed the threshold, senses I didn't realize had disappeared returned like a physical slap. My knee stung and my elbow hurt, along with the burning of my scraped face. My shoulder crunched every time I raised my arm, and the distinct smell of burlap buffeted my nose.

Then, all my various pains faded into the background again as I took a moment to orient myself to the ten-by-fifteen-foot space. In the middle of the room sat an eight-foot conference table with a chipped, fake-wood veneer top. A black, three-level delivery cart was stationed at one end of said table. A folding chair was shoved at a cockeyed angle under the table, and on the top of its top were four brick-shaped objects wrapped in brown paper. Much of the rest of the table was taken up with a burlap bag of coffee, and the weight of it made the table sag. One end of the bag was cut open, and unroasted, green coffee beans spilled onto the filthy surface, exposing the edge of another paper-wrapped brick buried inside.

Next to the chair, a waist-high, burlap-lined barrel three-quarters filled with green beans sat beside a pile of crumped burlap bags. I picked one up and held it in the light beam. A stamp on the loosely woven twine fibers read:

Producto De Guatemala
Cosecha San Marcos
FAIR TRADE
150 LBS SPAN NET
011-9735-0118

The number was called an ICO mark, the International Coffee Organization mark. The first part of the three-set code ID'd the origin country, the second set of numbers represented the export company, and the last set was the lot, the shipment number to which the bag belonged. The origin of this bag was 011, which was Guatemala.

I flipped the bag over to see another stamp on the back.

Specially prepared for Ochoco Creek Coffee.

Was the same stamp on the bag on the table? I directed Mr. Tim's light at it. Nope, not Guatemalan.

Café Limpio
003-5477-0998
70 KG NET

Not marked as fair trade. What country was 003? I wracked my mind, and then, wham! It came to me. 003 was Colombia. Oh, my god. Wasn't Colombia where most of the world's cocaine was produced? Were those bricks, sitting on the table not two feet from me, cocaine?

Holy Moses on a hell of a bender.

What were they doing? Removing the drugs from a non-fair-trade bag of coffee beans, then dumping the beans used to smuggle said drugs into the barrel with the Ochoco Creek bag, and then what? Selling the skankified beans under the Ochoco brand? The implications boggled my already boggled brain. Was Canavaro's entire coffee operation a sham?

Six more unopened burlap bags were stacked against the far wall. I flashed the top one. *Café Limpio.* They were probably all *Café Limpio.* If all six bags had drugs hidden inside, what a serious shitload of white snorty stuff.

Canavaro was working this *and* his little ammunition side-gig? Considering the ammo packed in Flying High coffee crates, he most certainly was neck deep in both, along with Bender, it would seem.

This was getting worse by the moment.

A deeper sense of foreboding than I'd yet felt crept up the back of my skull. The room suddenly came into sharp focus, as if I was nearsighted and put glasses on for the first time. My rattled brain settled. I had to pull it together to save my own keister, because no one was going to do it for me. I scanned the room again, saw another doorway on the far side.

No time like the present to investigate.

The space was only slightly smaller than the first. Two six-foot tables were set up in an "L" shape, on top of which at least thirty more bricks were stacked in neat rows.

That shit there added up to a shit ton of bad, bad, bad.

A third door led to a much smaller room. Three tinfoil baking pans half-full of whitish powder, and two pans of even more purely white powder sat on a scarred, plywood-topped, freestanding four-by-six-foot counter. A set of scales, spoons, and a mess of empty two-by-three-inch Ziploc type bags printed on one side with various colorful designs like smiley faces, dolphins, spades, dollar signs, running horses, and more were assembled next to the pans of powder. On a card table situated next to the island of nose candy were bags filled with preportioned amounts of the white stuff.

Yellow boxes of baking powder, five-pound bags of flour, and other plastic containers, contents unknown, were stored in a fancy, three-shelf bookcase complete with carved whirly-dos and bun feet. Straight out of the roaring twenties, or maybe even earlier. One surprisingly decent find in this subterranean hell hole.

Holy short skirts. I was in so much trouble.

What the hell had I run into by literally running into those damn crates? I should be back at the BOB, buzzed on free caffeine and loaded with coffee samples, happily ignorant of Randy Canavaro's side hustles.

Well, too little too late. The asshat king of West Coast organic coffee was a cheat, a drug smuggler, a gun runner.

And I was completely expendable.

As I gazed around the illicit drug factory, it occurred to me maybe I'd be worth more alive than dead if I had something they needed. They had to pay someone for the drugs they'd imported, right? If they didn't have the drugs, they couldn't make the money to pay for them. And much of that kind of owing led to great big problems. I returned to the first room and hefted one of the bricks. A couple pounds, not too heavy.

I squinted at the innocent-looking package in my hand. How many Benjamins could this one brick fetch? Once in a while, JT would talk about some of the drug busts she'd been involved with, but all I really knew was small packages added up to a whopping amount of money. If I hid the bricks, maybe I could use them as a bargaining chip for my life.

God. So dramatic. And unbelievably true.

All right then, where could I stash the stash? What had I seen on my journey to the center of the Earth?

The Pillar Room had potential with the junk stacked up along the wall. But the stuff was coated with hundred-year-old dust, and how easy would it be to catch a spot that'd been disturbed?

Nope. Move on.

The Door to Nowhere was out. What about the air conditioner? I charged out of the room and made a beeline for my silver friend. Two minutes later, after scouring it and finding no viable hiding spots, I scooted back to the Drug Room. Maybe staring at the contraband would help me come up with something. I closed my eyes and mentally retraced my steps.

Back, back, back, around the square I'd just trekked, through the tunnel, to its ragged entrance. The smack my head took from the low ceiling. Could I hide something in the tunnel's ceiling? The joists were exposed, but I didn't think they created any sort of a ledge where I could stash the bricks.

Wait. The pipe.

Maybe I could balance them on the crusty black pipe dangling from the ceiling by something akin to ancient wire coat hangers. I snatched up a couple bricks to experiment with and headed into the tunnel.

The space was still cobwebby, creepy, and oh, god, so very narrow. I hurried along, taking care not to bash my head again, searching for anything that'd work for my life-saving idea. I rounded the hairpin curve and spotted the pipe.

"Come on, work," I muttered as I attempted to balance one of the bricks atop it. Oh yeah, baby, it stayed put. But as fast as hope rose, it bottomed out. The bricks would be completely obvious to anyone squeezing through the shaft.

Desperation mounting, I continued to retrace my steps. Might as well keep backtracking. The light caught the opening in the wall leading into the first Pillar Room. Dejection slowed my steps. I swept the beam around one last time. On the upswing, it caught the hole someone had busted through the wall to allow the pipe to pass through. The gap between the wall and the conduit looked like it might be wide enough to slide a brick past.

What was on the other side? Did it matter? Hell, no. I stuffed one of the bricks under my arm and attempted to shove the other through the gap. It got hung up at the halfway point, but I pushed harder, and holy happiness, it squirted through the gap and disappeared, landing with a soft thump.

Hot diggety damn.

I deposited the other package, made the return trip to the Drug Room in record time and gathered up as many of the bricks as I could carry. Three round trips later, every brick I could get my hands on was now in its new hiding space. I reversed course once again, wondering what other trouble I might be able to cause. I exited the tunnel and stood, arching to stretch my back with my arms in the air. The light from Tim's phone flashed at odd angles against various surfaces and reflected brightly off the air conditioner as relief flooded through me. A small life insurance policy was way better than none.

Then I heard the muffled, very faint voice of a man shouting, "Little girl, come out, come out wherever you are."

CHAPTER FIFTEEN

Eddy

The pizza place they'd ordered from wasn't exactly Johnny-on-the-delivery spot. Rocky paced the room like a caged convict plotting his escape. Eddy figured he'd wear a path through the already worn carpet before the food ever showed up.

As if the gods of distraction read her mind, the magical, musical sound of an ice cream truck filtered through the cracks around the motel door.

Rocky's glum countenance morphed into wide-eyed wonder, and he came to a stop. "An ice cream truck! I must go and get my darling Tulip a Tweety Bird ice cream treat! She will like a Tweety Bird ice cream treat when she comes back to us." He dashed out the door.

Eddy peered at JT and Coop. "I don't think he has a cent left on him. But knowing Rocky, he'll con a free treat out of whoever's selling them. If so, maybe one of you might feel like eating a Tweety Bird ice cream treat if that there little mini fridge isn't up to keeping it frozen."

All three of them focused on the refrigerator as if it were the most interesting thing ever.

"Earlier," Eddy said, "Rocky mentioned he wanted to see Stark's Vacuum Museum on Grand, which, he informed me, is about a ten-minute walk away. If I can talk him into that, then maybe we can hit a fast-food joint when we're done and grab a bite. Better occupied than thinking too much. His poor brain is in overdrive, and there's not much positive for him to think about right now, considering."

"Good idea." JT checked her watch. "It's still three hours till we meet up with the Crescent City Creeps, anyway. You feel okay to go chasing after him?"

Eddy considered JT's words. "Yes, actually, I do. Huh. Guess I needed a little kick in the old carburetor to get me going."

"That's great," Coop said. "And don't worry, we'll save you guys some pizza."

"We'll be fine. Eat up." With a wave, she made her exit.

The sun was warm on Eddy's skin as she scanned the parking lot. A sea-blue ice cream truck was parked at the curb near the office, playing the newly revamped ice cream truck song. Thanks to Rocky, she knew the song was created in collaboration between Wu Tang Clan's RZA and Good Humor Ice Cream. She appreciated the significance of the change since the original ice cream truck music, "Turkey in the Straw," had racist roots. Although, if it'd been up to her, the new tune could've been speeded up a bit.

Excited kids and not so excited parents lined up to get their grubby mitts on a cool delight. She spotted Rocky's aviator hat third in line.

Eddy descended the cement stairs, crossed the lot, and slid into line with him.

The entire side of the ice cream truck was plastered with baseball card-sized pictures of what appeared to be every ice cream specialty known to humankind. She had to squint to make out the tiny pictures of the treats and their prices. The one thing she could see was a sign saying credit cards were accepted. Since she'd donated all her cash to the Save Tulip Fund, a credit card was all she had.

"Hello, Ms. Eddy."

"Hello, Rocky."

"They have a Tweety Bar, Ms. Eddy."

"I see that. Are you going to get yourself something?"

"Yes, I—" Rocky's eyes grew wide. "Oh no, Ms. Eddy. I do not have any money. It is in the Save My Beautiful Flower Fund."

"Not to worry." She handed him her credit card. "As soon as Tulip gets back, she'll want her Tweety Bird concoction."

"You are right, Ms. Eddy. Thank you."

"Tell you what. Once you have your treats, run them upstairs and stash them in the freezer of the tiny little pocket fridge in the motel room. Then let's go to Stark's Vacuum Museum. You can tell Tulip all about it."

Rocky brightened. "Sounds like a great plan, Ms. Eddy."

CHAPTER SIXTEEN

Shay

My breath hitched. I slapped myself into the corner made by the intersection of the tunnel wall and the plank Drug Room wall and attempted to become one with the ragged bricks and splintery wood.

I slid down until my butt hit my heels. Being a smaller target might be helpful. It took another second to realize the beam from Tim's phone still pierced the darkness. I somehow managed to kill it without dropping the device through my shaking fingers. Blackness settled like a blanket, comforting in its ability to disappear me and terrifying in its completeness.

"You goddamn little fuck. Where did you hide yourself?"

Canavaro. He wasn't close, but his bellow held an unmistakable snarl. I couldn't tell if the sound was coming from the other side of the tunnel or from somewhere on this side of my dungeon. The twisty tunnel and strange underground corridors screwed with the acoustics and made it next to impossible to pinpoint much of anything.

I pressed my head into the corner and clenched my teeth to keep from screaming. Where was the owner of that damn voice? And how had he gotten down here?

Think, Shay. Bags of coffee weighed in at close to a hundred-fifty pounds. So heavy I didn't think Canavaro and Bender would drop them through the trapdoor. It'd probably burst open on impact. I had no recollection of seeing a single coffee bean on the ground around Tim Burr. Not that I'd been looking for any such thing, but I figured a bean in the dirt would likely have caught my attention. So, going with that theory, there had to be another way into the fun house.

My brain was moving so fast I almost missed another muffled shout. "Should've taken her out before we dropped her." Hello, Bender. Then he raised the volume. "Go ahead and hide, bitch. We'll find you. The longer it takes the more it'll hurt when I cut you into little pieces."

Little pieces?

Canavaro's sick laughter echoed. They weren't making any effort to be quiet. Never a good sign. Either no one was around to hear anything, or, if anyone was in earshot, they were probably part of Bender and Canavaro's dirty-deals-done-not-so-very-dirt-cheap. Any hooligan in that position wasn't about to give a poor, terrified coffeemonger any assistance.

One thought oozed into another. What if others were down here after all, on the hunt but moving in silence? Sneaking around, waiting for me to make some mistake and reveal my position?

Come on, Shay. Stop it. You can only go with what you're sure of. And sure as shit, Bender and Canavaro were after my ass.

I refocused. Their cajoling and threats now clearly echoed through the tunnel, and they were coming closer and closer. Another access point had to exist on the other side, unless they'd lowered themselves to the basement through the hole in the floor, which I doubted. So, I needed to sneak back through the tunnel and find their access point before they found me.

An "Ow!" echoed even closer.

"Watch your head, Canavaro."

"Why didn't you make the goddamn opening bigger?"

"You hit your head on the rafter beam in the tunnel, not the bricks, dumb ass. Can't exactly raise the ceiling in here."

They were in the tunnel.

And I was four feet away from where they were going to exit.

My innards shrieked and I almost bit my tongue in half. I could make a break for it, most likely resulting in my capture and certain demise, or I could sit tight and take my pending dismemberment like a woman. Shitty choices all around.

Now I could hear their footsteps crunching over the debris of the tunnel floor. They must have rounded the switchback.

Holy duck a truck.

I braced one hand on the ground to balance myself and my palm hit a sizeable piece of rubble. I grabbed the rock shard, and it hefted nicely.

The steps grew louder yet. "You should install lights in here, Bender. All this crap on the floor is dangerous."

"I don't get in your end of the business. Stay out of mine. We wouldn't be down here in the first place if it wasn't for you."

"It was Burr's fault."

"You employed Burr."

"You're an asshole."

Jesus. They sounded like Eddy and Agnes when they got fired up. Did I have another ten seconds? Five?

Then, like a lightning strike, an idea exploded in my brain. I had no time to debate its merits because the wobbling glow of a flashlight was now visible through the ragged tunnel opening. One chance, and I better not blow it.

My heart drummed in my throat. Shit was about to get real.

Someone stepped out of the tunnel, promptly tripped over a pile of loose bricks. He went down with a yelp and not five feet from me. His flashlight sailed through the air, bounced off the far wall and rolled down the narrow hall toward the Drug Room door.

"Jesus Christ, Canavaro." Bender stuck one leg out of the hole, his beam of light painting the far wall in jagged zigzags as he extricated himself from the shaft.

Before he managed to complete the maneuver, I flung the rock as hard as I could toward the gap between the bulky silver air conditioner and the corridor which disappeared off to the left. The brick hit the wall with a solid thunk and ricocheted into the dark.

"Hey!" Bender shouted. He leaped over Canavaro's sprawled form and disappeared around the corner.

"Wait up!" Canavaro heaved himself to his feet and charged after Bender like a limpy rhino.

As soon as he was out of sight, I snatched up Canavaro's abandoned flashlight and pocketed Tim Burr's phone. Then I dodged into the tunnel, silently chanting, don't trip, don't trip.

I burst out of the tunnel into the Pillar Room. Took care not to repeat Canavaro's mistake and bolted toward the trapdoor of death and poor Mr. Burr. Those two bozos somehow managed to get down here and my life depended on figuring out how. As I ran, the flashlight beam hit the doorknob of the locked door I'd tried earlier.

Hold your Clydesdales, Shay.

I skidded to a stop.

What if?

I backtracked to the door and tried the knob. It turned. The door swung silently open to reveal an unlit, six-foot tall, three-foot wide corridor, its floor the same compacted dirt. Unfinished, gray-aged planks lined the sides.

I charged into the passage like a bull with a picador on its ass.

Hold that bull a second, Shay. Don't be stupid.

I slammed on the brakes and kicked it into reverse.

Why make it completely obvious I'd found their point of entry—or rather—my escape route? I hurriedly shut the door and shined the light around the knob. Lookie there. A deadbolt on the inside of the door. I shot the bolt home and fled.

After ten feet, the passage banked hard to the right. I hustled along, hoping I wasn't on a collision course with a dead end.

After maybe fifty feet, the corridor made a sharp left. Four long strides and it turned to the right. Ten yards and I was forced to hang another left.

Seven paces, one more right, and the passage opened into a space the size of a two-car garage. Well-worn wood shelving, reminiscent of the shelves in the basement of my dad's bar, lined three sides of the space. Boxes of various kinds and brands of liquor and beer occupied many of the shelves. Others had become a catch-all for junk a bar no longer had use for but wasn't ready to part with, like racks of dusty glasses and what looked like a broken fryer. Was this the Drunken Tankard's liquor locker? Or was I beneath some other bar?

Eight burlap coffee bags were stacked on the floor in front of a utility pushcart identical to the one I'd seen in the Drug Room. Oh, yes. I was most def in the right place. Bender or his minions probably used the cart to transport the bags through the Pillar Room to the tunnel and then from the other end of the tunnel into the Drug Room. I hated to think of the back pain the poor schmuck had to endure schlepping those bags through the narrow confines of the tunnel.

Part of the room was taken up with what had to be, at least, a century-old elevator. It could've come straight out of a steampunk movie. The front gaped open like a menacing mouth, and intricate, rusted wrought iron made up its interior.

A terrifying metal monster, lying in wait to eat its riders.

All aboard.

Hopes pinned on this rickety contraption, I hopped on. A brass dial with a cranklike handle was mounted to one of the elevator walls. Raised letters on the dial read Otis Elevator Company. This baby had to be one of their earliest models. I grabbed the handle and pushed it forward.

The elevator didn't move.

I pulled it backward.

Nothing.

My trembling hand shook harder. I muttered, "Come on, you mofo."

Most elevators had a door. Maybe that was the issue. I scanned the front of the contraption and saw two parallel, collapsed gates. I gave the outside gate a pull and it screeched closed. I did the same with the inside gate.

"Please work." I again took hold of the handle on the brass dial and shoved it forward. The elevator failed to elevate. I jammed the handle the other way. With a whir and a gentle jolt, the elevator actually began to rise.

It crept its way toward my salvation about a quarter inch a minute. Any second I expected the two goons to appear and shoot me in the knees as my torso disappeared into the enclosed part of the elevator shaft. Approximately two years later, I emerged into an industrial kitchen, and my ankles were still intact.

I hadn't thought of the possibility someone might be working in the kitchen until the elevator had bumped to a stop and I'd already slid both gates open. Somehow, my luck held, and the space was unoccupied. I slunk past a greasy Autofry machine—which must've replaced the fryer down below—and two refrigerators to a set of swinging saloon-style, louvered doors.

Beyond, a black-walled hall opened into a bar. Restrooms on one side and a closed door, probably to a storage area or an office, on the other. I caught a glimpse of the bar beyond the hallway, recognized the partially lit string of Christmas lights. Where was the bartender?

The soft whir of the elevator's motor registered in the back of my mind a moment before my conscious brain recognized what the sound meant.

Cheese and freaking rice. Bender and Canavaro were knocking on my ass. The one thing going for me was the elevator's incredible lack of speed. The antique machinery had to inch itself down before it would inch them topside. I had at least five minutes. Right? Unless they knew of a way to speed the apparatus up.

I wasn't about to stick around to find out. Through the swinging doors I went, took two steps and skidded to a stop when I heard the someone laugh out by the bar and another person spoke, but not loud enough for me to hear.

Fuckeroni. The bartender? And who? Instead of following my original plan and streaking past the bar and out the front, I detoured through the closest door, realizing at the last moment a sign on it read DICKS. Big surprise there. But if the Dick's room had a window, I might be in the business of a real escape.

My breath hitched and my eyes watered from the stench. The two-stall, one urinal john was deadly. And after a fast check, no window from which to escape.

Now what?

I had to get a message out. But how? I tried not to gag and locked myself in the stall furthest from the door. From the black slime on low the back wall and the buildup of god-awful gross gunk around the pipe behind the seat, I doubted any cleaning had occurred in recent memory.

Ew. Do not touch anything, Shay.

I grabbed my smashed phone out of my pocket and pressed the thumb sensor. The spiderwebbed screen still lit up. If only I could use my voice to make it function.

My voice. Voice activate it.

Siri. She could be voice-activated. Maybe enough of the phone still worked, and I could make Siri send a text to JT.

Wait a second. I was an idiot. Help was in my other pocket via Tim Burr's phone. I could call 911 and rouse the cavalry. Thirteen seconds later I swore under my breath and returned Tim's phone to my pocket. It was as dead as I was going to be if I didn't get my shit together. I must have forgotten to turn the damn flashlight off.

Back to Siri. What did one have to say to access her? "Siri," I whispered.

Zilch.

Maybe I wasn't speaking loud enough. I tried again.

Nope.

What the hell? "Siri, activate."

Stubborn little bitch remained silent.

"Hey, Siri."

A ta-ting sounded.

Yes!

Now all I needed to do was tell her what I wanted her to do. "Send a text to JT."

"Okay," Siri screeched at a volume I was sure would be heard all the way out to the bar. "What do you want it to say?"

I almost dropped the phone in the toilet in my haste to turn down the volume. Last thing I needed was to get caught in the skanky Dick's room because my artificial intelligence assistant had a big mouth.

Spit it out, Shay. "Big trouble at the Drunken Tankard. Send help ASAP."

She repeated who the text was being sent to and my then dictation, but now the sound was too low to hear at all. I raised it in time to catch her say, "Ready to send it?"

"Yes," I hissed.

"Okay, it's sent."

The door thankfully remained closed, and my breath came shallow and rapid. I jammed the phone into my pocket and tried to come up with a new escape strategy. How long had it been since I'd heard the elevator moving? A minute? Two? I couldn't stay here in hopes JT would sweep in and save me. The longer I dallied, the more certain my demise.

To hell with it. Mad dash time. Maybe the bartender would be too preoccupied to pay me any attention. I was fast. If I could make it out to the sidewalk, I'd be home free.

Go, now.

As I exited the stall, I caught sight of my reflection in the grimy mirror above a grimier sink. My hair stood on end. One side of my face looked like I'd skidded across a gravel road. Smudges of dirt covered my exposed skin.

Yikes.

I cracked the door open only enough for a quick hallway check. All clear. You're so close to a clean getaway, Shay. Stroll out as if you own the place and if anyone looks like they might leap up and give chase, then run like hell.

With a regrettably deep breath, I slipped out the door and set a walking pace of about seventeen miles an hour. I burst into the front of house and kept right on going. The stools in front of the bar were now unoccupied. The bartender was at the far end of the bar, face down in his phone. He glanced up as I came abreast. I couldn't not look at him, and as he met my eyes, recognition dawned.

Five long strides and I'd be out the door.

Four.

Three.

Two.

Wham! I heard a crackling and a guttural shriek of pain. Then I was sliding across the floor face-first. My body shuddered to a stop not two feet from freedom. I couldn't move. Couldn't breathe.

The pain receded as fast as it'd hit. My body still didn't want to work.

Shouting.

Lots of shouting.

Someone yanked me vertical, pinned my arms behind my back. My legs were so weak that if I hadn't been held up, I'd have fallen right back down.

Then Canavaro was there, all disheveled and wild-eyed. "Where are the drugs, you nasty piece of shit?"

I didn't know how he expected me to answer when I couldn't feel, much less move, my lips.

"Malcolm," Bender yelled, apparently to the bartender, "put the Taser away and get the duct tape and a rag."

Taser.

Oh.

Canavaro grabbed the hair on top of my head and shook me like he was cooking popcorn on the stove. My brain rattled. Now I knew what the kernels inside a pan of Jiffy Pop felt like. "Where'd you hide the fucking dope, bitch?"

When I didn't answer, he pulled an arm back and socked me smack in the eye. My brain rattled again. No compunction there not to hit a girl. Wanted to give him the finger if only I'd been able to. I did manage a "Fuck you," before he hauled off and tried to put his fist through my stomach.

I doubled over, struggled for air. Tried not to throw up. Holy crap, a punch to the solar plexus hurt.

Malcolm returned. He and Canavaro did a very efficient duct tape job—arms behind my back, ankles together—as if they'd done it before. Malcolm stuffed a rag in my mouth and wound tape across my face and around my head so I couldn't spit it out. The only saving grace to the fiasco was Malcolm's choice of clean towel for the job.

"That should do you," he breathed in my ear from behind. "Till I can do you." He pressed himself against me, up close and personal, his hot breath on the back of my neck and his crotch against my ass. I might not've had control over all my muscles, but I jerked my head forward and slammed it back into his face.

"OW!" he howled and let me go. "My fuging nose."

Hopefully I broke his "fuging" nose.

Canavaro grabbed my arm before I hit the floorboards again.

Bender laughed. "Bitch has a little fight left in her." Where'd he come from? It all happened so fast, from the initial tasing, to the trussing, to bashing Malcolm in the schnozz that my electrified brain was having a hard time tracking.

A phone rang.

Canavaro retrieved his phone without loosening his grip. "What?" He was silent a few seconds. "Jesus fucking Christ. I swear I cannot get a break. We'll be right there."

"What?" Bender asked.

"We need to get that shipment out of the conference center. Vendors are getting pissed because it's blocking up the storage area."

"That's a 'you' job."

"No, that's a 'we' job.

"Burr was yours, not mine."

"If we don't get the shipment, we can't sell it and if we can't sell it we can't pay for the drugs. We don't pay for the drugs, we're dead. You really don't want to piss her off, do you?"

I stiffened. Her? Seriously? The person at the helm of this evil, sordid, horrifying project was a woman?

"Oh, hell. No. What are we gonna do with this one?"

Bender raked me with the fire of hatred in his eyes. "Drop her again. When we come back I'll have a great time forcing the bitch to tell us where she hid the shit."

Malcolm hit the switch and floor dropped. Canavaro dragged me over to the edge of the hole and let go. I swayed. My leg muscles still didn't want to work.

"*Hasta la vista*, baby," Bender said, and gave me a shove.

Over the edge I went.

My feet hit the ground first. The shock of it sent splintering pain from my heels to my shins. I crumpled like an accordion, then tipped onto something sort of softish.

With utter horror I realized I'd landed on top of poor Tim Burr.

CHAPTER SEVENTEEN

JT

The Old Town Pizza delivery guy finally arrived. After she'd taken the first bite, JT was surprised at how hungry she actually was. She took a second bite and shoved it to one side of her mouth. "Wha kina pizza zith?"

Coop laughed. "I think it's the Ghost Pie. Alfredo, chicken, red peppers, mushrooms. Probably some special seasonings and secret ingredients. Other one's pepperoni."

Twelve minutes later, JT closed the lid on the now empty Ghost Pie box and set it on top of the small garbage can.

Coop flopped back on the bed, a hand on his stomach. "I think I could have eaten another one."

"Piece or pie?"

"Pie, of course."

"Of course. I swear you have two hollow—"

A snippet of the song "Sweet Emotion" sounded on JT's cell phone. "Text from Shay." She snatched the cell off the desk.

Coop was on his feet and beside her in the time it took the text to pop up.

I'm in big teeth at the Drunk Tank. Send help ASAP.

Their eyes met. JT wondered if the expression on her face was anything like Coop's. Confusion and annoyance colored with a tinge of anxiety. "Has Shay decided to become a lush and is locked up in some drunk tank? Or is she trying to tell us she's hammered at the Drunken Tankard?"

Coop pulled up Trip a Go Go. They watched the screen populate, and sure enough, Shay's avatar was right on top of the Tankard.

"For fuck's sake." The midlevel panic which had taken up residence in JT's gut subsided and anger bubbled like a now-active volcano. "Where's Mugs's number?" She shuffled through one pocket, then the other, before finding it.

Coop snitched a piece of pepperoni and stuffed half of it in his mouth. "Wha?" he said to the look JT leveled at him and swallowed. "Stress eating. Plus I need to keep my strength up."

"Sure you do, big guy." She dialed the number. Mugs answered on the second ring. JT explained the need for another trip to the dive bar.

Six minutes later, Coop and JT were on the way with Mugs driving as fast as she could considering the busy city streets. Four minutes later she pulled up to the curb outside the bar.

"Want me to wait?" Mugs cast a glance in the rearview mirror and JT met her gaze.

"If you don't mind."

"Nope. I'm dying to meet phantom Shay."

"You and me both," JT said. "Thanks."

As they entered the bar, two men stormed toward the exit. Baseball and Suit, the same two guys she'd seen earlier. Suit literally shouldered JT out of his way in his haste to leave.

"Excuse me," she called after him sarcastically, and added "asshole" under her breath. What was with people these days?

Once their eyes readjusted to the dimness, JT saw all the tables were empty. Coop walked over to check out the booths yet again.

The bartender was now perched on a stool behind the bar, holding a bag of ice to his face. Maybe Baseball and Suit's argument had erupted into fisticuffs, and he'd gotten between them.

"Checking in again." JT gripped the edge of the bar with both hands. "Any sightings of a woman with black spiked hair?"

"No."

"You sure?"

He flipped her off.

JT repressed the desire to rip his head off and met Coop at the hall leading to the restrooms and the kitchen. "Bartender still says he hasn't seen her. What a jackass."

"She's not in any of the booths or passed out under any tables. Let's check the bathrooms again."

Twenty seconds later they reconvened.

JT's previous level of relief had redevolved and she was fully and completely out of patience. "I don't know what kind of bullshit my fiancée is pulling, but I've had enough. Go Go showed her here. GPS doesn't lie." She spun on her heel and marched back to Ice Pack.

"Dude. We've been tracking my girlfriend for hours. Trip a Go Go says she's right here." Her voice rose. "Right in this goddamn bar. Where is she? You know—" JT was interrupted by a faint thudding coming from somewhere below their feet. "What's that?"

"What?" Coop asked.

"Thumping. Can't you hear it?"

Ice Pack mumbled, "I don't hear nothing."

Thump.

"There. That."

Thud. Thud thud. Thump. The sound wasn't loud, and it was hard to pinpoint where it was coming from. "For chrissake, what is that thumping?"

Thump, thump.

Coop narrowed his eyes as he cocked his head. "I hear it."

Ice Pack shrugged. "Old buildings creak and groan."

JT made a strangled sound and restrained herself from grabbing the front of Ice Pack's shirt. The effort made her shake. "What the flying fuck ever. Listen to me. Shay's supposed to be here. Where the hell is she?"

"You don't have to yell, crazy lady. Like I said, no chick's been in." Ice Pack stared apathetically at her.

Calm, JT, she ordered herself. She inhaled long and blew out slow, fighting the impulse to add more bruises to his face. "Show him, Coop. Show him she's here."

Coop glanced at his phone. "She is. She's right—uh."

JT cut him a glance. Her gut fell at his expression, and he handed her his cell. Where Shay's avatar had been, it was no longer. "Jesus Christ. We're in Portland's version of *Groundhog Day*."

"Told ya," Ice Pack said.

"Come on, Coop." JT spun and they swept out of the bar.

CHAPTER EIGHTEEN

Shay

I flopped around in a panic trying to wiggle myself off poor Tim, but it was harder than expected with the whole hogtie thing happening.

After a few tries, I managed to bounce onto the dirt floor. Then I put three additional flops between the two of us for good measure. My hands were going numb. I needed a pillow to prop my head up and take the strain off my neck. This so wasn't an appropriately ergonomic position. A good, long visit to a chiropractor and a masseuse were in my future, assuming I'd live long enough to have a future.

My brain ached. In fact, almost everything ached. The eye Bender blasted was swollen. I'd wound up with a bloody nose after wiping the floor with my face when Malcolm, good old buddy he wasn't, tased me. Mouth breathing was difficult with a soggy rag in the way, but luckily, my schnozz still worked even after the beating it'd taken. My cheek and forehead stung now that more grit was embedded in my flesh.

I closed my eyes. Why the hell was I so goddamn nosy? JT was always warning me about my overactive curiosity.

JT. What if I never saw her again? We'd never made our wedding plans. I hadn't told her I loved her the last time I was with her. I didn't tell her she was my heart, in fact, my entire world. I wouldn't get a chance to find out if Tulip really was pregnant, and I wouldn't be able to talk to Eddy about what was going on with her. My dad, Coop…holy shit, stop it, Shay. I needed to rearrange the direction of my thinker, stat.

I squinted at the faint outline of light seeping around the edges of the trapdoor. Eventually my breath evened out and the feeling I was about to expire eased. I tested the duct tape securing my wrists, but they'd done a fine job of applying it. The binding around my ankles was not as tight, but that wasn't saying much.

Exhaustion billowed through me like a top sheet settling onto a freshly made bed. I shut my eyes again. Might as well get what rest I could until the rollercoaster stopped click, click, clicking and I slid into freefall.

Present, past, future. It all twined together in the dark. I felt like I was floating and time as I knew it ceased to exist.

After a while, voices penetrated my daze. I wondered if I were dreaming. Then, loud and clear, a very familiar voice shouted, "We've been tracking my girlfriend for hours." My good eye sprang open.

"Where. Is. She?" echoed through the trapdoor.

Oh, my god. JT was right above me. I lost my mind, grunting, squealing, yelling, crying, anything to make enough noise to catch her attention. I slammed my heels on the dirt floor. I tried to send her psychic messages.

"Shay's supposed to be here. Where the goddamn hell is she?"

Oh, was she mad.

I screamed through the rag, flung myself wildly around, hoping to run into something I could bang against. My shins smashed into an immobile object, the pain momentarily all-consuming. Through the haze of agony, I realized it was a pillar. Where was it? The damn dark was too damn dark.

I found it again. Tried to hold myself on target, repeatedly ramming my feet against the wood as hard as I could. Would've worked better if I'd had hard-soled shoes on, but I still made some solid connections.

JT said something at a lower volume about a flying fuck. I doubled down, pounded the ever-loving shit out of that pillar, screaming her name through the gag. My breath came in jagged, snotty snorts.

Finally I could do no more. My muscles gave out, leaving me quivering. I screamed again, knowing it was useless, but couldn't make myself stop. Eventually my screaming became moaning, and then I didn't have the energy to do even that.

Tears of frustration leaked from my eyes as I strained to hear my lover's voice. Instead, the oppressive sound of silence sucked the last of the fight out of me.

CHAPTER NINETEEN

Eddy

"Ms. Eddy, Stark's Vacuum Museum is part of Stark's Vacuum, a retail store established in 1932 by none other than Mr. Clarence Stark himself!"

Eddy navigated a crumbled chunk of sidewalk as she and Rocky strolled the streets of Portland's downtown on the way to Stark's. She was incredibly relieved the prospect of investigating archaic cleaning devices was working to distract Rocky from obsessing about his wife.

His face lit up as he shared his prearrival research into what they were about to experience. "The museum is one entire wall! There is a historical timeline of dirt sucker-uppers, and real live antique vacuums mounted on the museum wall. Did you know, Ms. Eddy, the first carpet sweeper was invented in 1860? In 1901, Mr. Herbert Booth, of England, and Mr. David Kenney, of the USA, created the very first official sucker-uppers. Mr. Booth called his Puffing Billy. It looked like a fire truck. They needed a wagon and horses to pull it to appointments.

"Mr. Kenney's sucker weighed four thousand pounds. Which is two tons. Workers fed hoses into houses through windows and doors. And they had to feed the horses too, probably."

"My goodness. Sounds like a lot of work."

"Yes, Ms. Eddy. It does."

In two shakes and a wag of a boxer dog's tail, they found themselves at their destination.

The staff was kind and patiently answered all of Rocky's very specific questions. While he was busy investigating the ancient "sucker-uppers," Eddy test drove one of the modern Dyson models. It sucked the carpet like nobody's business and cleaned the wallet out as well.

When she finished, Rocky was still grilling Stark staff. She checked her watch. Only a little after four. An eternity till six. She hunted on her phone's map for someplace to grab a bite when they were done here. She found the Ranger Chocolate Company right on the other side of the block.

Less than fifteen minutes later the two of them emerged from the store, enriched with the knowledge of the vacuum cleaners ever so fascinating history. Eddy asked, "Rocky, would you like a snack at the Ranger Chocolate Company?"

He slid a finger under his aviator hat and scratched behind his ear as he considered the offer. "Ms. Eddy, I do not want to eat if my poor Tulip is not going to eat."

"You have to keep your strength up to help Tulip, Rocky. And who knows, maybe they are feeding your bride the Bugles she loves so much."

"Oh, yes, Ms. Eddy. I like it. Chocolate and Bugles. We have exactly one hour and fifty-seven minutes until six and I see my Tulip again. And we will have time to check out this strange and amazing Freakybuttrue Peculiarium before the agreed-upon time."

"Right on." Eddy crossed her fingers, toes, and would've crossed her eyes if she would have been able to walk without injuring herself. Whatever happened, she was sure she could talk some sense into the terrible, no good, very naughty duo.

They traipsed down Northeast Couch and made a right on MLK Jr. Boulevard. Rocky saw the entrance to Ranger before she did and dashed inside.

Minutes later they returned to the sidewalk. Ranger did as good a job cleaning out one's wallet as the Dyson, but the avocado and lemon ricotta toast was worth every cent. Eddy never had toast quite so delicious. Maybe Shay could add something like it to the Rabbit Hole's menu.

"Thank you, Ms. Eddy, for the most delightful Ranger cookie, my tall, cool glass of milk, and for allowing me to buy a sweet for my sweet Tulip." He clutched a fancy paper bag with twine handles containing a bag of chocolate-covered cherries.

"You're very welcome, Rocky."

They stopped on the corner of MLK and Couch to wait for their Ryde. Eddy had given Niccolo a buzz, but he was busy with a passenger, so she'd summoned another car while they ate.

Their Ryde scooped them up and, in no time at all, dropped them in front of a two-story, teal-gray brick building trimmed in hunter green. Two doors at either end of the edifice led up to what presumably were apartments. The front of the building was almost entirely plate glass, with the entrance—two solid, hunter-green doors—situated at the center. Above the doors, an orange banner with scrolled ends on a black background read "The Peculiarium," and below it, "Established 1972."

One of the doors was propped open, allowing passersby a glimpse of what awaited within. From the view without, Eddy wasn't sure she wanted to have what was certain to be one heck of an experience. Too bad Agnes was back home. She would've delighted in dragging Eddy into the confounding depths of the joint.

"Whoa, Ms. Eddy, check out the mannequin on the roller cart parked on the sidewalk in front of that sign." He squinted. "TODAY'S CURRENT ZOMBIE THREAT LEVEL. I think he has been zombified. He has a green, scaly, reptile head with shiny blue things on his very bulgy eyes." Rocky stared, his own eyes wide, at the collection of oddities occupying the space in front of the windows. "Holy wow. Look at the gigantic tennis shoe. I could fit inside of it if I scrunched up a lot. And the ax on the side of the sneaker. Did you know, Ms. Eddy, not everyone calls an athletic shoe a tennis shoe? Some people call it a sneaker and some call it a gym shoe, or a trainer. Or even just a plain old shoe."

"I certainly did not know that, Rocky."

"The red checkers decorating the shoe look like Paul Bunyan's flannel shirt. Maybe it is Paul Bunyan's shoe. Not sure I believe in Mr. Bunyan, but it is fun to imagine him."

Hoo boy. This visit was going to wear Eddy out for shizzles. Which, as she thought about it, was impressive because she wasn't already worn out. At the chocolate shop she hadn't even had a cup of coffee. Her energy level surprised her. She'd forgotten what it was like to not fall asleep whenever she sat her keister down. Plus, it was sure nice not to have to pee forty-eight times an hour.

Another mannequin in a 1920s wheelchair lounged beside a wood-slat bench situated on one side of the door. He could've been Lurch's older, bonier brother, and Eddy thought Larry was a good name for him. Larry sported a neon-green tuft of hair on top of his head and green tufts over both ears. His sharp features and hawklike nose gave him a "Terrifying Butler Risen From the Dead" appearance. Yikes. She decided the inside of the place was probably even crazier than the outside, and she'd hunker down with Larry to wait for Rocky. She paid the five-buck admission and watched Rocky happily disappear through a hanging gray curtain, which was nothing more than a sheet split down the middle. He was raring to view and interact with the collection of delightful and horrifying delights beyond, beginning with the anti-Santa Krampus she glimpsed before the sheet fell back in place. She knew from watching a movie called *Krampus: the Christmas Devil* a few years ago Krampus was half-goat, half-demon, a monster who scared kids into being good if he didn't kill them first.

She briefly perused the gift shop, waved to the friendly clerk, and settled in the sunshine beside Larry. He didn't say anything, but then again, he was most certainly a quiet sort. She extracted her phone from a pocket and checked the digital clock. An hour and fifteen to go before Tulip Time. She heaved a heavy sigh, opened *Grand Theft Auto III*, and resumed hijacking cars.

CHAPTER TWENTY

Shay

The sound of a door slamming against something startled me out of my stupor. My mouth was parched, and my jaws sore from chewing on the rag. Everything ached. Ignore it, Shay. Stay sharp.

Bender and Canavaro made no effort to be quiet. The glow of their flashlights grew brighter as they approached. Bender shined the light directly into my good eye and nudged me in the ribs with his foot.

I jerked.

"Yup. She's still kicking."

"Uk oo," I said.

"Canavaro, you get Burr. I'll carry the sassy one up." Bender thumped my side again.

I stifled the pained "oof" that rose in my throat. Hell if I was going to give them the satisfaction.

Bender bent over, his face six inches from mine. "Give me any trouble and I'll do more than shock you this time." The leer on his face made very clear his intention.

With a grunt, he hoisted me up and slung me over his shoulder like a bag of flour. Asshole was stronger than he looked. His shoulder jammed into my abdomen. So hard to breathe. For a fraction of a second, I entertained the thought of practicing my newly honed fish flop and making a very ungraceful dismount. But then I considered the potential consequences and changed my mind. My chances might be better when I was out of the dungeon.

I couldn't see Canavaro manhandle Tim Burr, but from the sound of it, he was having some difficulty.

Bender had taken three steps when an out-of-breath Canavaro said, "He's too fucking heavy."

"Jesus. Put him on the cart. I need to get this nosy bitch into the van before she breaks my shoulder."

Good. Hopefully I hurt more than your shoulder, you jack.

Bender made a beeline to the door leading to the elevator and staggered as he turned into the passage. I thought we were going to go down, but he rallied and lurched along until we made the storage room, a horror-filled déjà vu.

His breath came fast and hard. Maybe he'd have a heart attack.

Bender slid me off his shoulder and let me drop onto the metal floor of the elevator.

I half expected the move, landed hard but managed to avoid hitting my head.

He rolled the gates closed and we began to rise, a fraction of an inch at a time.

"Come here, bitch." With a fistful of my shirt, Bender dragged me to my feet and grabbed my throat, pinning me against the side of the elevator. His fingers were going to pierce my flesh and crush my windpipe if he applied much more pressure. In his other hand he produced a black stub-nosed gun and imprinted the barrel right between my eyes. The pressure banged the back of my head against the wrought iron.

A gun.

In my face.

Not once, but twice today.

I was going for a record.

"I'd like nothing better than to cap your ass right now, you drug-hiding fuck." His foul breath was hot. "You listen very carefully. I'm gonna cut the tape off your ankles and I hate making a mess."

"Ahhay." If he thought for one flipping second I wasn't gonna take advantage of having lower appendage mobility he was looney toons. As soon as the opportunity said "How do?" I'd reply "See ya," gun or no.

He ground the barrel against my forehead for emphasis then stepped back, fingers still digging into my throat. He stowed the six-shooter and replaced it with a switchblade, which he popped open. A finger's length of finely-honed, wicked sharp steel waggled an inch from my face.

I couldn't stop the flinch and detested the smirk on his ugly mug.

The bastard laughed. Caressed my cheek with the ice cold shank. "The things I could carve into your body. Just you wait." He reached down and with a flick sliced through the tape binding my ankles together.

He stood, pocketed the knife, and leaned in till we were nose to nose. He released my throat and placed his hands on my shoulders, fingertips compressing both sides of my neck. My vision narrowed until all I could see were the pores in his schnoz as my eyes began to cross.

"Don't fuck with me." He slammed me against the side of the elevator and let go. This slamming business was getting old fast. My head swam and my knees threatened to buckle as I tried to hoover oxygen in through my nose.

With a whir and a soft clank, we ground to a halt. My brain, only moments ago full of marshmallow thoughts, was now on fire. How was he going to get me out of the bar? Would he march me right past his patrons? Was there a back entrance I didn't know about?

Bender dragged me in front of him and twisted the back of my shirt in one hand, giving me a sharp jerk to remind me who exactly was in charge. Then I felt pressure as he pressed what was probably the gun against my spine. "Any funny moves and you'll wish you still had the ability to walk."

We exited the lift, and he directed me not through the swinging gates, but through a door I'd missed the first time around, hidden from view by the coolers, and propelled me into an alley. The van Canavaro had made me drive to the bar was parked near the door. The alley was deserted except for overflowing dumpsters and trash spilling from said dumpsters.

Damn. I was on my own.

"To the rear of the van." Bender continued to attempt to pierce my hide with the muzzle as we shuffled around the vehicle in lockstep. "Stop."

I stopped.

He circled around me to open one of the back doors. The gun was still in his hand, but at least it wasn't threatening to paralyze me.

Most of the cargo area was taken up by Flying High Coffee crates stacked lengthwise across the floor and piled almost to the ceiling. They'd left a four-foot gap between the crates and the back doors, where presumably they'd planned to stash Tim Burr.

And me.

If I wound up in that little slice of hell, I was a goner for sure, which would not do, not at all.

When Bender reached for the release to swing the other door open, I slammed my foot into the back of his leg and prayed I wouldn't topple over myself.

The impact smashed his knee against the bumper. He yelped and sagged sideways.

Quick as lightning I nailed his other leg before he could right himself.

He dropped to the ground with a shriek of pain.

How do you like that, you gnarly fuck?

I streaked away from the van. My escape ended about seven strides in when someone smashed into me from the side. We tumbled across the pavement and skidded to a stop next to one of the crusty dumpsters. A heavy body who needed a serious deodorant refresh pinned me to the gritty asphalt.

"Gotcha, ya fookin' floozy," a gleeful male voice growled. "I owe you for a busted nose." He dragged me to my feet, wrapped an arm tight around my neck. Hot breath sizzled against my ear as the arm tightened, cutting off my blood supply yet again. What was it with these guys and their disdain for respiration?

"Malcolm!" Bender yelled as my vision swam. "Stop it. We still need her. Get her in the fucking van and get back inside."

Ah, the tasing bartender was the one slowly dimming my world.

Malcolm eased up. I blinked.

Bender, rubbing his hopefully very damaged knees, stood straight. The snarly expression on his face turned him into a truly horrible Elvis impersonator. If a look could decimate, I'd be annihilated. Malcolm heaved me into the van like a bag of garbage and slammed the doors so hard the vehicle rocked. Good thing I'd jerked my legs in, or I'd be all set to hobble around without any feet.

The change from light to sudden dark was disorienting. I struggled to make out what was being said but the voices faded as I wiggled upright, hands jammed between my back and the crates. Something sharp scraped my skin and I jerked forward.

What was that?

I fumbled my fingers over the wood until I felt a hinge screw on the crate behind me that had come loose, protruding maybe half an inch. The edge of the screw was sharp, would rip up my arm if I wasn't careful. I shifted away from it, then froze.

Hold up, Charlie Brown.

If it could cut me, it could cut something else.

I rearranged myself and searched for the problematic hinge again. The movement was excruciating. My shoulders felt like they might pop out of their sockets. Luckily, it didn't take long to find.

As I tried to work the binding against the screw head, I had a vision of ripping out of my bonds like Bruce Banner busting out of his clothes as he morphed into The Hulk. Okay, maybe that was going a little too far, but the image gave me something to focus on.

Ignore the pain, Shay, and keep at it. Up, down. Up, down.

I felt the tape rip, then it began bunching instead of separating. Beads of sweat formed on my forehead. I fumbled with the screw to try and loosen it a little more but it wouldn't budge. Back at it, bunching or not. As I worked, I thought some thoughts. What were Bender and Canavaro talking about? What was their plan with the ammunition? Who were they going to sell it to? When were they going to squeeze me for the location of the blow? I didn't want to think about the how.

So many questions.

A sharp bang on the outside of the van scared the shit out of me.

Indistinct voices grew louder, then the rear doors opened.

Before my brain had a chance to scream "Get out!" Bender and Canavaro tried to hoist a burrito-ized Burr into the van. They'd rolled him in an old, ragged piece of carpet. Poor schlep looked like a giant Schwan's Bagel Dog, except his head and feet protruded from opposite ends of the bagel.

"Tilt him up." Bender's neck veins bulged from the effort. "I need to get his feet in. Asshole's too tall."

"Wait. Lemme get his head inside." Canavaro's face was stroke-out red.

"No, feet first. Then I'll bend his legs so you can cram his head in."

"It'll work better if—"

"Shut the fuck up and lemme do it. Fuck's sake, Canavaro."

Oh, my god. The two murderous, ammo running, coffee-switch-and-baiters bickered like Eddy and Agnes.

After more yapping, they managed to manhandle Burr into the van, the bulk of his body across my lap. They slammed the doors shut fast, probably in case he might reanimate and leap out like one of the walking dead.

"Jesus." I could barely make out Canavaro's words. "If that nosy little twat had kept her busybody self out of my business we wouldn't be in this mess."

"And if you hadn't lipped off to that coffee guy at the convention who was pissed at you for taking up so much room with the crates, he probably wouldn't have called the cops, you dumbshit."

"Jolly Lolly. Jackwad's had it in for me since I undercut his bid for the Kroger contract three years ago. Jolly Lolly's Java Juice. Worse than Flying High, and that's not saying much."

"How can you care about coffee at a time like this? You're an idiot, Canavaro. If you hadn't gotten into it with him—what the fuck kind of name is Jolly Lolly, anyway—fuck. It's done. Another five minutes and we would've been long gone. Instead, the 5-0 now have three loaded crates—with your goddamn logo—filled with stolen military ammunition. You know the first thing they're going to do is show up on your doorstep. Which will lead them straight to mine."

Silence.

Then Canavaro said, "We're both screwed. Fuck it. I'm gonna kill that piece of trash busybody right now."

"No, just cool your fucking jets. Let me think."

I worked the binds faster.

More silence.

Bender said, "We need to get rid of the evidence. The ammo and the collateral damage."

Were Burr and I the collateral damage? Of course we were.

"What do you propose?"

"Burn it down. Burn it all down. This bar. The entire Crook County Packing and Distribution plant. Everything. Burr can be kindling, and we'll incinerate the girl too. Let her feel what it's like to have flames licking at her flesh. Too bad I won't have time to play with that meddling piece of ass after all."

"That witch deserves to fry. What about the coke?"

"No time," Bender said. "We need to light up this place and get down to the distro center. I'll call Malcolm on the way and have him take care of this dump."

All my work hiding those drugs to use them as leverage was up in smoke. Figuratively, and apparently soon, literally. At least burning it would be better than being snorted up someone's nose.

"How are we gonna pay up without the drugs? Those people don't mess around, Bender."

"Never mind the money. We can deal with that later. Let's get moving."

Canavaro said something I couldn't make out.

"We'll get the fucking gas from the onsite pump. I'll start with the office and make sure the records get a good dousing. You do the outside. We'll meet to finish soaking down the interiors and the ammo and the two business busting assholes in the back of the van. Maybe leave a trail of gas back to the underground tank. Then we'll flick the Bic and watch it go WHOOSH!"

"Great balls of fire. When the ammo blows," Canavaro said, "it'll be the cherry on top."

"Right. Then we head for the border, cross at the tunnel. See if we can coordinate with Lauryn Grant to get transport out of North America."

Transport out of North America? What the hell? Were these two yahoos part of some kind of international...what? Kabal? Cartel? Street gang? And Lauryn Grant must be the woman in charge.

"Come on. We've got a three-hour ride," Canavaro said. "Pull off the Ochoco Creek Coffee signs and dumpster them. That'll buy us a little extra time."

Banging and a ripping sounds came from both sides of the van. The signs must've been magnetic. Once they were removed, it wouldn't be at all apparent what the van was used for or who it belonged to without the cops running the license plates. Of course, the plates might be stolen. Couldn't discount anything with those two.

The van rocked as they climbed aboard. We jounced along the pothole-filled alley and were soon cruising toward this Crook County Packing and Distribution place, wherever it was.

My legs had fallen asleep, trapped as they were underneath Tim. I gingerly shimmied out from beneath him and pulled my knees up tight against my chest. The movement caused Burr's carpet-wrapped body to roll toward the van doors.

The vehicle rapidly decelerated. Tim Burr reversed course and came to a stop wedged against my legs. No way could my knees remain bent as they were, practically under my chin, feet jammed under Burr. I pried one foot out, and then the other, and held my legs above the carpet roll, doing a great imitation of a V sit-up. Holy cannoli. I seriously needed to do some core work. My legs trembled. My abs began to shake. I couldn't keep my legs in the air. With a whispered apology, I lowered them into Burr. He was now a giant, person-shaped body pillow.

A body pillow?

Shay O'Hanlon, did you just call a dead man a body pillow? Horror suffused my veins. That thought had come unbidden, zipped through my brain nonchalant as could be. As if Tim Burr's life meant nothing. This guy hadn't harmed me. Tim is a—was a—human being, had people who loved and cared about him.

Probably, anyway.

Shame and fear welled, suffusing my chest, making my face hot. I soaked in those emotions for a while.

Then an image of Eddy wandered into my mind, her face stern but kind. She wagged a finger at me. "Child, Mr. Tim isn't here anymore. He's not scared or hurting. He's flying with the angels." Her face scrunched, even in my mind's eye. "Or dancing with the devil incarnate. Whichever, no matter. This here?" She jabbed her finger downward. "It's not Tim. It's a shell. He's gone. But you? You're alive. You do whatever you need to get yourself out of the hotbox of trouble you're in, or you're really going to be in one heck of a Sriracha-covered pickle."

A patch of rough road jolted me back into stark reality. Phantom Eddy was right. I was still alive. I needed to do whatever was necessary to save my own keister. I had no intention of winding up an extra crispy corpse. I had too many things to do, too many people to tell I loved them. One "I do" to accomplish. And so many Voodoo Doughnuts to try.

Back at it, then.

The more I worked the tape against the head of the screw, the number my hands became. I lost count of how many times I had to stop and squeeze my fingers into a fist to get the blood recirculating. Eventually, the intense tingling and the fact I could barely bend my fingers assured me this was as real as it got.

Come on, Shay.

Time ticked away like a countdown timer on a bomb. I leaned into my job with renewed energy. As I worked, I thought about my broken phone. Then I thought about virtual assistants. If I could free my hands, maybe I could try and make Siri call or text JT.

In a perfect world, if Coop's Trip a Go Go thing actually worked, JT would be able to see wherever the hell I ended up. When Canavaro and Bender finally stopped, the cops might be right there waiting, handcuffs at the ready.

I bit down on the rag in my mouth and went back at it.

CHAPTER TWENTY-ONE

JT

JT paced the room she and Shay shared, much as Rocky had done hours earlier. On the way back to the motel, she'd texted Eddy, who was doing what she could to distract the Rockster until the six o'clock rendezvous. They'd finished at the incredible, amazing, must be seen to be believed vacuum cleaner museum and were headed to some chocolate shop. Eddy had mentioned she'd tried a Dyson and liked it, although it sounded like she'd been traumatized by the price. JT filed the info away as a potential gift idea.

Coop lay on one of the beds, feet hanging over the mattress, refreshing Trip a Go Go every thirty seconds.

"Ice Pack is lying," she said.

"I don't disagree, but why would he lie? What's in it for him?"

"How the hell did you become so logical, Mr. Cooper?"

"I'm a geeky computer guy. We have to be logical sometimes."

Fair.

Coop shrugged. "Other than the pings, we don't have any proof Shay was even there at all."

"True. I seriously don't know if I should be as alarmed as I feel or if I should just figure she's in some drunk tank sobering up. But that would be so far out of character for her I can't see it."

"Agreed. Although maybe the wedding talk really did freak her out. Brides are known to lose their minds, or so I've heard."

JT raised a brow. "You've heard that, huh?"

He peered over his phone at her. "*Bridezillas* on WE TV. It's kind of addicting. Plus, I thought I'd get some insight into weddings for you and the Great Disappearing Act."

"*Bridezillas*? The Great Disappearing Act?" JT laughed, then narrowed her eyes. "Nicholas Cooper. Now I have the dirt on you. You now must bend to my every whim or I'll out you as a *Bridezilla* watcher."

"Idle threats. The extent I go for my best bud's wedding."

JT grabbed a pillow and chucked it at him.

He caught it and walloped her with it.

"Buster, it's on." She nabbed another pillow and took a whack.

"Hey!" Coop dropped the phone and secured his squishy weapon with both hands. He ducked out of the way of JT's next swipe and scrambled across the bed.

JT hopped on the mattress in hot pursuit and swatted his ass.

They laughed, on the edge of out-of-control, and damn it felt so good. Both of them needed a breather, even if it lasted only a few moments.

A couple minutes later, out of breath, they dropped side by side onto one of the beds.

Coop snagged his phone and did yet another refresh. He sat up fast.

Reflexively, she righted herself. "What?"

"Look."

She leaned in. Shay's avatar was back on the screen and was moving along Oregon 212, headed southeast. "This is all wrong. What the frankenfork?"

"She's almost to a town called Boring."

"And we're gonna be right behind her." JT fished out Mugs's card and dialed the number.

Mugs picked up on the first ring.

"Hey, it's JT. You up for a ride? We have a bead on phantom Shay. She's on 212, going through Clackamas."

"Hell, yeah. I love me a good chase. She's got what? Hmm. Maybe a twenty-minute head start. I'm dropping someone off. I can be there in ten."

"Thanks, Mugs." JT disconnected. "Ten minutes. I gotta pee. Be right back."

As she used the bathroom, her mind whirled. Should she call the cops? What exactly did she know? Nothing more than a stupid-ass dot representing the love of her life moving away from Portland in an app on the screen of a cell phone.

Maybe Shay did get cold wedding feet. But didn't her girlfriend have some responsibility to let the people in her life know what she was doing? And that she was okay?

Hell, yes.

When JT got her hands on her, she knew she'd be sorely tempted to handcuff Shay to her side.

On the other hand, if Shay really was in some kind of hot water, what exactly had she gotten herself into? At a coffee convention, no less.

JT washed her hands and peered at her exhausted, worried self in the mirror. "It's going to be okay," she told her reflection. She dried her hands and tried to believe that.

CHAPTER TWENTY-TWO

Shay

Sweat dripped down my face, stinging my eyes. The interior of the van was a sauna without the good sauna smell.

My shoulders screamed. The sides of my hands were chafed from rubbing against the crate as I rhythmically dragged the duct tape over my Lilliputian pseudo-saw. Periodically I tried to yank my wrists apart. I knew I was making progress because blood was flowing better to my fingers, but not quite enough progress to part the tape.

Canavaro and Malcolm must've used a gazillion layers. Jackwads.

I stopped again to catch my breath, air whistling through my nose. The snuffly sound reminded me of a Nat Geo Wild documentary of a rarely seen giant African forest hog being chased by a leopard. Whoever thought up gagging someone like this obviously never had it done to themselves. What if my nasal passages got plugged up? It'd be lights out.

"Shut up, Shay O'Hanlon. To get out of this you must get to work," Rocky's voice whispered in my brain.

Great. Now I was hallucinating Rocky. But his advice was sound.

Saw. Twist. Yank. Repeat. Time ceased to mean anything in the dark. Below my butt, the van's tires thrummed. Adrenaline had worn off, and the gag stifled a yawn. My jaw ached. I was so tired. Floaty and weak, again. One more try. Then I'd close my eyes and rest for a minute.

I leaned forward, ignored the pain, and wrenched the tape over the screw. On a downthrust, I felt the tape give, ever so slightly. It wasn't much but enough to kick me in the ass.

My pulse picked up. I repeated the wrist twist boogey and wondered when I was going to accidentally gouge a hand with the amount of pressure I was using.

The tape parted a bit further. I rammed my bindings against that damn screw in a frenzy. All at once the tape split apart. The gag stifled a victorious yelp.

Holy skipdoodles on a Ritz cracker! Adrenaline pounded. Freedom of movement was within reach.

My hands shook from the effort as I slowly peeled the tape off my right wrist, or rather, tried to peel my skin off the tape without leaving all of it behind. This stuff didn't feel at all like regular duct tape. Way too rubbery, way too much stick-um. It was like the tape Eddy brought home one day to wrap around the slivery handle of an old kitchen broom. Turned out she'd picked up Gorilla Tape, with double thick adhesive, two layers of fabric and a stretchy coating which was next to impossible to rip. You could slap that crap on a hole on the side of a ship and it would never sink.

My right hand eventually parted ways with the sticky shit from hell. I leaned against the crate and groaned. Tape still encircled my left wrist. The loose end flapped as I shook out my half-dead hands. My fingers felt like sausages. I ran the sausages over my Gorilla gag and followed its path across my cheeks, over my ears, and around the back of my head. Removing it was going to hurt like a bitch. Maybe if I ripped the tape apart at the corners of my lips, I could spit the sodden towel out of my mouth and leave the rest of the mess stuck until I had some help to remove it.

I worked a finger under the tape on one side of my mouth and slowly peeled it up. Big ow. This was going to end up a one-sided thing because peeling the skin off my face simply hurt too much.

Once I worked enough of the tape off my cheek, I pinched the edges between my fingernails and pulled in opposite directions.

The tape resisted.

I persisted. It ripped maybe a quarter inch. Halle-fricking-lujah.

Long moments later I pulled the disgustingly soggy cloth out of my mouth and tried to work up enough spit to swallow.

The rag gag dangled off my cheek. I was about to repeat the process on the other side of my mouth when it dawned on me it might be a good idea to appear as if I were still all bound up when Canavaro and Bender came to collect their loose ends. I'd buy a little time and that time might allow me to assess the situation before making any premature moves. It'd be easy enough to shove the detested rag back in my mouth and push the tape back on my face. If they looked closely, they'd realize something was weird, but better to take the chance than not.

I'd gotten so carried away with my sticky situation I'd forgotten my phone plan. I slid the phone out of my pocket and held my breath as I pressed the home button. The screen lit, glowing through the shattered glass like a kaleidoscope.

Hot diggety.

"Hey, Siri." I waited for the "ta tunk," which indicated Siri had initiated. Nothing happened. "Hey, Siri." Again nothing. What the hell? She'd worked when I whispered "Hey, Siri" at the Drunken Tankard, so why wasn't she working when I spoke the words? Did Siri only function if cell service was available? Maybe we were outside the coverage area.

Or it was possible the last tussle I had with good old Broken Snoot Malcolm might've done the phone in, even if it still had some juice left.

The sad fact was I had no idea where in the ever-loving hell we were and no way to find out.

Oh, come on, Shay, you know exactly where you are. You're in the back of a van with stolen ammunition and a dead body and your prospects for longevity aren't looking too hot.

Sometimes I hated my smart-ass brain.

I tilted my head back and rested it on the crate. Hope dissipated like a balloon with a pinhole, doing swirlies straight down the drain.

Stop it, I ordered myself. Pull it together. Think. You're not a quitter.

"Fine," I said aloud. "Inner self, you're one bossy bitch."

My inner self flipped me off.

All right then. What exactly did I know? We were headed for the Crook County Packing and Distribution center. Where was that? A three-hour drive somewhere outside Portland. As if I knew where much of anything was in Oregon.

Try the cell again. "Hey, Siri."

Nothing.

"Hey Siri."

Zipola.

I did three more Hey Siris. No response. The last dregs of my adrenaline dump dissipated. My bones ached. Everything hurt. I slumped against the crate, head in my hands. My eyes drooped as the swaying of the van lulled me into a fitful state of near sleep.

CHAPTER TWENTY-THREE

Eddy

An hour later, Rocky bounced out of the Peculiarium and threw himself on the bench beside Eddy, so full of tales of what he'd seen and experienced he was plum ready to burst. Eventually, he wound down until he sat silently beside her.

"Ms. Eddy, why did Tulip not tell me about the five thousand dollars she owes Pretty Boy Robbie and Scary Mary?"

"I have no good answer. Until we're able to have a conversation with your Tulip, we can only surmise."

"True." He leaned forward, fingers wrapped around the edge of the bench seat. "What happens when we give them the money but it's not all of it?"

Eddy held the silence a few beats. She'd wondered what would happen herself. "We'll cross that bridge in due time."

The hands on her watch inched closer to six, and seconds dragged on like hours.

The witching time came. The witching time went.

"It is 6:01 p.m." Rocky glanced up from his phone. "They are late, Ms. Eddy. It is no fun playing Monopoly by myself."

"I know it's not. We must have patience."

Seven minutes after six, Pretty Boy Robbie and Scary Mary appeared like phantoms from between two nearby buildings.

"Well, look who's here," Scary Mary said, her voice a sarcastic drawl.

Eddy wanted to say, well duh, of course we are.

"Where is my Tulip?" Rocky peered up and down the street.

"She's busy," Robbie said. "She sent us to pick up the money."

"I want my Tulip." Rocky stood, hands balled into fists at his side. "I want my Tulip. Right here. Right now."

Pretty Boy Robbie laughed in a way Eddy did not find at all amusing. "Give us the ching and we'll tell you where she is."

From her pocket, Eddy withdrew the wad of money and placed it in Scary Mary's outstretched hand. With any luck they'd be happy to take whatever she handed over. Eddy's heart knocked heavily in her chest.

"Don't let 'em leave," Scary Mary said to Pretty Boy Robbie. She walked over to an alcove alongside the building to count the money, probably so she wouldn't make herself a target for muggers. That would take the cake and the frosting too.

Rocky was statue still, for once not reciting a single factoid. That alone told Eddy how upset he was.

Scary Mary called Pretty Boy Robbie over for a brief conference, then they both came back. She gave Eddy the squint eye. "There's only one thousand three hundred and twelve bucks here."

"Don't forget the sixty-six cents," Eddy said.

"Whatevs. Where's the rest of the money?"

Rocky shifted beside her, and Eddy put a hand on his forearm. "We didn't have enough time to raise it all."

Mary glanced at Robbie, who gave her a nod. "We want the balance by 12:11 a.m. or we'll toss your little miss Tulip off the top of the Oaks Park Ferris wheel. She owes us. Meet us there with the dough. You call the cops, and you can kiss your animal-balloon maker goodbye."

The two con artist 'nappers retraced their steps and disappeared between the two buildings from which they'd emerged, like the snakes they were.

"Ms. Eddy, I do not want to kiss my animal balloon-maker wife goodbye. How are we going to come up with the money? We do not have any more. The banks are all closed." He literally wrung his hands. "Oh, my poor, poor, really poor, very poor Tulip. She must be so scared, and I am not there to comfort her."

"I know." She softened her tone. "Let me think a minute."

"Okay, Ms. Eddy."

She thought.

He paced, repeatedly checking his watch. "Ms. Eddy, one minute is up."

"Whew." She snapped her fingers. "One minute's all I needed. Look there how fast my mind worked. Like Crisco-ed lightning. I know exactly what we're going to do."

Rocky stopped. "What, Ms. Eddy?"

"Do you remember the loft above the garage at home?"

"Yes, I do. It's where Nick Coop hid when he thought JT was going to arrest him and put him in the klink for the murder of his very mean boss."

"That's right. I'm going to call up a wonderful lady named Carlee Doodle, one of the folks who was in desperate need during a desperate time. She rode the Knitter's Overhead Railroad in the loft some years ago, and she now lives in Gresham, a Portland suburb. Her boy's graduating from high school this year and she's doing great."

"Very nice, Ms. Eddy. Carlee Doodle is a funny name. Well, not her first name, just her last name. Does she like to doodle? Does she have a doodle dog? How can Ms. Doodle help us?"

"That there's a lot of questions. Never saw Carlee doodle, but you never know. Every person who comes out of our loft receives two thousand dollars to help in the next step of their journey, wherever they decide to go. We counsel each of our guests to tuck away at least an equal amount in cash in case they need to hightail it. The folks the Mad Knitters help are darn tootin' appreciative. I'm sure she'd be willing to give us a hand."

"We really need a hand, Ms. Eddy."

"Yes, we sure as shootin' do. I'll call Agnes and have her look in the Official Double DID Book for her contact information."

"What is the Official Double DID Book?"

"Dames or Dudes in Distress. The 'double' is there to make it more fun to say."

"You have a whole lot of Ds in that title, Ms. Eddy."

"Huh. I guess so."

Agnes answered on the second ring.

"Aggie, it's Eddy."

"I know, ya old coot. Caller ID. Are you still in the Pacific Rim?"

"The Pacific Northwest, Aggie, not the Pacific Rim."

"Oh, right. Somewhere above California. Remember the time we drove out to Tuba City? You got lost—"

"You were the navigator. You're the one who got us lost, not me."

"Can't help it if the map was wrong."

"It wasn't wrong. You were looking at the wrong map."

"Same difference."

"Forget the map, I need a favor."

"Course you do. What is it?"

"I need Carlee Doodle's address out of the Double DID Book."

"Okey doke. Hang onto your hooters and I'll be right back."

A couple minutes later Eddy wrote the address and phone number on the palm of her hand. "Thanks."

"You bet. What's going on?"

"We got us some troubles. I'll fill you in later."

"Sheesh. You can't even go on vacation without the T-word. Wish I was there."

"That's a truth." Eddy glanced at Rocky, who regarded her with a worried stare. "But everything's gonna come out smelling like the beautiful roses Portland is known for."

"I must say I'm not too fond of the smell of roses. But they sure are pretty. Lemme know if you need anything else."

"Will do. Later, tater." Eddy disconnected. "Aggie's a good doughnut."

"She sure is. Do you think we'll be near any Voodoo Doughnuts on the way to Ms. Doodle's house?"

"Dunno, but we can keep an eye out. Hang on now while I call Carlee."

After hearing Eddy's recitation of their situation, Carlee told her she thought she could round the cash up but needed a little time to make it happen. She lived less than fifteen minutes from the motel and agreed to meet them in an hour and a half. Eddy assured her she'd pay her back, which, of course, Carlee poo-pooed.

Next steps settled, Eddy and Rocky returned to the Eastside Lodge to regroup. The moment the motel room door was unlocked, Rocky made a beeline for the teeny freezer inside the tiny fridge and extracted Tulip's Tweety Bird ice cream treat.

"Rocky?"

"Yes, Ms. Eddy?" He ripped the package open and was in the process of withdrawing a very mushy Tweety.

"I thought you were saving Tweety for Tulip."

"I was. But when I get very upset and scared and anxious, it helps if I eat something sweet. I will buy Tulip another one. Or two. Or three. As many as she wants." He proceeded to chomp off the not totally melted remains of Tweety's head.

"There's a sound plan. When you're done decapitating your stress relief, why don't you lay down and see if you can nap for half an hour? We have places to go and a special peep to borrow money from."

"Okay, Ms. Eddy."

Three minutes later he was out, snoring softly.

6:45. Amazingly, Eddy was still awake. Her body was weary, but she felt...alive? It'd been so long since she'd been able to shift her caboose in gear, she'd forgotten how good it felt to assert control over her person. The last few months she'd been so intent on simply getting through each day she'd had no energy for anything else. What was wrong with her? Or what had been wrong? Her troubles began after Shay's near-death experience, and the revelation of a twenty-five-year secret affecting both her and Shay.

Huh. She'd have to think about it. She settled in the chair by the window with her Whacker in hand and watched over Rocky as he slept.

CHAPTER TWENTY-FOUR

JT

Mugs showed up in seven minutes instead of ten. They were on the road moments later. Once she'd been apprised of the situation, she said, "Your girl's probably about a half hour ahead of us. If you can see where she's going, I'm a dog on a T-bone. I'll get you where you need to go." Then she literally put the pedal to the metal, throwing both Coop and JT against the car's seat back.

JT was very happy she secured her belt as soon as she'd climbed in. "Thanks for coming so quickly."

"No problem. Every drive with the two of you has turned into an adventure."

"Adventure doesn't even begin to describe it." Coop scrambled to snap his own seat belt in place. "Wow, that's some acceleration you've got."

"You know it." Mugs sped past a gasoline tanker and swerved into the oncoming traffic lane to pass a truck. "I have a radar detector as well as a laser jammer. I got me six jammer transceivers, three in the front and three in the back. Cops mostly can't touch me."

JT figured it might not be a good idea to tell her she had a cop in the back seat. She didn't want Mugs to have a change of speeding heart.

Mugs braked hard, cut between two cars, and merged onto I-84 east. JT glanced at Coop, who met her with an "I hope we live to tell the tale" expression.

"Are they still on course?" Mugs asked.

"Hang on." Coop worked his phone with one hand and braced the other on the back of the front passenger seat.

JT's stomach twinged as she watched him. Good thing he wasn't prone to motion sickness. If she tried to look at her phone, she'd probably throw up.

"They're on Highway 26, still moving southeast."

"Hang on now." Mugs took the feeder onto Interstate 205.

They swayed to the left as she made the curve and hit the gas again. The ride was reminiscent of the Scrambler at Valleyfair back home in Shakopee, except here they had the luxury of a soft seat and belts, once you got the seat belt secured, of course.

Traffic was thick on a Friday at quitting time, and JT was grateful Mugs knew her way around.

"Shay's battery," Coop said, "is at twenty percent."

"Great." JT put a hand to her aching head. "We're about to catch up and her phone's gonna die before we get there."

"Don't you worry." Mugs glanced in the rearview at JT and then back at the road. "We'll catch up. They still on 26?"

"Yup," Coop said. "They just passed Sandy."

"Hmm," Mugs said. "Where could they be headed?" The woman was at ease racing down the freeway and carrying on a conversation without blinking. Or crashing. So far, anyway. "Let's see. After Sandy there's a couple podunk towns and then Government Camp. Great little alpine town if you like to play in the snow. Then not much till you get to Warm Springs and Madras, which are still pretty darn small. Talk is it's a great place to view an eclipse if you're into that kinda thing."

She skimmed past a Budget moving truck and hit the brakes as they came within sniffing distance of the rear of the car in front of them, then cut between the truck and the car with about six inches to spare on either end.

The moving truck blasted his horn and she waved as she pulled away. "Next town of note's Prineville. Home to Les Schwab Tire Centers, Crook County Packing and Distribution, and Facebook, with their controversial data center, controversial because it's run by coal. Then Apple showed up—coincidence, I think not—and decided to open a green data center, a flip-off to the Book of Face. Between the two of 'em, they've invested a shit-ton of dough in the area. A billion bucks a piece in a community of only ten thousand. Kinda like Oregon's own Area 51 minus the extraterrestrials. It's like they know something no one else does, what with all the money they've put up."

"Crook County?" Coop's eyes were locked on his screen. "Funny name."

Mugs's tone was thoughtful. "Does sound funny when you think about it. Like all the county has are crooks."

JT asked, "What does Crook County Packing and Distribution pack and distribute?"

"They do coffee. I think the Ochoco Creek stuff comes outta there, and I'm pretty sure they distro Flying High coffee too. Their jingle is hilarious." Mugs dropped her voice low. "'Flying High. Coffee your grandparents would love. Economical, plentiful, and tasty.' They say if you like Folgers, you'll love Flying High. I wouldn't know, though. I'm not a coffee fan."

Coop raised his head. "Ochoco Creek Coffee. That's Shay's coffee."

JT braced a hand on the front seat as Mugs made another quick lane chance. "Last time anyone saw Shay was at the Ochoco stand at the convention. An Ochoco Creek van was parked in front of the bar, and we hit on her location in that area. And now it appears she's traveling to a town where the very coffee she came to buy is packed and distributed? All of this can't be a coincidence. But why isn't she communicating with us?"

"We all know how Shay gets when she fixates on something," Coop said. "You can't hardly get her attention. Her phone is always silenced, so a text or a phone call often goes unnoticed. Maybe that's what's happening here." Coop grabbed the headrest again as Mugs busted another move.

He was right. One of the most exasperating things about her fiancée was her ability to tune anyone and everything out if she was concentrating on something. If it were the situation here, JT was absolutely going to dismember her when they finally caught up. And lecture her again about checking her phone more often. Especially when they weren't at home.

So, come on, she lectured herself. You're a detective. Detect. Go back to the beginning. "Let's run it down one more time, Coop. Do we even know she made it to the bathroom after she left you?"

"No."

"Next was the Drunken Tankard and that lying bartender."

"Maybe she ran into someone, and they offered to bring her right to the plant to…do what? With a pit stop at the bar?"

Maybe, JT thought, she should have paid more attention to the internal workings of the Rabbit Hole. Coffee and all things involving its production was in Shay's wheelhouse, not hers. "What could she do there that she couldn't do at the convention? Some kind of spectacular deal for checking things out in person?"

"Could be." Coop frowned. "Some of the vendors were offering tours of their factories."

"Did you notice if Ochoco was?"

"No, but it was so busy I could've missed it."

Mugs said, "Prineville's about three hours from Portland. Maybe your Shay is on a three-hour tour that went astray, like the castaways on *Gilligan's Island*. Seriously, though if she makes a stop in Prineville, or if you lose her altogether, how about we head directly to the distribution center?"

"Sounds good." A plan always made JT feel better.

Why didn't she feel better now?

CHAPTER TWENTY-FIVE

Shay

Something woke me.

I lifted my head. The darkness hadn't changed. I could hardly tell if my eyes were open or shut.

Yet, something had changed. I breathed deep. Be Zen. Figure it out.

Oh. Got it. The hum of tires. The hum that'd lulled me into a near catatonic state had disappeared. The van was stopped. At a stoplight? Or had we arrived at our destination?

The vehicle rocked. Both front doors slammed.

I stuffed the wad of disgusting rag in my mouth and pressed the tape against my face. Jammed my hands behind my back and did the best I could to resecure my wrists.

Then came the interminable slow-motion moment of in-between. In between inaction and engagement. Every muscle in my body tensed. Easy, Shay. Don't reveal your big secret too soon.

The in-between ended in a rush as the latch engaged and the door creaked open to reveal the hulking form of Randy Canavaro. Both his hands were free of weaponry. Great sign.

He squinted at me.

I squinted at him.

He said, "The bitch's still here and Burr is still dead."

I tried to peer past him to familiarize myself with the canvas of my impending escape, but Bender hovered behind Canavaro, blocking the view. I couldn't tell if he was armed or not.

"Outta there, you pain in my ass." The Can Man grabbed the front of my shirt and yanked me over Tim Burr with a little too much enthusiasm. I used the momentum to launch myself into him. Canavaro crashed backward into Bender. They went down like a couple of human dominos, and I landed square on top.

For a second, we were all too stunned to move.

Then I rolled off Canavaro, ignored the pain as my ass impacted gritty, worn asphalt. I tried to yank my hands apart so I could use my arms to get up, but, goddamn it, my wrists were once again stuck together by the devil tape.

With a heave up, I lurched to my feet and swayed as my legs remembered what it felt like to stand.

Bender pounded on Canavaro. "Get up, you fat fucker." Canavaro flailed atop him like an upside-down lobster.

I did a lightning location survey as my legs stabilized. Three tan-colored, two-level, corrugated metal buildings were connected to create a U-shaped nook the width and depth of a hockey rink.

My instincts screamed "Stay outside and run like hell." I left the two horizontal hotheads shouting at each other and trundled away, working feverishly to pull my wrists apart.

The asphalt extended twenty feet past the ends of the buildings and became a road. Dead ahead, past the end of the blacktop, a three-strand, barbed wire fence stood between me and a herd of black-and-white cattle not fifty feet away.

Jesus. I could dodge to the right or left, but I had no idea where either route would lead. We could be in a fenced compound. If so, either direction would be a waste of time. At least I could see freedom straight ahead, and safety in numbers, even if the numbers had cloven feet. They wouldn't dare shoot at a cow, would they?

Who was I kidding? I sent a "save the cows" prayer into the universe and took off.

The barbed wire loomed. Three paces from the fence I planted a foot and leaped. In high school, I'd tried out the high jump. One broken nose later I retired that idea. Time for redemption.

I sailed over the fence with a foot to spare. Tucked my head as I hit the ground, somersaulted, and slid feet first through something mushy before I came to a stop. The one good thing about hitting the ground so hard was the force of the impact knocked the gag out of my mouth. Suddenly it was a whole lot easier to breathe. I rolled to my knees and managed to stand, trying desperately to rip my wrists apart.

Canavaro was in the process of pulling Bender up.

Run, Shay! What are you waiting for? I pivoted and charged awkwardly toward the lot of chill, cud-chewing cattle, my gag swinging wildly from the tape still attached to one side of my face. I figured livestock almost always equaled a nearby farmhouse. Hopefully a farmhouse occupied by someone who wasn't involved with Crook County Packing and Distribution.

Forty, or seventy, or maybe a hundred four-legged, furry methane emitters enjoyed the deceptively nice evening, blissfully unaware of the trouble in their midst. The cows huddled in bunches on muddy ground around a galvanized, oval water tank. Some animals stood ankle deep in mud while others further out grazed contentedly. If I could get to the other side of the watering trough, I'd have a tiny bit of protection from the hail of bullets I was certain was coming my way.

A backward glance almost cost me my balance. I stumbled, caught myself. The two mad men were at the fence trying to figure out how to get over it.

The first cow I bobbled past gave a low, throaty moo. The second peered at me with huge, friendly brown eyes and mooed louder.

The closer I got to the water tank, the softer the ground became. The air seemed to thicken, ripe with the cloying scent of cowpies and sludgy muck.

More cows picked up the call and soon all I could hear was the collective baying of suddenly unhappy cattle.

I threaded my way between sets of closely grouped beasts. Maybe hanging at the trough was the bovine equivalent of gossiping around the water cooler.

From the rapidly increasing decibel level, I figured the herd was probably pissed I'd interrupted their between-meal snacking. I slowed to take another fast assessment of Bender and Canavaro's whereabouts. I'd lost sight of my pursuers, and if I couldn't see them, they probably couldn't see me. Hopefully. I was about to pick the pace back up when a truly gigantic black cow stepped in front of me. I pulled up short, three inches shy of his slimy sniffer. Pointy, six-inch horns jutted from his forehead.

Instead of a polite moo, his head reared back, his eyes bulged, and he let loose a bellow louder than anything I'd ever heard a cow make. Not that I had a lot of experience with cows. Or bellowing. What I did know was this cow was one unhappy mofo.

The small hairs on the back of my neck stood on end. Holy shitcakes. If I wasn't in human trouble, I was elbow-deep in cow trouble. I took a step back. The mud underfoot threatened to suction the shoes right off my feet. "Hey, big guy, take it easy."

Mr. Horns bellowed again and lowered his head like a bull about to charge a picador. And right now, that picador was me.

His breath came in quick, frantic bursts.

My breath come in quick, frantic bursts. I retreated another sticky step.

He eyerolled, and pawed the mud.

The slop underfoot became slop over foot as my shoes sunk into the muddy cow poo.

He snorted. Snorted again. His sides began to heave. The cattle behind Mr. Horns began to congregate around me in a semicircle, their movements agitated and uneasy. The closing of the ranks obliterated my escape route.

The only way out was the way I'd come in. Maybe I could encourage my unhappy new friends to trample Canavaro and Bender instead of me.

Mr. Horns huffed, the wild look in his eyes growing wilder yet. I tried to back up, but my shoes were now solidly cemented in the Oregon earth. They weren't going anywhere. The idea of running for my life in my socks wasn't nearly as bad as running for my life through cow shit in my socks.

Mud poo flew as Mr. Horns pawed the ground again and roared.

Oh, hell. Who cared about cow shit? I popped my feet out of my shoes, spun, and took off the way I'd come, simultaneously trying to run and free my hands from the goddamn Gorilla Tape. If I hadn't had to concentrate so hard to remain upright and alive, the thought of a half-hogtied person bobbling along as fast as they could from a horde of enraged cattle would've been freaking funny.

The cherry on top of today's lesson in Murphy's Law was the fact that the crazy herd was driving me right back toward the men I was attempting to ditch. How would you like to die today, Shay? Trampled, shot, or burned to death?

Another ungodly bellow from no more than two feet behind urged me to haul ass even faster. I swore I could feel hot bovine breath on my neck.

Ahead, Canavaro had managed to crawl through the barbed wire into the pasture and was holding two of the strands apart for Bender. Bender saw what was roaring toward them and shouted something. Canavaro half-turned. An expression akin to Edvard Munch's *The Scream* appeared on his face. He scrambled back through the strands of barbed wire he'd been holding.

Enraged mooing filled the air. I couldn't run-wobble one step faster. My breath came in bursts and my lungs burned. Wasn't sure I could gather enough steam to leap over the fence a second time, but what choice did I have? Twenty feet, ten, five feet to go. The gruesome thought of being run over by hundreds of hooves gave me one last bump of adrenaline. I flew over the damn fence and crashed on the blacktop not ten feet from Bender and Canavaro.

Before I could separate myself from the asphalt, the two goons were on top of me like bees on a honey-filled hive.

"See, lady," Bender said, "you were meant to die today. And for chrissake, you really fucking stink."

CHAPTER TWENTY-SIX

Eddy

Carlee Doodle lived in a '50s style, bright yellow, or neon green, depending on where the sun was in the sky, ranch-style house with an attached two-car garage. The color almost matched Eddy's super-favorite, super-lucky high-tops. Too bad she'd left them at home. Never did she expect to be knee deep in these sorts of shenanigans in the land of coffee and rain. The phrase "Sit back and smell the roses" had no place here, even if Portland was the City of Roses. It was a good thing she'd brought her Whacker in case things got out of hand. Initially, the mini baseball bat had fallen right out of her pants pocket when she tried to stow it at the motel. So, she'd stuffed it down the back of her pants, under her shirt. Last thing she wanted was to worry Rocky.

He trailed Eddy up a stone and concrete pathway blackened by years of dirt and moss and maybe even Oregon fairy dust, liberally sprinkled with sticky pinkish-tannish-brownish leaves fallen from a dogwood tree shading half the front yard.

"I sure hope your friend has the money," Rocky said as they ascended the porch steps. "Oh, Ms. Eddy, what if she does not?"

"Shush now. She will. You wait and see." Eddy wasn't at all sure, but better to keep that worry to herself. She rang the bell, her hopes pinned on the moment at hand. This was their Hail Mary. Please, all gods and goddesses, let it end in glory.

The door swung open to reveal a fresh-faced girl in her teens with a happily yipping sheltie on her heels. Bright purple hair floated atop her head and her sides were so slicked back and shiny Eddy figured she must've used half a bottle of Dippety Do. Her colorful hair starkly contrasted with her very pale skin and the black Portland Timbers hoodie she wore. If Eddy's memory served, this was probably Harper, who'd been about three the last time she'd laid an eye on her.

"What's up?" the kid shouted over the dog's excited barking.

"We're here to see Carlee," Eddy hollered.

"Mom!" The kid trounced off, leaving them standing in the doorway guarded by the vociferous mutt.

A six-foot, slender woman with incredibly magenta hair, a bright smile, and a deep dimple in one cheek arrived almost instantaneously. Like daughter like mother. She bellowed, "Zapper! Quiet." Remarkably, Zapper hushed midbark. "Oh, my goodness, Eddy, it really is you. I can't believe you're standing on my front porch. Get in here."

The scent of fresh-baked cookies tickled Eddy's nostrils as Carlee pulled her inside and crushed her in a fierce embrace. Eddy thought of herself as a good, solid hugger, but not even she could compete with Carlee's enthusiasm. The woman had enough charisma to light up the entire Vikings' football stadium, and probably the Seahawks' too.

Eddy made quick work of introducing Rocky to their hopeful savior, who enthusiastically squished the stuffing out of him as well. When Carlee released a rather stunned Rocky, his aviator cap sat askew on the top of his thinker. In slow motion, he tugged it back in place.

"Please, sit. I'll be right back." Carlee zoomed around the corner of the room and disappeared.

The living room was directly off the front door and was a comfortable, lived-in space, with a picture window overlooking the front yard. A built-in bookshelf filled with a hodgepodge of books took up one wall. *The Oregonian*, Portland's newspaper, lay open on a coffee table next to a half-filled coffee mug. The table also held a haphazard pile of magazines and a clear bowl filled with Dove dark chocolates. The bowl was covered by a fancy lid with whoopsie-dos all over it, which was good. Dark chocolate was bad for any hound. On the other hand, for humans, it was essential.

A couple recliners, a rocker, and a mission-style, walnut-colored futon encircled the coffee table. Eddy settled on the futon, which was situated across from the picture window, and Rocky sat beside her.

"Do you think Carlee would mind if I had a chocolate, Ms. Eddy? Maybe it will help me not worry about Tulip."

"I think she certainly would not mind. Go ahead."

Rocky lifted the lid and grabbed a piece of the foil-wrapped candy. "Oh! Look, Ms. Eddy, look outside." He pointed at a red feeder hanging in front of the window. "Hummingbird."

A pinkish hummer hovered next to the feeder and then zoomed out of sight. Something in the back of Eddy's head relaxed. Hummingbirds were a sign of happiness and joy. Boy, oh boy, they could use some joyful luck right about now. "It's a good omen, Rocky. Things are gonna work out fine."

"I hope so." He sat back, unwrapped the Dove.

Eddy patted his knee. "You watch."

A couple of minutes later, Carlee returned, bearing a platter of chocolate chip cookies, which looked and smelled suspiciously fresh and probably right from the oven. She shuffled the newspaper and magazines out of the way and plunked the goods on the coffee table.

"Carlee, you didn't need to go to the trouble."

"Hey, when trouble's afoot, everyone needs a little comfort food. Besides, when the dough comes in a package and one simply has to break it apart and bake it, it isn't any trouble at all."

"Ms. Carlee, how did you know my absolute very favorite, most yummy in the tummy cookie in the whole wide world is chocolate chip?"

Eddy glanced at Rocky. His eyes were wide, his expression delighted. The cookies were the perfect distraction. "Those look even better than the Dove chocolates."

Carlee picked up a round disc of deliciousness. "I think most people who eat cookies love the chocolate chip version, Rocky. Help yourself." She took a big bite.

For a few seconds no one spoke as cookies were consumed.

"These are very, very warm and gooey, Ms. Carlee," Rocky said through a mouthful. "Even better than Dove. Thank you so very much. Eating something yummy always makes me feel better. Did you know Ruth Wakefield, who ran the Toll House Inn in Whitman, Massachusetts, and her bestie, Sue Brides—well, I do not know if she was her bestie, but I hope she had a bestie—invented the chocolate chip cookie to go along with ice cream? It was not an accident, like some people think. Ms. Wakefield knew exactly what she was doing. I am very glad she invented these. And I'm glad you made them." He grabbed another and stuffed it in his mouth.

Carlee eyed him. "You're welcome." To Eddy, she said with amusement, "What a recitation. He do that often?"

Eddy nodded and glanced at Rocky, affection softening her gaze. "You never know what's going to come out, but whatever it is, he's always right."

They shared a few more moments of companionable cookie chomping.

Carlee dusted crumbs off her hands. "All right. We've tamed the sugar beast, now let's get down to business. I have your dough." From a side table drawer, she withdrew a bulging six-by-nine manila envelope. "All three thousand six hundred eighty-seven dollars and thirty-four cents."

Eddy had been pretty sure Carlee'd be able to pull the money together, but there was always the chance she couldn't. Delight surged inside her that at least one of the lessons the Mad Knitters tried to impart to their Overhead Railroad passengers had taken root. She accepted the thick envelope Carlee handed her.

"I listened to you back then, Eddy, and I still heed your advice to this day." Carlee shot Eddy a triumphant grin and scooped up another cookie. "It's quite a wad. Do you have something to carry it in?"

"Stopped using a purse when I travel, not that I travel much. So I guess the answer is no. Hadn't thought about needing a money carrier."

"Hold on a sec." Carlee popped up and darted out of the room. She was back before Eddy could blink twice. "Here."

She thrust a neon-pink fanny pack with navy straps at Eddy. A logo was screen-printed on one side. The words Carousel and Bingo were wrapped around a white carousel horse.

"Well, knock me over with a dabber. Me and Aggie used to go to Carousel Bingo in Brooklyn Park every Friday night for a little bingo and maybe a few too many pull tabs. Heard they closed in 2015."

"I worked there for a little while before you and I met up. Interesting place."

"Sure was." Eddy wagged the money at her. "Thanks for the hookup." She wrapped the mesh belt around herself, clipped it, and tucked the money away. Because of the strap, the knob on the grip part of the Whacker pressed harder into her back, which she didn't mind. In fact, she felt better knowing her peacemaker was right there.

Rocky sighed. "Those wonderful cookies were very tasty. Thank you, Ms. Carlee." His face drooped. "I wish my Tulip was here to try them."

"You fix what needs fixing," Carlee said, "and bring your wife to me. I'll whip up a brand-new batch just for her."

Her words perked Rocky right up, and he snatched another cookie. "That would be most wonderful, Ms. Carlee. I think my Tulip will like you very much. And I know she would like to talk to your purple-haired person who answered the door. And meet Zapper."

Eddy looked around. "Speaking of, where is the pooch?"

"I sent him in with Harper. Harper doesn't much talk to anyone except her friends, but Tulip would be welcome to try. Zapper the Yapper, on the other hand, would love to meet your wife, Rocky. He's quite the boy. Harper's been taking him to agility classes and turns out he's a natural. I think they might even do some competing."

After some more small talk and cookie munching later, Eddy said, "Carlee, thank you for the floater. I can't exactly explain what's going on right now, but when I can fill you in, I will. And I want you to know I'll pay you—"

"Don't you even say it." Carlee wagged her head. "I am so grateful for you and the rest of the Mad Knitters. You saved my life, and Harper's too. You kept us safe. I'm more than thrilled to return the love. That kid of mine's always been my number one priority, and though she might be a challenge right now"— Carlee threw her hands in the air—"she's doing exceptionally well. Truly, it's all thanks to you."

"Pshaw. You did the hard work. We just gave you some space to breathe." Eddy looked at her phone to check the time. "We'll get out of your hair now. I need to rustle up a Ryde."

"You don't have a car?"

"No. We're supposed to be at the Big on Beans Convention all weekend and wasn't s'pose to need transportation."

"I have the perfect solution. Follow me."

Carlee led them through the galley-style kitchen into the garage and flicked on the lights. Parked by the door was a Subaru Forester. Carlee led them around the Forester toward the shadowy side of the garage. "I bought Hummer the day after I left your loft, Eddy. I've been saving her for Harper. She runs like a shaky charm if you don't need quick acceleration."

Carlee had a Humvee? Eddy hadn't expected her to own a ginormous military-like vehicle, but whatever floated her boat was fine as long as the engine worked. They stopped in front of a tarp-covered vehicle nowhere near big enough to be a Humvee.

"And here's Hummer." Carlee whipped the tarp off.

Definitely not a Humvee, which she might've preferred over...this. Her mouth opened, but no sound came out. She tried again. "Oh. My."

"Isn't she beautiful? Vintage 1972."

Rocky ran a finger along the door. "This is a very well-preserved Ford Pinto, Ms. Carlee. With an amazing paint job. You have kept this antique auto in very good condition."

"Thank you, Rocky."

Eddy was glad Hummer wasn't a Hummer Humvee, but she vividly remembered the fiery history of the Pinto in the early '70s. For a short amount of time, a matter of months, if her memory could be trusted, she'd had a Pinto with a Green Glow paint job, a color remarkably reminiscent of baby poop. This deathtrap was bright yellow. A giant hummingbird was painted in stunning detail on the top of the car: head on the hood and body on the roof, with wings extending over the car doors on either side. The bird's head was iridescent purple, blending into a shimmery pink at the neck. Probably would be even more stunning outside in the sun. So long as it didn't blow up.

Carlee laughed. "I can see the worried expression on your face, Eddy. Don't worry, the explosive problem with Hummer's hinder was fixed long ago." She patted the car affectionately. "She'll get you wherever you need to go in one piece, I promise."

CHAPTER TWENTY-SEVEN

Shay

Canavaro and Bender dumped me in a second-floor mop room and went off to do whatever prep needed to be done to torch the place. In their hurry to take care of biz, they'd left the light on, which I very much appreciated.

I was exhausted, my feet hurt like a bitch. My white socks were now black. I thought about taking them off, but then figured they provided the tiniest amount of protection, so left them on.

Regardless the state of my socks, I was alive. My girl and I had a wedding to plan, for Pete's sake. If this little bout with mortality did anything, it was to wake me up to the fact I needed to stop stalling and get on with proclaiming my love for JT to her and the world. Although the thought of the multitude of details we needed to navigate was pretty much worse than cleaning the bathroom floor with a toothbrush.

The scent of bleach and urine cakes brought me back to my present predicament. I had to admit the blend was better than the obnoxious smell wafting off me. No way did I want to see what my clothes were covered in. I took a couple of slow, calming breaths through my mouth instead of my nose. Thanks again, yoga.

The room was narrow, maybe five feet wide and eight deep, lit by one bare overhead bulb. Metal shelving with cleaning supplies lined one wall. In the far corner, a mop bucket was parked by a floor drain, and a handle with a shriveled mophead hung on a hook nearby.

What could I use to cut the tape off my wrists? I scanned the rack, muttering, "Come on, come on, there's got to be something."

The top shelves held huge bottles of various kinds of cleaners, garbage bags, rolls of toilet paper, hand towels, and a dogeared old *Playboy* magazine stuffed between the TP and towels. None of it was going to be any help.

The bottom shelf was loaded with unopened cardboard boxes. Left, forgotten or not, on top of one of the boxes, was a green metal box cutter.

My first real break of this entire fucking fiasco. I kneeled and waddled backward toward the box the cutter rested on and gingerly felt around for it. Where was a backup camera when I needed one? The last thing I wanted to do was knock it to the floor.

Thirty seconds later, my hands were free, and I worked to slice the tape between my cheek and the gag. After much sawing, the tape parted and I tossed the disgusting, soggy, Gorilla-covered rag into the mop bucket. I was sure I looked like an idiot, with tape still adhered to either cheek and wrapped around the back of my head. But, I was alive, and that's what mattered.

All right. Next move. Call for help. I patted my pockets, then did it again, this time more urgently. Neither my cell nor Burr's was anywhere to be found. I must've lost them somewhere in the pasture. Bumblefuck on a cowpie.

Well, do what you gotta do, Shay, I told myself. Get the hell out of this room and the hell out of the warehouse before I become a statistic.

Of course, the doorknob didn't budge when I tried it, so I decided to pull a Derek Morgan from *Criminal Minds* and bust the sucker open with a totally awesome foot plant. Then I remembered my shoes were stuck in the pasture.

I spotted a dusty red toolbox behind three bottles of WD-40. I popped it open and rummaged through the contents. A hammer and assorted screwdrivers.

Sweet. I went to town on the doorknob mechanism with my tools, and before long managed to unscrew the handle and pull the knob off the door. Then I used a flat head to pull the latch back and then gave the door a push. To my surprise, it swung open about two inches. At the rate my day had gone, I never expected the easy fix to work.

Smoke seeped in, and I quickly used my fingers to pull the door shut. Dammit. I blew out an anxiety-filled breath. Were Canavaro and Bender nearby?

Whatever you do, Shay, do it with gusto.

I stiff-armed the door and burst out of the supply closet like a horizontal jack-in-the-box. I was about halfway down a hundred-foot hall fast filling with swirling, dark smoke. It was, however, devoid of bad guys. The staircase my kidnappers led me up was situated on one end of the long hall, and on the other end, an exit sign glowed red as thick smoke seeped in around a door leading who knew where.

A distant pop pop popping was drowned out by an incredible explosion, followed by rapid, deeper booms. I dropped to the floor and covered my head. The pops and booms didn't stop. It dawned on me the heat from the fire was probably causing their ill-gotten ammo to explode.

I scrambled up and scrammed toward the stairs, figuring I'd be safe enough using them since the flames were on the other end. Except, the closer I drew to the stairs, the thicker the smoke in the air became.

Shallow breaths, just take shallow breaths.

Black smoke boiled up the stairwell in huge waves. My eyes watered so badly I could hardly see. I was trapped, in dire need of an alternate plan, stat.

I'd passed five or six doors on the way to the stairs. All I needed was a room with a window. I backtracked to the previous door. It opened. I fumbled for the lights.

A moment later, a row of lights burst to life, dimly illuminating a room the size of my high school cafeteria. Not a window to be had. At least a hundred Ochoco Coffee crates were stacked on one side of the expansive space and Flying High crates were heaped haphazardly on the other. Four heavy-duty, eight-foot plastic tables were arranged in a square with chairs tucked all around.

Burlap bags filled with coffee beans, or maybe drugs and coffee beans, or hell, maybe even ammunition, were piled waist-high at the far end of the tables. The setup was reminiscent of the one in the little room under Bender's bar where I'd swiped the bricks of drugs. This appeared to be a contraband assembly line on pause, waiting for workers to show up Monday morning.

They were gonna be in for some bad news.

I backed out and shut the door. In the short amount of time I'd spent in the contraband assembly room, the hall had grown even smokier.

Panic welled, and for a second, I froze.

Stop it. Get a hold of yourself. No time to freak until you're out of the pyre. I gritted my teeth and forced a couple of breaths through my nose.

Move on.

The next door was locked. The one after opened to a warren of offices. I made a quick search, struck out again. Escape routes were hard to come by in this joint. Who'd want to work in an office without any kind of a view? People who didn't want to chance being seen from the outside, that's who. The bad guys who smuggled dope and guns and bullets and who knew what else.

This whole thing had to be a nightmare. I was going to wake up, snug and safe with JT at my side. Everything would fade away as we headed out for the Big on Beans Coffee Convention. My eye stung as a drop of sweat rolled into it.

No denying it, the nightmare was my reality. And the temperature was rising. Even the floor beneath my filthy socks felt warmer. Move your caboose, O'Hanlon. I bypassed the supply room from which I'd escaped and made for a door on the left. It was unlocked. I flicked the light on to reveal a dormitory. Ten bunkbeds, five on either side. Once again, no light source except two parallel fluorescent bulbs overhead. Sheets and blankets from a few of the beds lay half on the floor, as if whoever'd been sleeping had leaped out of bed in a hurry.

Two round tables held crayons and coloring books and a bunch of Legos. Some of the crayons and colorful square bricks were scattered on the floor. Beyond the tables was a bathroom. What'd Canavaro do, work his staff twenty-four hours a day? And he allowed them to bring their kids? It made no sense. Where were they, if that was the case?

I pivoted to leave when I heard something other than the nonstop bang, bang, bangs. I froze, held my breath. Nothing. After all I'd been through, I was probably losing my marbles. Scoot before it didn't matter how many marbles were left in my brain.

Then I caught it again. An abruptly cut off half-sob.

The hairs on the back of my neck sprang to attention. Someone was in here.

My heart kicked it up a half-million notches. Good guy? Bad guy? But bad guys wouldn't cry, right? If whoever it was didn't get out now, they were probably going to die in a not good, very horrible way.

Fuckity fuck.

"Hey, who's there?"

No one answered.

"I heard you, I know you're in here. You gotta get out. The building's on fire."

Nothing. I hastened into the bathroom. Other than pee on the seat, pee on the floor, a dirty, rust-stained sink, and a moldy shower stall, it was unoccupied.

The only other hiding place was under the bunks. Could someone be that cliché? "If you're under the bed, get your ass outta there."

This time I heard a very juicy snork. No doubt, someone was in here with me.

My tone sharpened. "I'm not kidding. We don't have time for games."

Still nothing. Fucking A.

"Whoever you are, out." I stomped over to the first rumpled bed and flipped the blankets up and took a gander underneath.

No one.

I moved on to the second bed. Nothing but dust bunnies and a worn-out, kid-size tennis shoe.

Last option. I yanked the covers away and dropped to my hands and knees. "I know you're under there."

Terrified dark eyes met mine. All at once I realized the who was a little girl. "Oh, shit." I grabbed the waistband of the kid's pants and dragged her out. She burst into tears and scrabbled away from me, cowering against the leg of the bunk. She couldn't be more than four or five, her hair shiny-black, her skin dusky. The child was dressed in a stained Grinch T-shirt, raggedy jeans, and wore only one shoe, a match to the sneaker I'd seen under the other bed.

I held out a hand.

She flinched.

"Easy, kid, I'm not gonna hurt you." I was probably a terrifying sight with all the tape stuck to my face, my filthy clothes, and no shoes. "Hey. Come here. It's okay."

The kid hesitantly moved toward me, eyes narrowed.

"We need to get out of here. The building's on fire."

Something in the way she held herself so stiffly struck a chord. What in the flying fuck a duck was Canavaro doing? Was that son of a bitch trafficking kids? Enslaving them? Kidnapping them for ransom? Or could it be as simple as the fact he allowed his staff to bring their children to work? Why had this one been left behind?

More softly, I said, "Where are your parents?"

"Dey come took eberyone away." Her voice was husky. "The hurty men. Dey had *pistolas*."

"The hurty men?" I echoed.

"*Si. Mi hermana* push me under *la cama*. Dey took her and *mi madre* and eve'rbody away."

"Did these men hurt you?"

She looked down. Her expression said everything I needed to know. Canavaro could add abuser and maybe human trafficker to his list of indiscretions. The slumbering Protector who lived deep inside me was now wide awake, trembling with rage. I welcomed her burst of white-hot fury.

"I'm going to get you out of here, okay?" I held out a hand. The kid placed hers in mine. I couldn't help but pull her into quick a hug. Initially she resisted, then melted into me as if I were the first safe human contact she'd had in a long time.

Goddamn it.

I scooped her up and stood. She clung to me, wrapping her arms around my neck, legs around my midsection. "What's your name? *Su nombre?*"

"Lira."

"Okay, Lira. I'm Shay. Do you know of a room on this floor with any windows? *Las ventanas?*" My high school Spanish teacher, *Senor* LaBudd, would be proud I remembered that.

Her face scrunched up and she wiggled until I let her down. "I show you."

I followed Lira into the hall. She grabbed my hand as we both tried not to cough. "Come."

She pulled me toward the no-go exit door, which was now so hot the air around it shimmered. I was close enough to see the window was reinforced with mesh, and through it the flames danced yellow and a deep red-orange. Thick plumes of acrid smoke now squirted through the gaps between the jam and the door. The good news was the door still held the flames at bay, but I doubted it would last much longer. As we approached, the increase in temperature was stunning.

For a second, I thought Lira was going to try and lead me straight into hell until she stopped in front of a door less than five feet from the devil's entrance. I moved to grab the doorknob and just as quickly jerked my hand away. The knob radiated heat. However, no smoke seeped under the door, so I assumed the proximity to the fire itself was the culprit.

I pushed Lira behind me and tried used the hem of my T-shirt as a potholder. I screeched as the hot metal seared my fingers through the cloth.

Too fucking hot. Damn it.

"Be right back." Lira spun and charged down the hall the way we'd come. In a matter of seconds, she was back with one of the blankets from the bunk room. The kid was a tiny genius.

This time the hot knob didn't burn my hand. I pushed the door open and tossed the blanket aside. The fire had not yet eaten its way into the room, and the best news was the large picture window illuminating the interior.

Lira darted around me, and I slammed the door shut. The space was a breakroom, with a table, chairs, microwave, fridge, a well-used couch, and, ta da! The window to the outside world.

Holy shitballs. "You did it, Lira."

She gave me a big smile.

I edged over to the window and glanced outside, careful not to expose too much of my body. The breakroom overlooked the parking lot where I'd tried to make my grand, but failed, escape attempt. The van in which Tim and I had arrived was still there, but I didn't see anyone lurking about.

The window wouldn't open. Canavaro probably glued it shut with Gorilla glue. Well, then, time to take matters into my own hands.

I glanced at the kid. "What do you say we fly out of this coffee coop?"

She vigorously nodded. I picked up one of the chairs and heaved it through the window. The glass shattered and the chair dropped out of view. I snuck another cautious look outside in case the chair's appearance caught the wrong person's attention. Luckily, all was quiet on the pasture front. I knocked out the remaining shards of glass and leaned over the edge to see what we could use to get the hell out of here.

The ground-level window was too far away to be of use. The corrugated siding was smooth, with nothing to offer as a hand or foot grip, so simply climbing down wasn't an option. Two dumpsters, blue for recycling and green for garbage, were pushed up against the building. I hadn't noticed them when the

Can Man yanked me out of the van, but then again, I'd been rather preoccupied. The black plastic lid on the blue container was up, leaning against the structure's wall. It was almost full of flattened cardboard, sheets of paper, and other recyclable junk, maybe five feet to the left and seven feet below the window.

It was probably our best chance. Maybe our only chance. All we needed to do was perform a lateral jump at a crap-ass angle and hope to hell we landed in the dumpster.

"Come here, Lira." I scooped her up and sat her on the sill. "Listen carefully, okay?"

"Okay."

"I'm going to take your hand and lower you out the window. When you're down as far as I can reach, I'm going to swing you back and forth. I'll let go once you're close to that blue recycling bin. Do you see it right there?"

She looked, nodded again.

"You're going to land inside the bin."

"Si."

"Then move off to the side as fast as you can and I'll jump, okay?"

"Si, Shay."

I didn't want to give Lira time to think and freak, because then I'd freak. "Let's—"

A loud explosion directly below us made the building shudder.

Lira shrieked.

I crushed her to me, afraid she was going to tumble backward out the window. Once I was sure we were stable, I leaned us forward and stuck my head out to see what happened. Flames and smoke roiled out of the window below us like mystical, angry snakes. The popping sounds were louder now too. Canavaro must have stored ammunition throughout his complex.

Super cool. Nothing like getting shot by heat-fired bullets. We needed to scram before this place blew up or collapsed.

Lira clung to me like a second skin. She shuddered a couple of times, then arched far enough away from my face to look intently in my eyes. Fear danced in hers, but they didn't reflect the terror I felt.

A breathy "*Por favor*," came out as *poo favoo.*

"Yes?"

"Do not dwop me."

My heart about snapped in half. "Lira, I won't drop you. I'm going to swing you back and forth three times and then let you fly like a bird. You'll land on the cardboard in the dumpster, okay?"

"Si."

I held onto her wrist for dear life and carefully lowered her out the window. For a fleeting second, I wondered who I thought I was. I could kill this kid. But if I'd left her hiding under the bed, she'd be dead for sure.

You can do hard things, Shay. Do this hard thing now. Holding the girl with one hand was more difficult than I expected, and I tightened my grip. If my arm didn't rip out of its socket, she wasn't going to fall. I needed to send the kid sailing with the right amount of force.

"On three, okay? *Uno.*" I swung her toward the dumpster and then back. "*Dos.*" I added more speed. "*Tres!*" I let go and watched her soar.

Lira landed in the dumpster, and it was just like I knew what I was doing. She scooted into the far corner and waved frantically at me to hurry up.

I crawled through the window and balanced on the four-inch ledge. Heights didn't usually bother me, but my last nerve was frayed beyond the brink. Don't look down, Shay, you'll be fine. I braced one foot against the casing so I could push off it like a sprinter using starting blocks. If I miscalculated, there would be no sticking this landing.

I pushed off with as much force as I could and flailed my arms for a never-ending, eternal second. With a thwomp! I hit the cardboard and rolled to my back. For a moment I lay still, eyes wide, staring up at the blue sky. I was alive. Lira was alive. Holy fucking shit.

Our combined weight compacted the contents of the dumpster by a good foot, and if we stayed hunkered down, I was pretty sure we'd be invisible from the ground. I rolled over and pulled myself to the edge of the bin. Lira crept next to me, and together we took a cautious peek.

Smoke and flames spewed from the breached first-floor window. The loud rat-a-tatting had slowed. I wondered if the ammo was spent or if the fire hadn't yet reached additional projectiles.

A door on the other side of the fiery window burst open. We ducked in tandem. Lira pressed her little body against mine and buried her head in my side. I wrapped an arm around her and peered over the edge.

Canavaro charged through the door, trailing smoke. His arms were full of plastic-wrapped whitish blocks about the same size as the drug bricks I'd hidden under the Drunken Tankard. He was headed for the van and his path would send him right past our hidey-hole.

The Protector inside me roared. That bastard put me and this poor kid through two different kinds of hell. Her hell I couldn't even begin to imagine.

Come on, my rather irritating voice of reason argued. Stay calm and get the hell out of here.

But wait, the Protector whispered seductively, you could get him back for what he did to you and Lira. Even better, make sure the slimy reptile paid for what he'd done. It was sin enough to exchange organic, fair-trade coffee with run-of-the-mill cheap beans. It was another matter entirely to smuggle drugs, kidnap me, murder Tim Burr, probably traffic humans, and attempt to snuff me and Lira.

Are you crazy, rational me roared. Who knew where Bender was? Jump Canavaro and if Bender shows up you're dead. How many lives have you already used up today? But the thought of Lira, and who knew how many kids, entrapped by Bender and Canavaro's devious plots tipped the scales.

"Stay here." I nailed Lira with my best "do as I say" glare and jabbed my finger at the cardboard under us.

"Okay."

As Canavaro passed, I vaulted out of the dumpster and crashed down on him like a lightning bolt from the sky.

The plastic-covered packages were jarred from his grip as we hit the blacktop.

Then the Protector shoved me out of the way and took over. All I could hear was an incredible roaring in my ears. My fist connected with Canavaro's nose and what little restraint I'd managed to maintain completely vanished. A red veil of fury descended, and I lost it.

Tears and snot flew as I watched myself work him over.

"Hey. Hey!"

I barely registered someone yelling.

"Shay, stop!" This time words seeped into my lizard brain, but I was too far gone to understand, much less respond.

Then somebody was pulling me away from my punching bag. I shrieked as arms wrapped around from behind and dragged me off Canavaro.

"NO!" I bellowed, squirming to break the hold.

"Shay. Shay, come on."

The voice. So familiar.

"Breathe, baby, I've got you."

I inhaled once, and again. The seething, all-encompassing wrath eased. I shuddered. The world returned.

Coop. Right in front of me. His mouth was moving. How'd Coop get here? Maybe I'd shifted from a dream state to hallucinations. Behind him, a cop was in the process of peeling a bloody Canavaro off the asphalt.

I couldn't stop shaking.

"Shay, it's okay. You're okay."

JT.

JT's arms were around me.

JT was here.

In a split second, my bones dissolved. I collapsed against her. "Lira," I gasped. "Get Lira out."

"Baby, who's Lira?" Her familiar, warm voice made me want to cry.

"Lira." I pointed at the blue bin.

JT shouted, "Check the recycling dumpster."

A moment later someone hollered, "There's a kid in here."

"Don't hurt her!" My words were drowned out by raised voices as police surged the dumpster. Firefighters appeared, shouting orders, and dragging hoses every which way. It was chaos. My exhausted, overwhelmed brain couldn't keep up.

"Come on, Shay," JT said, "you're a walking disaster. And holy nasty, what's that smell? Oh, never mind, let's get you checked out."

"Not without Lira."

JT yelled something else and then Lira was there.

I grabbed her hand.

JT grabbed mine.

I allowed her to guide us to the front of the building, where several ambulances were staged in the back forty of a large parking lot. I glanced behind me at Crook County Packing and Distribution. Fire trucks surrounded the complex.

Flashing red lights. Yellow flames. Orange flames. Red flames. Black smoke. So much smoke.

The act of recycling was like turning coal into diamonds. It transformed one thing into something else entirely. Something better. Something hopeful. Maybe by dragging Lira out of a burning building I'd given her a chance to recycle her short life and start anew.

Fifteen minutes later, Coop and a woman named Mugs quietly hovered as a paramedic worked to patch me up. I wasn't sure if Coop's prolonged silence was because Mugs was there or because he was taken aback by my bloodied, bruised, stanky, Gorilla-taped self.

Two uniforms had whisked Lira away after she'd been given the go-ahead by one of the medics, presumably to be questioned about why she was here, who she'd been with, and what she'd been through. I felt awful but they assured me she'd be well taken care of.

Still, my insides were edgy. Somehow, in those few minutes between finding the kid and sending her flying out of the window into the recycling bin, we'd bonded. I had never been one to pay much attention to the younger set, and in fact, usually thought of children as booger-nosed knee grabbers. But Lira wasn't one of those. Not at all.

I'd hugged her. Watched her square her shoulders and walk away, so small between the two hulking law enforcement officers. She was the bravest squirt I'd ever met.

JT stood a couple yards away, talking in low tones with an Oregon State Police detective named Stephanie Weaver. She'd arrived not long after I landed on a stretcher, and I gave her an extremely condensed rundown of what had happened and named the names I knew.

When Detective Weaver had walked up, JT had greeted her like an old friend. From their conversation, I gathered they'd met at one of the FBI's National Academies JT had attended. She eventually introduced Weaver as one half of Stephanie Squared—apparently her wife was also Stephanie. That had to get confusing. Maybe one was Steph and one was Stephanie. Or maybe one of them went by their initials.

Steph, Stephanie, SW, or whatever, was maybe five-six, with silvery-blond hair and piercing sapphire eyes. Her blue-gray getup differed from the Minnesota State Patrol's maroon and gold, which I was used to seeing when they pulled me over for speeding. A black tactical ballistic vest with lots of interesting pockets covered her uniform shirt. The five-pointed silver star pinned to the vest was mesmerizing, a good distraction from the painful poking, prodding, and wound cleanup and tape detaching the nice but no-nonsense medical professional performed on my person.

"Okay." Patty the Semi-Sadistic Paramedic gave my shoulder a pat. "I've done what I can with bandages and spit. I'd recommend staying away from Gorilla Tape."

"I'll do my best."

JT turned away from Weaver to focus on me. "How is she?" she asked Patty.

"Pretty much in one piece. I don't think anything is serious enough for an emergency room run. Watch the shoulder. If it doesn't improve in a couple days, might be something to have checked out. A shower as soon as possible might be a really good idea. Otherwise, I've done as much as I can for her various—and I mean wildly various—injuries. Aside from a black eye, numerous scrapes and contusions, probable pulled back muscles, strained shoulder ligaments, and mild smoke inhalation, I think she'll live. Ice what you can, ibuprofen will probably help. She'll be sore in a day or two, so expect that. Get her in to her primary doctor when you get home and have her checked out. You can have her back now."

Normally I'd be mad the medic wasn't directing her words to me, but I was so absolutely done I was more than happy to let JT field the medical direction.

"Thanks." My wife-to-be glanced at me with a relieved smile and returned her attention to Stephanie-not squared. "Steph, thanks. We'll get Shay in for a statement tomorrow."

"Sounds good. Later." Steph headed toward a gaggle of law enforcement honchos milling near a black RV with SWAT painted in big white letters on its sides.

After I'd been plied with a bottle of water, some Mountain Dew, two Snickers bars, and a bag of Cheez-Its, I desperately needed a bathroom break. We piled into Mugs's car and hit the Chevron station on the way out of town.

Once the necessities were taken care of and Mugs filled up the gas tank, we were back on the road. I was totally confused about how Mugs and Coop and the light of my life had managed to show up in the nick of time. JT assured me they'd explain, but she wanted to know where I'd been the last nine hours. I was about to launch in on an abbreviated version of my impossibly crazy-ass day when JT's phone rang.

"It's Eddy," she said. "We have another situation on her end."

Oh, boy. How much could've happened in the amount of time I was gone? Did the situation have something to do with her depression? Thoughts whirled through my brain at crackerjack speed.

JT answered the phone. "Eddy! We've retrieved Shay." She glanced at me, her dark eyes softening with affection. "She's a little banged up but okay." Eddy said something else and JT's scowl returned. After a few more uh-huhs, I sees, and Jesus Christs, JT said, "Okay. Let me check. Mugs, a question."

Mugs glanced in the rearview. "What's up?"

"How far are we from Oaks Amusement Park?"

"Oaks Amusement Park?" Mugs echoed.

"Yeah."

"Damn and dominos, riding with you all is a like living an episode of the *Twilight Zone*. Love it. Okay, hang on." She one-handed her phone. "About two hours forty-five. Is the park our next destination?"

Coop twisted around in his seat to look back at us as JT repeated the ETA to Eddy and listened a little longer. "All right," she said. "We'll be there with a few minutes to spare. Should be able to get inside and find you in plenty of time." She paused. "The Ferris wheel. Got it."

This weird ass convo did a good job of pulling me out of my stupor. "What's going—"

JT held up a finger. "Okay. See you soon." She disconnected.

"Now what?" Coop asked.

"You don't want to know." JT sighed deeply and reached for my hand. "Tulip's in trouble. You're not going to believe what's happened."

On a different day, I might've agreed. "After the shitshow I've been through, I'm willing to believe about anything."

CHAPTER TWENTY-EIGHT

Eddy

Eddy pulled her Whacker from behind her back and tossed it into one of the rear seats with a sigh of relief. She took a few moments to refamiliarize herself with the five-speed standard transmission and managed to back the car onto the street. After only two killed engines and a few jackrabbit starts, they were cruising down 182nd headed for Interstate 84.

Like the excellent direction finder he was, Rocky already had the map to Oaks Amusement Park pulled up on his phone. "In one mile we will take I-84 south. You know, Ms. Eddy, I really liked Ms. Carlee. She is funny. She bakes very good cookies." He paused. "It is getting very warm in here."

Eddy had noticed the temperature in the car was rising, but she'd been so busy concentrating on remembering how to use the stick shift she hadn't paid much attention to how warm it had become. Now that Rocky brought it up, the car suddenly felt sweltering in the eighty-something degree heat. "Roll your window down." She grabbed the crank and gave it a twist. The window lowered about two inches before the crank ceased to crank.

Rocky's face turned red as he struggled with his window. "I can only make it roll halfway down, Ms. Eddy."

"Well, heck and holy holly. We might be in for a steamy ride." Carlee had mentioned Hummer was temperamental about a few things but had forgotten to specify what they were. Apparently, the windows were one of those things. "Take it easy before you give yourself a heart attack. Hopefully neither of us has the toots."

Speaking of gas, she glanced at the dashboard to check the gasoline level. It would be par for the crazy course to run out of go-juice now. Two nostalgically familiar, circular gauges showed her speed on the right and the gas indicator on the left. She was happy to see the needle quivering on full. To the left of the steering wheel were two chrome knobs, one for the headlights and one for the wipers, right where she remembered them. She pulled on the knob for the lights and the dash illuminated. Driving in the dark was a coming certainty and you never knew when the Oregon sky might decide to cry.

"Ms. Eddy, do you mind if I turn the radio on?"

"Go ahead and give it a twirl."

The AM/FM radio with its brown-with-age plastic-covered dial was situated between the front seats on the lower half of the dash. Rocky bent close to study it. Good thing he was short and his eyes still sharp, because she'd have to contort herself into a pretzel to see the radio dial clearly, and besides, she didn't have her readers along for the ride.

The car hit an unexpected bump and the ashtray beside the radio dropped open, nearly bonking Rocky in the face.

He jerked away with a yelp. "Holy cowzer, Ms. Eddy, I almost got beaned in the thinker."

"Good thing you've got finely honed reactions, young man. I'm surprised the roads here are so rough." Road hazards in this burg were surprisingly plentiful for a place which very rarely went below freezing in the winter. Eddy wondered if they had roadwork season here like they did back in Minnesota.

"It is a very, very good thing I have fast reflexes." Rocky slammed the tray shut and returned to his perusal of the radio. Two seconds later the tray fell again. He closed it. This time it dropped open almost immediately.

Eddy reached over and gave the ashtray a good, healthy bang shut. "Guess that's one of those quirks Carlee mentioned."

Rocky turned the radio on. Fuzz filled the stuffy interior. After some twisting of the tuner, he locked in a peppy jazz station.

Eddy tapped her thumbs on the wheel in time to the music. Good way to keep one awake. Awake? Whoa. Hold on a minute, old lady. She still wasn't painfully bone tired as she'd been feeling for weeks now. Hadn't obsessed about Red Bull once in the last few hours. Nor did she need the bathroom every few minutes. Score at least three in her win column.

Rocky straightened. "After all that, I am very hot now, Ms. Eddy."

"See if air-conditioning is an option on the temperature controls. If it is, maybe the little bugger still works."

"Okay." He leaned forward to study the levers. "Ms. Eddy, the car does have air-conditioning." Rocky adjusted the sliders and held his hand over one of the vents. "We will be very warm by the time we arrive at the Oaks Amusement Park if this does not work. Oh! I think I feel cool air."

"Anything cooler than this would be sorely appreciated." Eddy dragged an arm across her forehead. "Remember, we've been through worse." She glanced at her charge, who was now slouched against the unbreathable vinyl. "We'll be okay. Everything always ends up just the way it should."

"I know." Rocky stuck his lower lip out. "But I am tired. I want my most darling Tulip back. I want Shay to come home from wherever she went. I want to eat some most delish food and have a Voodoo Doughnut and go to sleep."

"I know, Rocky. I know." His wishes were hers.

The tires thumped over uneven pavement and the ashtray fell open again.

"Leave it be, child."

Rocky heaved a full body sigh and glanced at his phone. "You must take Interstate 5 south in one half of a mile, which is one thousand two hundred and eighty feet."

"Roger that." The exit loomed and Eddy took it. As she came off the ramp to merge onto I-5, she stomped on the gas pedal. Hummer's engine howled. Accelerating from thirty to sixty took forever plus three point two days. Cripes, might as well cut a hole in the floorboards so she could propel the car forward with her feet like Fred Flintstone. Yabba dabba doo.

They crossed the Willamette, passed the edge of downtown Portland, and exited onto Oregon 43, paralleling the river.

"In two point three miles we must make a left onto the Southwest Sellwood Bridge. I wonder if they sold wood on the bridge in the olden days. What do you think, Ms. Eddy?"

"Sounds reasonable to me."

Rocky guided them back over the Willamette, instructed her to make a couple of left turns and then a right. "Now we follow this road—Oaks Park Way—and the amusement park is on the left."

"'K. We gotta get to the Ferris wheel. Can you use your fancy Google Earth thingamabob to help us figure out where we should park?"

Rocky sat up straight. "Oh, yes! Yes, Ms. Eddy, I can do it."

Eddy continued puttering slowly along Oaks Park Way. The ribbon of roadway disappearing into the dark was almost more eerie than the ghostlike trees lining the drive. She didn't think they were too far from the city, but it was dark as hardened lava out here. Everything was…creepy. Chills having nothing to do with the semi-cool air blowing out the vents periodically ran down her spine, but she didn't want to let Rocky know how nervous she was. Wouldn't do to add more worry swirling around his aviator hat-covered brain.

"We have arrived at the land of fun and amazement almost two hours early." Rocky did a triumphant wiggle-jig.

As Eddy thought about it, maybe he wasn't doing so much a triumphant wiggle as he was attempting to repress a need to pee. Lord knew she'd been in that position more than a few times. Then she realized with utter delight she still didn't need to use the can. She hoped she wasn't becoming dehydrated. Eh, who cared? She soaked in the amazingness of not to having to hunt down another lady's room. Yet, anyway.

"Okay," Rocky said, "I have a very good place for us to park and spy on the Ferris wheel. It is right at the edge of the parking lot. Then we will see JT and Shay and Coop if they get here before Scary Mary and Pretty Boy Robbie and my most darling Tulip."

"Always a good idea to get the drop on your friends and your adversaries, Rocky. I like your plan." Eddy sure hoped her kids would make it before what had better be the final confrontation with those two shysters. It'd sounded like they were a good two hours and some away when she'd spoken with JT. At least she no longer had to worry about Shay, though she really wanted to know where that girl had gone and why. After she hugged the ever-loving innards out of her she was going give Shay a piece of her mind. Disappearing like that and worrying everyone, she knew better.

They passed three parking lots divided by rows of what appeared to be maples, but it was so dark it was hard to tell. A full moon instead of a quarter one would've been mighty helpful. The amusement park did a good job saving electricity, because as far as Eddy could tell, there was not a light to be seen. Well, except for a single glowing Coke machine outside one of the buildings.

Rocky's excited bouncing rocked the entire vehicle. Felt like Hummer might need some new springs added to the growing list of half-working things. Momentarily, Rocky directed Eddy into a lot and around to the far side of an oval, mulch-covered oasis in the ocean of blacktop. As she pulled in, Hummer's headlights illuminated a few waist-high shrubs amongst the mulch, and a gnarly tree whose branches grew in asymmetrical directions.

A circular tent with a green-and white-striped top, maybe ten feet in diameter, was erected next to it, protecting a picnic table. A purple wrought iron bench was positioned nearby, along with a thirty-gallon garbage can. Maybe the area was Oaks Amusement Park's idea of a break room.

On the other side of the tent, the parking lot abutted two corrugated metal, pole barnlike buildings, probably used for maintenance and storage and who knew what else. The parking lot in front of the building had become a repository for concrete blocks, old tables, and two contraptions that looked like movable storage containers.

Eddy eyed the shrubs and the sad, arthritic tree, which probably weren't going to provide them much in the way of cover, but their choices were limited. As in almost zero. She shifted into park and let out a long breath.

Maybe fifty yards away, her headlights illuminated a part of their target, the Ferris wheel. A fourish-foot, black fence surrounded the wheel, and was hooked to a chain-link fence separating the parking lot from the park itself.

She killed the lights and the black of night settled. She could barely make out the outline of the Ferris wheel against the slightly lighter night sky. Maybe once her eyes adjusted, she'd be able to see at least a little more clearly. Her nerves were a-frazzle, but she was still on her game, and still didn't have a hankering for Mello Yello or the Bull. Eyes on the prize, lady, she reminded herself. You're doing great.

Huh.

Felt good to be proud of herself. Hadn't had much to be proud of lately. Self-talk was all the rage these days, and maybe there was something to the theory.

"Ms. Eddy, this is perfect. We are sort of hidden and now we will know when those two no good, very bad, not-friends of Tulip's show up. And Shay and JT and Coop."

"Yup." Eddy stifled an unexpected yawn. "Good golly. I'm not all pooped out like I have been, but I think exhaustion is catching up."

"It is okay, Ms. Eddy. If you would like to close your eyes and rest for a little while I will keep watch, like they do on *Law and Order: SVU*. Did you know *Law and Order: SVU* has been on television since September twentieth, 1999? That is one year before the year 2000. 2000 was the year the dot-com bubble burst."

Eddy allowed her eyes to drift shut as she listened to Rocky enlighten her with new century trivia.

A snort from Rocky jerked Eddy out of her stupor. For a few seconds she struggled to orient herself. Her heart raced as adrenaline jacked her veins. She had no idea where she was. Maybe she'd jumped from one dream into another.

Rocky snort-snored again, and everything came rushing back. They were in the parking lot of Oaks Amusement Park, waiting for Pretty Boy Robbie and—holy cooties, what time was it? Had the kids arrived? They would've come right to the car if they had. So probably not yet.

What if they'd accidentally slept through the doofy duo's deadline? Ohmigod. She jerked upright and scrabbled for her phone. It wasn't on her lap where she thought she'd left it. Desperation ratcheted up like a weed-covered Nessie emerging from Scotland's Loch Ness as she desperately patted her legs, the seat, and ran her fingers between the seat and the door. She leaned forward to check the dash. On her second swipe her hand brushed what could only be her cell.

Thank the heavens. She slapped a hand to her chest to hold in her galloping heart. The time, Eddy. Check the time. Fingers trembling, she lit up the phone. 12:15 a.m. What time were they supposed to meet again? Scary Mary's scary voice played like a ghost in her head, *"We want the balance by 12:11 a.m. or we'll toss your little miss Tulip off the top of the Oaks Park Ferris wheel."*

Oh, holy rollers, no.

"Rocky." Eddy shook his arm. "Rocky, you gotta wake up."

After a second, he mumbled, "Ms. Eddy, please stop."

"Come on, it's time to find Tulip."

"Is it eleven minutes after twelve midnight?"

"Well, maybe a touch past."

He stiffened under her hand. "Oh no, oh no, oh no, oh no. I fell asleep. I did not mean to fall asleep. We cannot be late. Pretty Boy Robbie and Scary Mary will throw my Tulip off the top of the Ferris wheel at exactly eleven minutes after twelve in the dark of night!"

"Let's go." Eddy reached into the back for the Whacker. Now was the time she'd need it if she needed it at all. She forced the image of Tulip splayed askew on the ground out of her mind. Before Rocky had a chance to devolve into the panic zone, she opened her door and stepped out, tucking her Whack-a-bad-guy stick away once again, and made sure the pink fanny pack was secure.

Rocky followed, just as she hoped. She scanned the lot for a car, for any indication of Shay and the rest of her flock, or Tulip and Dim and Wit.

Nothing.

Rides and buildings and ticket booths were no more than ghostly objects she could sense rather than clearly see. As they hustled across the pavement, Rocky broke into a run. Eddy squinted into the night, willing good guy headlights to appear. Maybe they'd parked somewhere else. Or they weren't here at all. Good grief, come on, already. This bull pockey needed to end, and end now.

The Ferris wheel loomed large as they approached, a circular sentry guarding the grounds of amusement.

Rocky pulled up short in front of a fence encircling the ride. "Ms. Eddy, I do not see my bride. I do not see Scary Mary or Pretty Boy Robbie." His voice pitched higher than she'd ever heard it.

Wow, was she out of shape. Eddy's breath came in short bursts. "Hard…to see…in this dark. I—"

"You're late." An apparition stepped out from behind a three-by-five-foot, shingled booth situated between the fence and the Ferris wheel. The apparition solidified into Scary Mary. Dear Jesus-on-a-stick. Mary was even scarier because she had two gouges across one of her pale cheeks. Eddy hoped Tulip inflicted the damage.

With Mary accounted for, where was Robbie? Were he and Tulip actually on top of the wheel? She couldn't recall hearing the Ferris wheel fire up, but who knew how hard she'd slept, and they were not exactly parked up close and personal.

Rocky said, "Where is my Tulip, you no good, very scary, super mean, horrible terrible person? I want to see my Tulip. Right now!"

Scary Mary's laugh was thin and harsh. The sound grated, shooting cold tendrils of fear down the nape of Eddy's neck.

"You want to see your oh, so lovely lady?" Mary sneered. "Show me the money, as they say." She rubbed her fingers together in a circular motion.

It seemed as if their tardiness wasn't yet considered a mortal sin. Thank the gods of Graceland. Eddy said, "I've got it. Every last penny. You'll get it when we get Tulip. Where is she?"

"Show me the moolah first."

"Give me my Tulip!" Rocky hollered, hands fisted at his sides.

"No dough, no dolly," Scary Mary returned at equal volume.

"Calm yourselves, for cripes' sake," Eddy said. "I told you I have the gosh darn cash." The two of them were bound to have an attack of one sort or another if they didn't cool it. She jerked a thumb at herself. "Money for you." She jabbed a finger at Mary. "Tulip for us. Same time."

Scary Mary glared. After a few seconds of consideration, she muttered, "Fine," and disappeared into the booth. A generator rumbled to life. The Ferris wheel's mechanical parts squealed and groaned as it began to move.

Imagine that. Both she and Rocky had slept through the din. The screeching metal was loud enough to raise the dead. Good thing there weren't any cemeteries around, Eddy thought. Then she realized she had no idea if there were any eternal resting places nearby. Hopefully the answer to that was a vigorous no. Funny how one's mind could run in weird directions during times of great big trouble.

After maybe thirty seconds, the wheel ground to a stop. Both Pretty Boy Robbie and Tulip were visible as the car they sat in rocked gently back and forth over the loading area. Eddy put a reassuring yet restraining hand on Rocky's shoulder in case he decided to charge. With her other hand, she reached back and wrapped her fingers around the Whacker and slid it free. She didn't know yet what she might use it for, but best be ready for anything.

The rumble of the generator stopped, and Mary exited the shed. She waved at Robbie, who then released the safety bar and sent Tulip over to them.

She pivoted to Tulip and shoved a finger in her face. "Not a word till we're done with business."

Tulip nodded.

Pretty Boy Robbie peeled himself out of the Ferris wheel seat and limped toward them. She took a closer look at Rocky's bride. Her right eye looked swollen, but it was hard to tell for sure in the dark. And was that a fat lip?

"We meet again," Pretty Boy Robbie said. "Where's the money? We held up our end of the bargain. Can't wait to unload this bitch." He reached over and thwapped the back of Tulip's skull, snapping her head forward.

Shay was usually the one to see red and lose her mind when the proverbial poop hit the fan. This time Eddy was the one firmly embedded on the express train to the land of retribution. How dare these good-for-nothing twerps hurt Tulip. How dare they kidnap her and demand a ransom. How *dare* they?

Major Tom, control's lost.

Eddy whipped out her Whacker and whapped Pretty Boy across the nose. He dropped to his knees with a screech, hands to his face.

Like a Cajun Ninja, Tulip leaped on Scary Mary, who staggered under the impact.

Rocky glanced at his wife dangling off Mary's neck, at Eddy, and back again. His scowl morphed into full-fledged fury. He charged Scary Mary with a roar worthy of a medieval warrior, and upon impact, all three of them hit the ground. Tulip and Rocky gleefully hogpiled on top of a squawking Mary. Mary tried to throw the wonder twins off, but they weren't having it.

Eddy took another swipe at Robbie Not So Pretty and gave him a healthy tap on the back of his noodle. He kissed the ground with a grunt. "You're lucky I can give Carlee back her money now, or I'd have to bonk you even harder." Every time he tried to move, she rang his bell again.

Tulip whooped. "How do you like this, Scary Mary? You're not so scary anymore. What are we going to do with these two ruffians, Ms. Eddy?"

"You hold your ground"—THWACK!—"young lady."

Laughter from somewhere behind Eddy made her freeze, arm raised mid-bonk. She twisted around to see the distinctive outlines of Shay, JT, Coop, and a woman she'd never seen before. Shay had a hand to her mouth but couldn't smother another amused outburst.

"What took you so long?" Eddy plopped her keister on Pretty Boy Robbie's back. "We started the party without you."

CHAPTER TWENTY-NINE

Shay

I couldn't stop laughing. Eddy and Tulip and Rocky taking care of biz was the best sight ever. They didn't need us, they were johnny-on-top of it. And people. JT practically held me up as I howled. Once I regained control and could stand on my own, JT said, "Let's give 'em a hand with cleanup."

I carefully pulled Tulip off Scary Mary and whispered, "You okay?"

Tulip glanced at me, expression puzzled, which puzzled me. "Maybe a little banged up, but I'm fine."

I lowered my voice even more. "But your secret."

"What secret?"

I put my lips to her ear. "I know you're expecting!"

Tulip's eyes went wide. "What?"

"It's okay. I won't say anything until you guys are ready to tell everyone."

She screwed her face up in thought. "But I'm not expecting anything."

"It's okay. Like I said, I won't say a word." I pinched my thumb and pointer together and zipped them over my lips.

"About wha—"

"Bring Mary over here," JT called. She and Coop had Pretty Boy Robbie backed up against the side of the generator shack. He dejectedly rubbed his head.

I gave Tulip a lopsided smile. Even my mouth was exhausted. "We can talk about it in the morning."

She gave me a weird look. "Whatever you say, Shay."

Mugs appeared, and I tucked thoughts of baby bumps and bottles into a metaphorical diaper bag and stowed it in a corner of my brain. Mugs took one of Mary's arms and I grabbed the other. Together we hauled her to her feet and marched her over to JT's virtual interrogation room.

We formed a semicircle around the two of them, sort of like human prison bars.

"Tulip," JT said, "what would you like to do with these two law busters?"

She eyed them a long moment. "If they've learned their lesson, I'd very much like to let them go, as long as they go far away and never call me again. Mary thought I was talking about money when I told her I had all the riches I could ever need on the phone a few weeks ago."

"But, Tulip," Rocky said, his voice trembly, "they hurt you. Your eye. Your lip. They hurt me."

Tulip stood up straighter. "How did they hurt you, my love?"

"My heart. I thought it was going to break. I was so worried about you, my lovely Tulip." His bottom lip quivered.

Tulip wrapped her arms around him. "Oh, Rocky, my adorable hubby, it's okay. My eye will heal and so will my lip. Those happened before Robbie and Mary understood what I was talking about when I spoke about my riches. I meant the love we share, and the love we have from these people who are like family. Besides"—she leaned into him—"I kicked Robbie right between the legs after he hit me in the eye. His voice sounded like a little girl's for a while."

"You did a wonderful job, my darling." Rocky's shoulders dropped and he exhaled. "I will trust you, my most wonderous, beautiful, wickedly excellent punter."

Tulip plastered a big kiss on his cheek.

"Not to interrupt, but, Tulip," JT said in her serious cop voice, "do you want to press charges against these two?"

Tulip stared at the two of them for a long moment. "I think they've received enough damage. Although I will say if I ever see either one of them again, I'm going to do some more kicking and then I'll call you, JT."

CHAPTER THIRTY

Shay

The Mad Greek Deli on Burnside was an eccentric soccer sanctuary for the Greek foodie. Dozens of colorful scarves hung from the ceiling, brandishing the logos of more soccer teams—or football clubs as they were known in the soccer world—than I'd known existed.

The place was colorful, bright, and cheery. Something about the deli, aside from mouthwatering aromas, calmed my innards and made me feel less scattered. After surviving the last twenty-four hours, we all could use some peace.

A sea of mahogany tables and mission-style chairs filled two-thirds of the restaurant. Televisions on every wall offered a clear view from almost any vantage. The rest of the delicatessen held an ordering counter, a food warmer showcasing some of the deli's more popular offerings, and a U-shaped bar with a white top. Rows of liquor bottles and beer cans were neatly organized on shelves behind the bar. Some trophies from whatever sports the deli sponsored—probably soccer—graced the top shelf along with more bottles and cans of booze.

I did a double take when I noticed a *A Christmas Story* leg lamp tucked against the far side of the liquor shelves. Portland. Definitely weird.

The weirdness continued with an eye-popping shrine to the Portland Timbers. The display graced a good twenty feet of wall space on the far side of the bar. A TV was suspended from the ceiling between two flags. One of the flags was green, yellow, and blue, and looked like the Swedish flag in the wrong style and slightly off-kilter. The other was blue, white, and green with a thin black pine tree running down the middle.

On the upper left side of the shrine, aligned with the top of the TV, were white, twelve-inch letters on a black background spelling out RCTID, whatever that meant. On the right, the words NO PITY balanced things out. Maybe the Timbers were renowned for not showing mercy to their opponents. Or maybe they were too nice and needed reminding to kick some soccer ass.

Directly below the boob tube was a two-foot Timbers logo with green and yellow stripes. The whole display was a bit dizzying.

A chest-high wall separated the bar from the main dining room. Me, Coop, Eddy, Tulip, and Rocky were seated next to the wall at two tables which had been pushed together. JT was outside on the phone with Detective Weaver.

On our tables, dinner plates, or rather, brunch plates, since it was only ten thirty, were scraped bare and scattered between mostly empty serving dishes.

Niccolo, a Ryde driver Eddy had befriended, had made numerous trips to the kitchen and back, bringing us different varieties of Greek delicacies to try. Eddy told us his cousin owned the joint, and apparently said cousin didn't mind we were served what appeared to be some of everything on the menu.

I carefully threw my napkin on the table. Every inch of my body felt like it'd been run over by a moving truck. The tip of my nose was the only thing that didn't feel broken. "I am so done. If I try to stuff one more thing in me, I'm gonna explode. But," I assured a hovering Niccolo while trying not to burp out loud, "this is the best Greek grub I've ever had."

He clapped his hands. "I am so glad."

"Greek cooking"—Rocky waved a half-eaten piece of baklava—"is one of the very first fusion cuisines. It has influences from the Romans and the Turks and Europe and India."

"Yes!" Niccolo boomed. "So many flavors, so many sumptuous meals. Did you know the first cookbook was written by a Greek cook? His name was Archestratos."

"In 330 BC, which means before Christ." Rocky stuffed the rest of the baklava in his mouth.

Niccolo nodded gravely. "You are a very knowledgeable person."

Coop laughed. "He's smart, and now he has unfettered access to the Oracle. You can't beat him."

Niccolo stroked his chin. "The Oracle?"

"Google," Eddy said.

He laughed, the rich sound coming from deep down. "No, you can't beat that. I'll be right back with more desserts."

As he disappeared into the kitchen, the front door opened, and my sister, Lisa, strolled in.

"Lisa," Tulip called, "we're over here."

With a wave, Lisa threaded her way to us and dropped into a seat between Eddy and Coop.

"Child"—Eddy gave her a poke with her elbow—"where have you been?"

Lisa sighed and slid her sunglasses up to rest on top of her head, then tucked her long hair behind her ears. I now recognized the move was something she did when she was stressed. It hadn't been long since I'd found out she was my sister from another mother. I'd had a hard time reconciling the fact my dad had a brief relationship with her mom after my own mother had been killed in a car accident when I'd been a preteen. The passing of time did help, and these days it was a lot easier to accept. She was a good human, and sometimes I could still be an ass, mostly without meaning to, but I was trying.

She glanced at Eddy for a second, then focused on me. "Back when I was in college out here, I got into some trouble."

"Hey." Coop flicked his hand in dismissal. "Who doesn't get into trouble in college?"

She gave him a weak smile, which was more of a grimace. "You have a point." Her eyes took on a faraway look. "So, I was at a party at the Lovecraft Bar. Which I've found out is now known as the Coffin Club."

"The Coffin Club?" I asked. "Seriously?" Holy shit. My sister had some crazy weird in her too, just like the rest of us.

"Yup." Color rose on her cheeks.

"Lovecraft, as in HP?" JT asked and rested a hand ever-so-gently on my shoulder. She'd snuck back in, and I hadn't even noticed. "He's one of the fathers of horror, science fiction and fantasy."

I glanced up at her, shocked my betrothed would have any idea who Lovecraft was at all. Horror, sci-fi, fantasy…none of it was her style. She gave me a soft smile. "I did a report on him for an English class in high school."

"Yeah. That's the one. I was young and dumb and got nailed with a pocket full of pot."

"But marijuana is legal here!" Rocky's eyes widened in indignation.

"True, Rocky," she said, "but back then it wasn't. It was under an ounce, but that was a Class B felony. When the state legalized pot, they eventually passed Senate Bill 420, allowing for marijuana offense expungement. I've spent a couple of months working with an expungement lawyer from home, and it was like divine timing, you wanting to come here, Shay. The last two days I met with her and spent some quality time at the courthouse finalizing the legal stuff. Good news is, as of right now, it's like the charge never happened."

"Congrats," I said. "That's great. Why didn't you tell us what was going on?"

"Because"—Lisa reluctantly locked eyes with me—"I feel like we've had a pretty rocky go of things since I came into your life. I didn't want yet another thing to make you think even less of me."

Hoo boy. That was honest. And if I were honest, she was absolutely right. I needed to get over myself. My life hadn't been easy, but then again, neither had hers. JT's fingers tightened on my shoulder. I squeaked and she rapidly released her grip. "Lisa, I'm sorry I've been a complete—"

"Stop. Let's start this whole thing over." She held out her hand. "Hi. I'm your sister, Lisa."

Her palm was warm as I grasped it. "Lisa, I'm happy to meet you." I cracked a hopeful smile. I was going to do better. It was time for me to let go of my preconceived notions. Lisa wasn't trying to steal my father out from under me; she was looking for family. After my harrowing adventures of the last day, after finding little lost Lira, after reconfirming how important the people in my life were to me, it was time to lay down my fear and embrace my sister. I stood, circled the table, and hugged her. It was a little awkward—okay, maybe a lot awkward—but it was right. We parted, and her lips curled up, reflecting my own smile back at me.

Before either of us could say anything else, Niccolo approached our tables with another—oh, god, please let it be the last—tray. "These are Pasteli, honey sesame bars." He held the tray out to Lisa. "My dear, you haven't had a chance to sample the deliciousness of the Mad Greek Deli. Please."

Lisa accepted a bar and soon we were deep in caramel-like honey and sesame.

As I chewed the gooey treat and ruminated on the complicated situation between me and Lisa, I thought more about my father. The man who I felt was the obstacle between Lisa and me was actually the bridge between the two of us. We'd come a long way, my Pop and I, but I still harbored some deep-seated anger, which surfaced now and then.

Life should be about love, not anger and resentment and fear. It should be about our commonalities. So many in the world were terrified of those with black and brown skin, of folks of different orientations, the differently abled, the neurodivergent. On and on it went.

Damn. What a grown-up thought.

I glanced up as Eddy laughed at something Lisa said. She seemed a whole lot peppier than she had when we'd first arrived in Portland. Maybe this trip was good for her, after all. But I still wanted to check in on her emotional barometer. There it was, the dumb emotion business again. Yup. Maybe we both needed a little therapy. Together. And maybe on our own too. Guess we each had plenty of luggage to sort out.

The sweets had disappeared and so had Niccolo, satisfied he'd taken care of every possible edible need we might have.

Tulip, who'd launched into a retelling of her adventures, said, "I still can't believe Scary Mary and Pretty Boy Robbie would do such a thing."

"I told you, my most dearest darling," Rocky said, "I had a very, very, very bad feeling about those twins of evil."

Tulip leaned over and smooched his cheek. "I think it was the Witch's Castle you had a bad feeling about, my love."

Rocky's face scrunched. "Might be true, but I still had a no good, very bad feeling."

"Yes, you did." Tulip hugged his arm and Rocky's face scrunch was replaced with a beaming look of love. Sometimes love could be so easy. It was humans like me who didn't want to deal with emotion, didn't want to face the BS life shuffled up, who managed to throw a screwdriver in the works.

Keep things simple, O'Hanlon.

"All right, Shay"—Eddy eyed my scraped and bruised face— "aside from the obvious, what in the world happened to you?"

Last night we'd made it back to the motel and did nothing but drag ourselves to our respective rooms. I was so exhausted it was all I could do to climb the steps to the second floor. On the ride back, I'd given a rudimentary rundown of events to JT and Coop, but even they hadn't heard the entire unbelievable saga. For the next forty minutes, I detailed the accidental discovery of ammunition, the shystering of the coffee, bad boys Canavaro and Bender. The tunnels under the Drunken Tankard, Tim Burr. All the frustrating times I thought I'd have cell service only for it to disappear before anything went through.

"Oh, my god," JT said. "No wonder we could never find you. Every time I thought we had a lock on you, you disappeared. I admit I got a bit hot."

Coop laughed. "I don't think hot is quite the word for it."

"Maybe not." She kissed me. "Continue."

I opened my mouth to follow JT's directions when Rocky looked up from his phone. "Those tunnels under the ground, Shay O'Hanlon, they are called Shanghai Tunnels. Do you know why they are called Shanghai Tunnels?"

"No, I don't."

"They are called Shanghai Tunnels because legend says the tunnels stretched all the way to the river, through Chinatown, and underneath various business establishments. Opium dens were set up in various rooms in the tunnels too." He bent his head to the phone. "Men who probably had too many alcoholic beverages in the local taverns were said to have been dropped through a trapdoor by the bar into a holding cell." He looked up at me. "That is what happened to you, Shay O'Hanlon. Then the men would be conscripted onto ships bound for Shanghai. It took something like two years for them to return if they ever did at all. That is a very scary thought."

I thought back to the jail-type bars I'd seen and the rat maze I had navigated. The primitive rooms, the buildup of years of dust. The strange room where I'd found the drugs. "Interesting. So, if I would've found the right tunnel, I might have made it out to the river?"

"Yes, correct, Shay O'Hanlon. But, according to my Oracle, most of the tunnels have been cut off because concrete walls from many of the buildings were extended through the tunnels and set even deeper to help stabilize the structures above when the earth quaked."

"Huh." Eddy met my eyes. "You do get yourself in some interesting jams, Shay."

"I know I do."

"Holy moly." Lisa's eyes were saucers. "What happened next?"

I launched into the story, earning a few gasps when I told them about my almost escape from the Tankard and ensuing tasing, and my return trip through the trapdoor in the floor, and then the excursion out of town.

The van ride to Crook County Packing and Distribution on top of Tim Burr freaked Rocky out. "You had to sit on him?"

"Well, my legs were resting on him."

"That is very gross." Rocky shuddered. "And I feel very badly for Mr. Tim Burr too."

"Me too, Rocky. I felt terrible using him like a foot stool, but I didn't have a choice."

"True." His mournful expression morphed into the bright look he got when he was about to enlighten us. "Do you know how long it takes for a body to decompose, Shay O'Hanlon?"

I held a hand up. "I love you, Rocky, but that is something I would like to know nothing about."

He sat back. "It is okay, Shay O'Hanlon. I understand not everyone can stomach those facts. I do not like to think about it either. What happened next?" Decomposing bodies aside, Rocky leaned forward again, his eyes wide and expectant.

By the time I got through the cow pasture escape attempt, the dead body tension had eased, and laughter ensued when I described being chased by a herd of pissed-off bovines.

"Wow," Coop said, "no wonder you had no shoes and"—his upper lip rose—"had such a…funk about you."

"That smell was beyond funk." JT shuddered. "Poor Mugs, our amazing Ryde driver. She put up with our craziness and Shay's unfortunate, horrifying stench."

"She was awesome." Coop bobbed his head. "Happy to do whatever we asked. I think she got a kick out of it. Wish there were more drivers like her in Minneapolis."

Rocky said, "It is too bad we don't have Ryde at home. They pay better and the company is very nice to their workers."

"I'm glad to hear it." I smiled at the Rockster. "Those ride-share companies suck the life out of the drivers. And, by the way, it wasn't my fault the bad guys built their evil enterprise next to a cow pasture."

After groans rounded the table, I continued my virtual tour. I brought everyone into the packing and distro center, explained how fire forced me to backtrack, described the shock of finding Lira, and our semi-miraculous escape. Now that I really thought about it, if I hadn't gone back, Lira might not have made it. I swallowed hard at the lump that formed in my throat.

JT realized I'd been hit by an emotional tornado, and, like a good almost spouse, saved the day. "Good news is Lira'll be okay." She squeezed my knee, gently this time. "When I finally laid eyes on Shay and saw she was beating the holy hell out of someone, I could hardly believe it." JT cut me a sideways glance. "Then again, I should know better when it comes to what this one finds herself involved with. She's a shit magnet. Literally." JT snickered. I bounced my fist against her thigh. She caught my hand and interlaced our fingers.

Eddy's face was stone. It was the look she had when she was furious. "What happened with poor little Lira? That's a surefire rotten thing for her and her family, and who knows how many others, to go through. I'm of a mind to visit that bozo in the clink and take my Whacker after his sorry behind. First lying about his coffee, then drugs, to murder and people trafficking? Hard to add additional naughty business, but I'm sure if the cops look, they'll find even more to toss at them." She crossed her arms and harrumphed, then peered at JT with a scowl that would make an inchworm squirm.

Holy mahoney. This was the most Eddy-like Eddy'd been in weeks. Something I didn't realize I'd been holding between my shoulders released.

JT said, "Lira's supposedly in good hands in foster care, according to a social worker I talked to this morning. They're working with the cops to figure out where her family may have been taken when they were evacuated from the building. I guarantee there'll be a full investigation into all the goings-on at Crook County Packing and Distribution."

Coop jabbed a finger at me. "Look at what happens when Shay has to go to the bathroom. She winds up breaking up an ammunition and drug and human smuggling operation practically singlehandedly."

Snickers all round. He was right. What a coincidence it was I had to use the facilities at that time and knocked over that particular crate of not-coffee. If all that hadn't happened, I wouldn't have been dropped into the basement of the bar and then carted to Prineville. I didn't even want to think about what had been planned for Lira and her family. On the other hand, maybe there weren't any coincidences at all. Maybe the universe put people in the right place at the right time. Wow, Shay, you can actually have some deep, perplexing thoughts once in a while. Then I bopped myself in the forehead. "How could I have forgotten to ask about Bender? I assumed he'd been scooped up with Canavaro. Did they get him?"

"No." JT shook her head. "He slipped away during the chaos. But they picked up his bartender, and it sounds like Canavaro is singing like the jailbird he's going to be, so I think they'll find Bender soon enough."

Lisa rolled her hand. "What's next?"

"I rearranged it so Shay can go in this evening at six to give her statement." JT smiled devilishly. "I figured she might want to get back to the Big on Beans Convention and order coffee for the Rabbit Hole since we don't know what will happen with the order Coop placed."

Oh, my god I loved this woman. I was coffeeless, and she'd given me the space to correct a not-so-minor issue. It wouldn't do at all to come all the way out here for new and different coffee and go home empty-handed.

"Yeah, that damn Ochoco order." Coop banged the table dramatically with a fist. "I better get a refund."

JT patted his fist. "Call your card company and tell them what happened. They will probably reverse the charge, considering."

"I'll do that."

Tulip tapped the tabletop with much less vigor than Coop to catch my attention. "Shay, you might want to pick a different brand to bring home."

"You know it. But that's okay. I have a few other coffee bean ideas. As long as they don't come out of Crook County, they'll be great."

"Amen," JT said. "Detective Weaver's going to keep me in the loop. Shay, you might have to come back here to testify."

"Food carts. Voodoo Doughnuts. Putting those dickheads away. Fine by me."

CHAPTER THIRTY-ONE

Shay

Uptown Minneapolis was flush with coffee fiends, and the Rabbit Hole Coffee Café had been busy enough; I'd done nothing but run all day long. Kate had taken over the caffeinated wheel and would dock the SS Rabbit Hole at eleven. I wearily slumped into a chair at one of the round café tables out front. We'd been home three days and I was sore, tired, and happy to get back into a regular routine, free of kidnapping, drugs, murder, human beings as a commodity, and shystery ammunition.

With a yawn, I scanned the shop. The Rabbit Hole occupied half of an old Victorian house Eddy owned. She lived in the other half, and Rocky and Tulip kicked back in my old apartment above the café.

Artwork from local artists graced the walls, which were a variety of soothing, swirling, warm reds, oranges, and yellows. Half of the eight three-foot-round French café tables were in use, and no one sat in either of the two overstuffed chairs flanking the hearth. Even if no fire was burning, both Dawg, our boxer, and Bogey, our flunky ex-K9 bloodhound—he still couldn't restrain himself from burying his head in whatever crotch was handy—were sound asleep on the rug in front of the fireplace. Dawg sprawled upside down, and occasionally one of his sizeable paws twitched as he probably had better dreams than I'd been having. All was as it should be, and that, at least, made me feel better.

Condensation dripped down the glass of iced coffee on the table in front of me. It contained my hopefully new favorite drink, a butterscotch mocha made with my newly-imported-from-Portland Tortoiseshell Blend coffee from a company called Dapper & Wise. They advertised the blend as having notes of brown sugar, buttered toast, and nutmeg. I'd sampled the coffee at the Big on Beans Convention and their description was right on. I took a long swallow and let the concoction roll over my taste buds. With the addition of the butterscotch and chocolate, it was decadent.

Aside from the coffee, I particularly liked Dapper & Wise's philosophy of paying above the fair-trade minimum and making it a point to encourage friendliness and fun as a company culture. Exactly what Kate and I strived to do at the Hole.

D&W was the number two roaster on my list after Ochoco Creek, or maybe I should call it Flying High crap coffee. In hindsight I should've put Dapper & Wise first and would have avoided the entire murderous debacle. On the other hand, I did help take down a couple nasty villains and sort of rescued a kid, so there was that. I also needed to make sure Coop was reimbursed for all the Ochoco coffee he'd purchased at the Big on Beans Convention if his credit card company refused to reverse the charges. As we waited to board the plane in Portland, he'd called the company and put a stop on the transaction. Considering Ochoco's situation, I didn't know if the stop would work or not, but I wasn't about to leave him in a financial lurch.

My shoulder was moving better, and the bruises were fading. Considering the unbelievable misery I'd been through, I had to admit I was honestly lucky to be alive. After what happened in Portland something seismically shifted inside me. It was the first time I truly realized I wasn't invincible. It wasn't like I didn't know I was human, like the rest of the world's population, but now, in this moment, life seemed so incredibly fragile. Maybe it had something to do with Lira and how small and world-weary she'd been. Or maybe I was getting old.

The prospect of not seeing JT, Eddy, my dad, Coop, or Rocky and Tulip, and, yes, Lisa, ever again, shook me. The very concept was almost too much to bear. How could a single thought suck all the oxygen out of the room and make it difficult to breathe? The choking feeling brought me back to how truly vulnerable I'd been. Kidnapped, tased, and trussed up like a Thanksgiving giblet.

Vulnerability. I hated that word. Exposing feelings better buried so deep they should never see the light of day was akin to death. Maybe this was how Eddy had felt since her most secret of secrets had been ripped open for all to see.

Ick. Ick, ick, ickity ick.

Opening up to anyone had never been an easy thing for me. How JT had ever broken through my self-imposed island of misperceived safety, I'll never understand, but I was so glad she'd persisted.

Then my brain returned to tiny, adorable Lira. She was such a small tyke, all alone in this big, crazy world. With luck, the situation would only be temporary.

God, I hoped she was okay.

Even if her social worker and foster family were vetted, whatever that meant, the system in general didn't have the greatest track record. Considering what had happened to the Turpin kids in California after they were rescued from their abusive parents and placed in a horribly abusive foster home, social services all over the country were probably iffy at best.

Intellectually, I knew there was nothing I could do about Lira's missing family but wondered for the ten millionth time what has happening with them. My innards were unsettled, ungrounded. I hated the feeling.

I took a sip of my coffee, then idly rolled the sweating glass back and forth between my palms as I considered the state of my feelings. Maybe, I mused, I was off-kilter because I was finally going to say "I do" and suddenly my relationship with JT would become more real than it already was. Marriage was no joke. The legal right to marry and all the benefits and responsibilities which came along with the institution had been a long, ugly battle for both interracial couples and the LGBTQIA+ community. Marriage meant way more than a Brittany Spears fifty-five hour "Let's get hitched, um, oops, I didn't mean it, let's get an annulment" moment. The privilege of being straight and white was vastly underrated.

Maybe my dis-ease was linked to the same events Eddy was having problems processing.

A new development were bad dreams. Every night since we'd been home, JT had to shake me out of the grip of a nightmare on rewind. Every time, I found myself back in the Shanghai Tunnels, desperate to find a way out. I'd get so close to escape, and then something inevitably happened to thwart my flight to freedom. I'd been in a lot of scrapes in my life, but none had brought on repeated night terrors like that. The whole thing exhausted me.

Enough of the depressing and distressing. Better to think about something pleasant. Like my adorably hot wife-to-be. She'd be stopping by soon, hopefully with an update from Detective Weaver about how the investigation in Portland was proceeding.

I breathed deeply, allowed the familiar aromas of Kate's specialty cinnamon rolls, brewing coffee, and the unique scent that could only be a well-established café settle over me like a soft comforter. The usual buzz of conversation, the whiny whirr of the coffee bean grinder, and the high-pitched whistle of steaming milk were a balm.

Maybe I honestly did need real help processing my issues. I made a face at the thought.

"There you are. What's with the sourpuss mug?" Eddy placed a cup of coffee on the table and settled in a chair across from me, looking perky and way more alert than me. "I would've grabbed you something to drink but it looks like you've taken care of that yourself." She eyed the iced concoction in front of me.

"I'm good, but thanks." I gave her a smile and leaned toward her on my elbows. "How are you?"

"Pretty well recovered. Our trip was much more exciting than I ever expected. Shanghai Tunnels, Witch's Castles, dead people, Ferris wheels at midnight. I don't know how you kids manage to find a tangled web wherever you go."

"It's a real talent." Now or never, Shay. You've been waiting to talk to Eddy. Do it. "How are you, really?" I paused a beat. "Before we left you couldn't rouse yourself off your recliner, and if you did it was to make a trip to the bathroom."

Eddy squinted an eye, much like an elderly-ish Popeye minus the extra-large muscles. "You know, your coffee trip was just the ticket. Knocked me out of my melancholy. Didn't even realize I was melony schmelony."

"JT and I've been worried about you."

"Oh, child. You don't need to worry about this old lady."

"But I do."

"I know you do." She rolled her eyes in mock indignation.

"I was wondering if you might be willing to go talk to someone with me, and maybe together we can sort through some stuff."

She gave me a confused look. "Sort through what?"

Oh, for Pete's sake. I didn't want to make her mad, but I did want to be honest. Look, Ma, I'm turning over a brand-spanking new leaf. "Well, after the fallout in March when what happened to Mom and Neil, and...all that came out, you kind of...shut down. You weren't interested in your television shows, you had to drink Red Bull or Mello Yello to function. You didn't even want to go to your Mad Knitter meetings." I figured it wouldn't be prudent to say anything about her need to use the bathroom every six seconds.

"Well, I certainly had no energy, that's a true thing." Eddy's expression grew thoughtful. "The color in the world faded out somehow. Everything was gloomy and gray. But things look brighter now."

"I'm happy about that. But I was thinking." I glanced at Kate talking to a customer at the counter, instead of looking at Eddy.

"Glad to hear your brain is working. Spit it out, child."

I forced myself to meet Eddy's eyes. They brimmed with love and kindness, and maybe a hint of wariness. "I think you were—are maybe—I dunno, depressed."

Eddy peered at me as the moment stretched too long. The last thing I wanted to do was insult her or hurt her feelings. I shifted uncomfortably. "Never mind. Forget I said anything."

"No, no." Eddy's shoulders sagged, and she rubbed her eyes. "You're right. I have been stewing."

"Maybe…you might want to do some therapy. And I might need a little brain tune up myself. I've been having nightmares." I sighed, slow and deep. The worst was now out in the open. "Maybe we could do some of it together. Work out what happened. And I dunno. Maybe you should talk to someone on your own as well, in case there's things you need to get off your chest you'd rather I wasn't there to hear. Maybe I should too."

We sat in silence for a couple of minutes, me kicking myself for saying anything, and Eddy, who knew what was on her mind?

Then she bobbed her head. "You're right." She grabbed my hand and gave it a squeeze. "Talking all this out with someone is a fine idea. I guess we both have some funny business to chew on."

Well. Some things go better than expected. Maybe I wasn't the only one feeling a sea change coming.

The front door chimes jingled. In traipsed Coop, carrying a brown paper bag. He approached and placed the bag in the middle of the table.

"What's that?" I asked.

"Figured you could use a treat. Merry Christmas in June."

With affection, Eddy watched me grab the bag and peer inside. "What's—ohhh," I groaned in delight and glanced up at Coop. "If only I wasn't gay."

"I know, I know. You'd marry me for the ice cream."

"It's not just any ice cream." I pulled three pints out of the bag along with three white plastic spoons. "Sebastian Joe's. I love you forever, Coop."

"You already do."

"Beside the point."

Sebastian Joe's was, hands down, my favorite ice cream. The shop of deliciousness was down the block from the Hole, on the corner of Hennepin and Franklin. If you needed something from me, score me some banana-y vanilla-y caramel-y Pavarotti and I'd be putty in your hands.

Eddy asked, "What kinds you got?"

Coop pulled out a chair, flipped it around, and sat with his arms propped on its back. "I got Shay's Pavarotti. Oreo for JT, and a new one called Henry by the Lake, just for you, Eddy. It's made for a fundraiser for University of Minnesota's Masonic Children's Hospital." He held out the container to her.

"Very nice." Eddy took it and pried the top up. "What's in it?"

"I sampled it. Good shizz." Coop licked his lips. "Caramel ice cream, coconut, T-Rex cookies, and chocolate chunks. I bought a double-dipper and ate it on the way here."

"What's a T-Rex cookie?" Eddy asked but wasted no time putting spoon to ice cream, and I did the same. God, so freaking good.

"Not sure," Coop said, "but it was tasty."

The front door clanged again, and my nearly betrothed strode into the Hole, shoulders back, a smile on her face. Her dark hair was up in a ponytail, and a lightweight blazer covered her badge and gun. She looked capable and oh, so very hot, and not hot in a sweaty, gross way. Hot in a I-want-to-take-you-home-to-bed hot. This woman took my breath away. This sizzling chick wanted to marry me. It still stunned me. Holy hoosgow, how did I ever get so lucky?

"Whatcha got there?" The object of my love and admiration kissed the top of my head and pulled a chair up to the table.

Coop passed her the carton of Oreo.

"You are my favorite man-human, Nicholas Cooper." Five seconds later JT was knee-deep in chocolate cookie and cream bliss. "This is what I want for my last meal." She swallowed and scooped out another huge bite. My girl was headed for an ice cream headache if she wasn't careful.

"Thank you, Coop"—I poked my spoon at him—"for making dreams come true."

"Call me the dream maker, but I'm not a love taker, so don't call me Pat Benatar."

"You're a funny man." I shifted to face JT. "What's the 411 on our Portland coke and murder buddies?"

She wiped her mouth. "It's complicated. So Canavaro hid ammunition stolen from a military base in Idaho in crates of coffee beans at the Crook County Distribution and Packing plant, which were sent south, to Mexico. As a rule, he used unmarked, unlogoed crates. Somewhere along the line there was a colossal mix-up, and a load of the ammo wound up in Flying High crates and those crates were shipped to the Big on Beans Convention. Shay managed to tip over the right, or I guess if you're Canavaro, the *wrong* stack."

I was quite good at doing the one thing that'd cause a ruckus. "How did he manage to heist ammunition from a military base?"

"Tim Burr was a weapons supply tech. He diverted partial shipments, coordinated the process of stealing the ammo, loaded the crates, and shipped them out. Because of an error on his end, the wrong crates made it to the convention."

"Wow," I said, and licked my spoon before taking another bite of ice cream. "No wonder Canavaro wanted to—did, actually—kill him. How was Bender involved?"

"I'm getting there. But back to the crates. Canavaro, or, most often, his minions, would bring the crates down south, transport them via a quarter-mile-long tunnel under the border into Mexico, and then hand them off to his contact there. Then the crates would eventually come back full of non-fair-trade coffee beans and drugs, mostly sourced from Colombia. The crates were then brought back to Portland."

"Wow," Coop said, "Canavaro was good at diversifying his illegal businesses."

"Right on, Nicholas," Eddy said. "That man had his fingers in a whole lot of badness."

JT set her container of Oreo awesomeness on the table and pointed at what was left of my drink. I nudged the cup toward her. She picked it up and tipped it at Eddy. "Canavaro partnered with Bender, who owns the Drunken Tankard, to take the drug shipments, and Bender used the tunnels under the bar to process and break down the bricks into saleable packages. He turned the packs over to Malcolm, the bartender, to dole out to street-level sellers." She finally took a sip of my iced coffee. "Hey, this is pretty good."

"Holy shit. I really did stumble into a wasp's nest."

"You did," she said. "It was the perfect setup. Canavaro used the money from the sale of ammunition to buy the drugs, and after taking a portion of the proceeds, the rest of the money went to buy more ammo. I guess they're still working on what happened to the ammunition once his Mexican connection took it. The connection's a woman, they think a South African arms runner who's been so elusive they aren't even sure what she looks like."

I glanced sharply at JT. "That's right. I heard those two knuckle knockers talking about a woman who'd have them by the short hairs if they didn't deliver."

"All right, there you go." JT plunked my now empty cup on the table. "If they can link her to the scheme, Shay, you can say you nearly singlehandedly broke up an international, illicit weapons ring, along with a drug smuggling operation."

The table was silent a few moments as we considered my not so heroic heroism and continued to demolish the best of Sebastian Joe's. Time for a subject change. I sucked a fortifying breath and glanced at JT. She put her hand on mine, met my eyes, and nodded. The time had come. "In other news, JT and I finally set our wedding date."

Coop's head whipped fast toward me.

"About darn time," Eddy said. "When is it, child?"

JT squeezed my fingers and looked at me in the special way she did. I felt her love in my veins. "November 26th."

"Nice." Coop gave us the thumbs-up. "Not too soon and not too far down the road. Why that date?"

I couldn't stop a grin. "My mom's birthday. JT and I decided it would be a nice way to honor her."

"Great choice," Eddy said. "Perfect. She'd love it."

"We have a couple requests." JT pinned Coop with a pointed cop look. He and my father, of all people, had decided they wanted to be the party planners.

"Shoot."

"No dresses. No pink. Friends and family only."

"Noted."

Eddy patted my arm. "I'm pretty sure you're going to be in good hands with those two."

Getting word of the wedding out in the world made me feel lighter already.

"Ms. Eddy! Shay O'Hanlon! Nick Coop! JT Bordeaux!" Rocky's voice floated through the café as he scurried out of the hall connecting the Rabbit Hole to his apartment and Eddy's place. "Where are you?"

"Out here, Rocky," Coop called.

Rocky dodged around the front counter and skidded to a stop right before running full tilt into our table. "We were expecting!"

"Were?" I breathed the word and set my Pavarotti down. Did something happen to Tulip? If those two boneheads hurt Tulip or her baby, I'd track their sorry keisters down and—hand to my Minnesota nice heart—let them have it in a decidedly non-Minnesota nice way. But then, almost instantaneously, I realized Rocky wasn't upset.

I glanced sharply at Eddy. Had anyone dropped the baby bomb on her yet? With all the chaos of the last few days I'd forgotten about this turn of events.

"Expecting what?" Eddy asked. "A package?"

Nope, apparently, she was none the wiser.

"No, Ms. Eddy we were not expecting a package! We were expecting a baby!"

I didn't think I'd ever seen Eddy at a total loss. She opened her mouth and closed it again without a word passing her lips.

"We are now parents!" Rocky put two fingers to his lips and whistled loud enough customer's heads swiveled in our direction.

I glanced at JT in alarm. She shrugged, the look on her face as confused as mine.

Tulip came around the front counter, arms filled with a bundle wrapped in a fuzzy blue blanket.

Christ on a coaster, did Tulip give birth upstairs, in that tiny apartment, without any medical attention? Horror warred with fascination.

"Hey, everyone." A smile accentuated Tulip's dimples. "Rocky and I have some amazing news."

Here it was. Hold onto your skivvies, folks, shit was about to get real.

She stopped beside Rocky. "We'd like you to meet the newest member of our family."

I felt like I might pass out. Could this really be happening? JT made a strangled sound and Coop's spoon was frozen in midair. I couldn't tell what Eddy was thinking, but her eyebrows were tickling the top of her hairline.

Rocky gave Tulip the sweetest look of adoration. "Show them, my most darling of all. Show them our baby."

Tulip pulled the blanket down. Only the back of a head was visible, blond hair standing on end, turning brownish by the ears. "We'd like you to meet our daughter, Josi!"

I blinked. Then blinked again. That was a mighty furry kid.

"Is that…" Eddy leaned forward and tugged the blanket down further. "Bless my stars. It's a puppy."

Tulip lay the blanket and its contents on the tabletop. I grabbed my empty glass and our ice cream containers and set them on an adjacent table.

Sure enough, a little furball, all whitish-tannish baby fuzz with the longest black lashes I'd ever seen, kicked her way out of the confining folds and shook herself so vigorously she almost toppled.

"Oh my," Eddy breathed, "look at the little squirt."

"She is very tiny, Ms. Eddy." Rocky beamed as if the puppy were his firstborn. Which, I guess, she kind of was.

"Josi, huh?" JT gently picked up the puppy and cradled her. "You may be the cutest puppy I've ever seen." Big dark eyes peered up at her and Josi wagged her tiny tail.

The familiar sound of two dogs doing the wake-up shake, rattle, and roll pried my attention away from the fuzzball on the table. Bogey and Dawg must've smelled the interloper and decided to wander over to investigate. Our table was suddenly crowded with wet noses and curious customers. Coop took fuzzy Josi from JT and cradled her against his bony chest. The wee pooch was passed around, garnering many oohs and ahhs, as the proud parents looked on.

I glanced at JT, feeling a bit shell-shocked. She caught my eye, and I bobbed my head the direction of the kitchen.

We both pushed away from the table and exited the happy gaggle.

I rounded the counter and told Kate to go check out the new arrival. She hustled over the canine mosh pit. No one was interested in coffee when there was a puppy to play with, so I continued into the kitchen.

Dishes were mostly done, and the red-clay-colored floor tiles were barely damp from a recent mopping. I leaned against the stainless triple sink and crossed my arms. "Expecting. Holy shish kabobs, JT. I was sure Tulip was pregnant."

JT settled beside me with a sigh. "Me too. I must admit I'm relieved, but the thought of a kid running around here was sorta, kinda interesting."

Yikes. I studied the floor. "You…want a baby?"

She was quiet. Then, "No. Oh, hell, I don't know. Our life is too complicated, too unpredictable."

"True." I felt in no position to think about adding a kid to the mix. Not right now, and I wasn't sure if I'd ever be ready for that. Good god, we hadn't even done the wedding thing. Then Lira popped into my mind. I remembered her sweet grin, her bravery, her solid body wound tight around me. The thought of what had happened and what could happen to the poor kid made the Protector in me rear up and steal my breath, then retreat just as quickly. My gut clenched.

"It's nothing we've ever really talked about." JT shrugged. "It's hard enough to coordinate life with a couple dogs. With a baby? It'd be even harder. But wouldn't it be fun to have a little one bouncing around on a contact caffeine high?"

I laughed. I loved the way she could defuse my emotional moments when they needed defusing. "I dunno. Come here." I snagged her elbow and pulled her around to stand between my legs. "I don't know what to say about mini humans right now. But maybe"—I looked up at the ceiling for a second and let out a deep breath of air before meeting the beautiful eyes of my love—"maybe we could keep up on what's happening with Lira. I'd like to know how she's doing."

JT kissed my nose, then my lips. "I'll do my best, baby. The Oregon State Police are doing everything they can to find where Canavaro or Bender took the rest of the people they were holding and whoever else might have been with them. With luck, they'll be able to reunite Lira with her sister and her family. We'll see what happens." JT rested her forehead against mine. Both of us knew that even if Lira and her family were reunited, it didn't necessarily mean a happy ending. "Let's concentrate on one thing at a time."

The look she gave me seared my heart in so many ways. God, I loved this woman.

"You're right. One thing at a time." I gave her a rakish grin, stepped back, and grabbed her hand. "Come on. Let's see if Josi likes ice cream as much as Bogey and Dawg."

In the end, everything boiled down to family and love, be it family of origin or family of choice. Or both.

We had that in spades, hearts, diamonds, clubs, and now, in puppies.

Bella Books, Inc.

Women. Books. Even Better Together.

P.O. Box 10543
Tallahassee, FL 32302
Phone: (800) 729-4992
www.BellaBooks.com

More Titles from Bella Books

Hunter's Revenge – Gerri Hill
978-1-64247-447-3 | 276 pgs | paperback: $18.95 | eBook: $9.99
Tori Hunter is back! Don't miss this final chapter in the acclaimed Tori Hunter series.

Integrity – E. J. Noyes
978-1-64247-465-7 | 28 pgs | paperback: $19.95 | eBook: $9.99
It was supposed to be an ordinary workday...

The Order – TJ O'Shea
978-1-64247-378-0 | 396 pgs | paperback: $19.95 | eBook: $9.99
For two women the battle between new love and old loyalty may prove more dangerous than the war they're trying to survive.

Under the Stars with You – Jaime Clevenger
978-1-64247-439-8 | 302 pgs | paperback: $19.95 | eBook: $9.99
Sometimes believing in love is the first step. And sometimes it's all about trusting the stars.

The Missing Piece – Kat Jackson
978-1-64247-445-9 | 250 pgs | paperback: $18.95 | eBook: $9.99
Renee's world collides with possibility and the past, setting off a tidal wave of changes she could have never predicted.

An Acquired Taste – Cheri Ritz
978-1-64247-462-6 | 206 pgs | paperback: $17.95 | eBook: $9.99
Can Elle and Ashley stand the heat in the *Celebrity Cook Off* kitchen?